Dark River

IJ Benneyworth

Also by IJ Benneyworth

The Amanda Northstar Mysteries

Dark River

Heads Will Roll

Queens of the Steal

The Name of the Game

Sisterhood

With thanks to Mum, Anne, Cathy and so many others over the years, not least my grandfather who predicted I would become a writer. It took a while Taid, but here it is.

*Follow IJ Benneyworth
on the web and social media:*

Web: www.scribecorps.com

Facebook: IJ Benneyworth Books

Twitter: @scribecorps

CHAPTER ONE

The full moon cast its cool glow on the glassy water of the Hudson River. The earlier wind had softened to a gentle breeze. At such a late hour, traffic was rare, so the only sounds were subtle cricket chirps and an owl's occasional hoot as it hunted in nearby trees. As Judy Sterling began her slow walk to the center of the Saratoga Bridge, an aging suspension structure similar to the southerly Bear Mountain Bridge, she considered all this and cracked a slight smile. As things went, it was not such a bad night to die.

Judy had parked her car in a lay-by just on the bridge's western side, near the entrance to a forest trail popular with walkers. The Saratoga Bridge was one of the major crossings over the Hudson. Therefore it wouldn't take long for someone to find her car and the note she had left in the glove compartment. Judy knew it would provide small comfort to her husband, Raymond, and son Jason. Still, perhaps it was better than the alternative. That way only led to heartache for everyone.

The path she had decided to take was easier, or at least that was what she had been telling herself since the decision had been made. Was she being selfish? Yes, if she was honest with herself, but it was that honesty that had caused her to finally realize that she simply couldn't continue living life as she had been. It was a lie that had to end.

She had certainly experienced moments of doubt, usually centered on Jason. However, they had become increasingly rare as her plans had advanced, until they had vanished altogether. Like a traveler shedding baggage, the journey had seen weight lifted from her shoulders until this moment, where she felt she could just as easily fly to the center of the bridge as walk. But there was no rush.

Judy checked her watch. There was time to spare, time to enjoy the view of the glimmering Hudson and of the lights of Independence town, only a few miles downriver. She would miss the friends who lived there, asleep now in their beds, unaware that their most recent encounters with Judy Sterling would be their last. They would be shocked, mourn, speculate, gossip, and eventually forget, or at least discuss it in passing once or twice a year over tea or book club meetings.

She reached the center of the bridge and stopped. All she now possessed in this world were the blouse and skinny jeans she wore, and a cashmere coat Ray had bought her for their anniversary three years previously. She had left her purse and phone behind, also in the car glove compartment, easy enough to discover. They would help with identifying the owner of the vehicle. Besides, she wouldn't need them where she was going.

Judy felt for her wedding ring, something she often did unconsciously when nervous. But she had put it in the envelope that held the note. It had belonged to Ray's mother, and Judy felt it was not her right to take it. It hadn't ultimately served her well, but some future Sterling ought to benefit from it.

She rechecked her watch. Not long now. She took a deep breath to calm herself. There was no going back. Then, in the distance, the rumble of a car engine, coming from the Western side. She turned in the direction of her own car, just about visible in the moonlight, and focused on the road beyond it. The engine's sound grew louder until she finally saw the car it belonged to emerge from behind a bank of trees that obscured the road.

Its speed was ferocious, and within seconds its wheels had met the surface of the bridge, but then it began to slow as it approached her. It was getting close enough that Judy was able to make out the details of the car. It was one she recognized, one she had seen countless times. As its headlights washed out Judy's surroundings and made a white ghost of her, her eyes widened in shock and disbelief as she gradually came to recognize the driver behind the wheel.

CHAPTER TWO

Amanda Northstar woke a few seconds before her alarm clock was scheduled to beep. She didn't know why she still set it, as her body clock had always preempted the electronic version since she had been eighteen. No doubt being woken up at the crack of dawn, or more often before, by an army drill sergeant banging an empty trashcan had ingrained the instinct into her. Now, twenty-seven years later, it was still as sharp as ever.

She reached out and switched the alarm off before it had the chance to sound. There was no sense risking waking Max up, who was a light sleeper. In seventeen years of raising her son, she had learned most of what there was to know about him. This included things he no doubt wished she didn't, such as the stash of pornography DVDs hidden under the base of his wardrobe, which she had kept quiet about. Better that than marijuana. One of the things Amanda had learned the hard way, through tantrums during his early years to periods of moody sullenness in more recent times, was that Max needed quality sleep, as did most boys his age. If he was allowed that, he was as charming, sweet, and conscientious as she could have wished. If he were denied it, his Jekyll could give way to his Hyde.

Not that she indulged his grouchiness or temper one bit when they did surface. Since his birth, Amanda had mixed a mother's love with a father's authority. In the absence of the real thing, she had no choice. She praised him when he merited it and chastised him when he deserved it. Considering how other young men without fathers had turned out, Amanda liked to think she had done a decent job. In just under a year, she'd know either way when Max flew the nest and, she hoped, headed for college.

She turned over and gazed for a while at the empty side of her bed. Amanda always slept on the left side. It wasn't out of any particular preference, but simply because that was the side she had ended up on when she had started to sleep with Max's father, who shared his son's first name. That was the point of her choosing it, after all. It was to honor a father who would never meet his son and to remind the son that half the union that created him had lived, breathed, and existed beyond pictures on walls and in photo albums. Reflecting that partnership, Amanda had passed her own surname on to

Max. She was an only child and did not wish to see the Northstar name end with her.

She had long come to terms with Max Senior's death and had since dated other men without guilt. Seventeen years was a long time to be alone, and Max hadn't resented it. It had helped that that handful of men had all been kind and considerate, capable of sustaining an intelligent conversation, and enjoyed outdoor pursuits as Amanda did. She was not one to rush into relationships and had carefully vetted them in her own cautious way. But each had ended, some amicably, some less so, and all before things had become too serious or involved. Truth be told, there had been nothing wrong with any of them. The main thing they lacked was beyond their control. They simply weren't Max Sr.

Amanda wasn't one to believe in love at first sight, but she couldn't deny that she and Max's father had sparked in a way she had not experienced before nor since. Within a year of leaving the United States Army, she had returned home to Independence, met Max, and had become engaged to be married. A few months later, she had fallen pregnant with their son. It had been a whirlwind of events compared to a decade of careful routine in the army, transforming from Staff Sergeant Northstar to Amanda, housewife and mother-to-be.

Amanda had been perfectly happy to embrace that future. Unfortunately for all of them, the brain aneurism that had killed Max Sr. in minutes, during one of his high school football coaching sessions, had changed everything. She had started down another path that day. It was one that led to the here and now, where she needed to swing herself out of bed and get ready for another day serving and protecting the good people of Independence County, New York, as their duly elected sheriff.

***

Amanda changed out of her pajamas into shorts, a t-shirt, and running shoes and quietly made her way downstairs and out into the back yard through the rear kitchen entrance. Dawn had only broken a few minutes before, but it was light enough to find the way to her studio. To call it such imbued it with a grandness that was not really warranted, for it was no larger than the average garage. It was big enough to hold the canvasses and other painting equipment she had gathered over the years, as well as a solitary treadmill and a weights bench in the corner. Nevertheless, Amanda had built it with her own hands several years ago. She had designed it so that one full side of the building was comprised of glass and had a fine view of Independence below the ridge her house sat upon.

When the light was right, Amanda would spend time painting the panorama before her, which remained static but far from uninteresting. The colors on display changed with the seasons. The forests beyond the town and adjacent Hudson River would transform from green to orange and gold and then to white. Fall had started, and the trees were beginning to surrender their greenness. Amanda had set up her latest canvass on an easel. The town and river were already painted, but blank white space still awaited the forests to be added.

She had decided to wait until the trees had fully turned. It would take a few weeks more, but she didn't mind. She had always been patient with her art, enjoying the process as much as the end result. Though her friends had always told her she was too modest, Amanda didn't consider herself a skilled artist. Still, even on tour in the army, she had carried a small drawing pad around to sketch scenes of interest. There had been some beauty in Kuwait's flat deserts during the first Gulf War, with even the burning oil wells providing their own chilling but captivating spectacle.

As Amanda entered the studio, painting was not on her mind. She headed for the treadmill as she did every morning and set it at a moderate pace, enough to work up a sweat. She would increase the speed every few minutes until she sprinted and held it for as long as she could before hitting the stop button. After a minute of rest to catch her breath, she would bench press some light dumbbells and call it a morning. Sometimes she would go running through town or hiking in the Catskill Mountains with Max, but she found this morning routine enough to keep her fitness where she wanted it.

However, Amanda was not averse to a little vanity. She considered herself to be in good shape for a woman in her mid-forties. Possessing of a slim build, a decent bust, and flowing dark brown hair, she might not have had the opportunity to show it off in her uniform, but she was happy to maintain her figure, even if just for herself and the occasional lucky guy who had the rare fortune to see her in a dress.

By the time she had finished with the weights, the sun was up, and the studio basked in warm light. She checked her watch. Max would be up soon. Thankfully he had reached an age where he was just as capable of making them breakfast as she was, though she imagined she would always have to remind him not to forget his school books or brush his hair until the day he flew the nest.

Amanda left the studio and headed back to the kitchen. She instantly saw the huge St Bernard ambling around the yard, sticking his nose in various bushes and slobbering over the leaves. He turned his head towards her and bounded up, tail wagging in delight. Amanda scratched the sweet spot behind his ears and smiled, always pleased to see Boomer because it meant her mother was close by.

CHAPTER THREE

Amanda left Boomer to roam the yard and entered her
kitchen through the back door. She was instantly met by
the smell of bacon and accompanying sizzle. Humming
to herself as she poured several spots of pancake batter
into a separate frying pan, was Maggie Northstar, her
silver hair tied back into a bun, her shirt sleeves rolled
up. Amanda spotted Maggie's coat folded atop one of
the breakfast bar stools. She had clearly been for one of
her early morning walks with Boomer, rising at dawn
with an abundance of energy. Like mother, like daughter,
Amanda supposed. Maggie turned around and threw a
cheerful smile.

'Morning, hun. Breakfast is up in five.'

'You know you don't have to do this,' Amanda said
with a phony sigh, secretly glad that she wouldn't have to
rustle something up for Max and could jump straight
into the shower. That said, Amanda had already
scheduled a later breakfast meeting, so she would have to
cram in two helpings with a smile on her face. It looked
like the treadmill would get a second session that
evening.

'Always a pleasure, never a chore,' said Maggie with a dismissive wave of a spatula. Her attention returned to the rapidly browning pancakes.

As Amanda headed for the stairs, Max appeared at the bottom, rubbing the sleep out of his eyes. Tall and lean, he had inherited her body shape, but took after his father in most other ways, from the handsome angular face to the mop of black hair that paid tribute to James Dean when properly styled. He had passed her height last year and seemed to be adding another inch every few months.

'Morning trooper,' she said, ruffling his hair playfully as she climbed the stairs. She knew that the clock was ticking before such displays of affection became embarrassing for him, if they hadn't already. 'Grandma has breakfast on the go.'

'Really?' Max said, instantly perking up as he made his way to the kitchen.

Amanda headed into the bathroom, dumped her sweaty kit into the laundry basket, and grabbed a fresh towel from the linen closet. She turned on the water in the shower cubicle and waited a moment for it to warm up before she stepped in. As the hot spray gently loosened her muscles, she closed her eyes and let her mind drift for a second, visualizing her schedule for the day.

Once she was done with her first breakfast, she would drive into town and commence her second, courtesy of her predecessor as sheriff, Glenn Shepard, her friend and mentor ever since her post-army return to Independence. Despite being heavily pregnant and emotionally scarred, Glenn had seen her potential and, after a suitable amount of time following Max's birth, had recruited her as one of his deputies.

Before retiring to realize his ambition to own a sports-themed bar and grill, Glenn had repeatedly prodded her to consider running to replace him. He had given her purpose and a future during one of her darkest periods and so Amanda ensured that she always made time to see him. This enabled her to remain close to Glenn and occasionally solicit advice about the job, which he was always happy to provide.

After chewing what was surely to be actual as well as conversational fat with Glenn, she would then head over to the sheriff's department building and drink copious amounts of coffee while reviewing paperwork. That was pretty much all the day had to offer, bar a welcome reprieve of visiting the elementary school to give a safety talk to the children now that the evenings would be getting darker earlier.

Such quiet days were both the curse and the blessing of Independence, both the town and the surrounding county. Baghdad-on-the-Hudson it was not. It had allowed Amanda to get by with a tiny department of just herself, two deputies, and an administrator. However, if the budget ever came through for one or two more of each, she wouldn't refuse it.

Amanda finished washing her hair and toweled herself dry. She returned to her bedroom, dried her hair with a hand dryer, and tied it back into a neat bun. She applied some basic makeup and put on her uniform, a sharp outfit of boots, pants, long-sleeve shirt and tie, all black, with a golden sheriff star and name tag pinned either side of her chest. When she left the house, they would be joined by her gun belt, leather jacket, and 'Smokey the Bear'-style stetson hat.

She headed back down to the kitchen, where she found Max sitting at the breakfast bar, tucking into a small stack of pancakes and bacon, both drizzled with syrup. Maggie was pouring him a glass of orange juice. Amanda's mother assuredly knew her way around the kitchen, which was no surprise as it had been hers until only a few years ago.

When Max Sr. had died, and with a baby due imminently, Amanda had moved back into her childhood home, the house having been in the Northstar family since the early 1900s. Her father, Maggie's husband Adam, had died of cancer when Amanda was in her early twenties, and so Maggie had welcomed the company and the chance to help raise her grandson.

It was an arrangement that had worked well. However, following her retirement as a high school history teacher five years previously, Maggie had decided that it was time to give Amanda and Max some space. She had found a small cottage nearby to suit her needs. They had protested, but Maggie's mind was settled. She had always said that there was never any single owner of the Northstar house, just caretakers until the next generation took over. Now it was Amanda's turn to do with it as she wished until it came time to pass it on to Max. That had not stopped Maggie from visiting often, though, as this morning had demonstrated.

Amanda sat next to Max as Maggie laid a fresh plate in front of her. Amanda hadn't realized how hungry she was until the blend of sweet and savory smells hit her nostrils. She eagerly began eating.

'Thanks, Mom, I appreciate it. I'm a little pressed for time this morning,' Amanda said between mouthfuls.

'A busy day on the cards?' enquired Maggie as she sat down to her own plate.

'I arranged to see Glenn on my way to the office, promised that we'd have a coffee to catch up,' replied Amanda, omitting that coffee would likely be joined by more carbohydrates, fat, and protein.

Maggie turned her attention to Max, who had finished his plate and was halfway through his juice.

'And how is school treating you, Max?'

'Well, we're only a few weeks into the new year, so it's a little slow so far, but that won't last for long.'

'Are you signing up for any teams? You've only a year left, and it all looks good for the college applications,' Maggie prodded gently.

Max quickly glanced in Amanda's direction to see if she had any reaction to the question, but she was mopping up the last of the syrup with a folded wedge of pancake on the tip of her fork.

'Eh, I may just carry on with the track team. But it would be nice to try some new things too,' he said, a slight hesitation in his voice.

It did not escape Amanda's ear, and she looked over to him, curious.

'Oh, like what? Academic or athletic?'

'The world's my oyster, Mom,' he said with a wink.

He quickly finished the rest of his juice and glanced over to the wall-mounted clock.

'I gotta get ready, Chelsea'll be pissed if she has to wait for me again.'

'Watch your language, young man,' protested Amanda, unamused as Max hopped off his stool. 'Especially in front of your grandmother.'

'Don't worry about me, kiddo,' said Maggie playfully. 'I heard much worse from your mother's mouth when she was a teenager.'

'Yes,' Amanda acknowledged. 'And I had the two-week groundings to show for it.'

'Better than the wooden spoon on the ass I had when I was short with my mother,' Maggie retorted.

Max looked on at their exchange with amusement.

'I guess sass runs in the Northstar women, huh?'

'You got that right,' said Maggie with a nod. 'Just the same as charm runs through the Northstar men. Not that you need me to tell you that, what with young ladies picking you up at the door.'

'Chelsea's just a friend, Grandma,' Max said, shaking his head.

'That's how they all start out, dear,' replied Maggie with a wry smile as she forked a small piece of pancake into her mouth.

Max sighed and shook his head again, grinning. He headed for the stairs and bounded up.

'I may be home late, depends which teams I try out for,' he called down.

'Okay, just text me,' Amanda replied just loud enough to carry upstairs.

She looked over to Maggie and raised an eyebrow.

'You know if you're going to play Cupid, Valentine's isn't for another five months.'

'Oh, he knows I'm just having fun,' Maggie said with a wave of her hand. 'Besides, he doesn't need my prodding. I wouldn't be surprised if he's having to beat the ladies off with a lacrosse racket.'

'Speaking of which, did you notice how he was a little evasive about the new activities he's thinking of? That wink has always been his quick exit in any conversation.'

'Amanda, he's a young man, with the emphasis on man. He's going to be evasive about most things, especially with his mother. I'm sure you kept a few secrets at that age.'

'More than a few,' acknowledged Amanda sheepishly.

'Well, there we are then. Anyway, you head off and see Glenn. I'll clean up and finish walking Boomer. I'll be at the Historical Society most of the day if you want to stop by.'

Amanda nodded, stood up, kissed Maggie on the cheek, and headed into the hallway. She grabbed her jacket and hat from the hanging hooks near the front door and checked herself over in the mirror. She was ready to take on the day, despite what little promise of a challenge it held. It had all the makings of another quiet shift.

CHAPTER FOUR

Keith Billings parked his SUV on the small gravel parking area and turned the engine off. He stepped out and stretched with a satisfied groan. In his forty years on Earth, he had journeyed to the rainforests of the Amazon, the savannas of Eastern Africa, and the deserts of the American Southwest. Wherever there was fascinating wildlife to film, he had visited.

By comparison, the drive from New York City to the Hudson Valley was regularly underwhelming. Billings was a local and had driven around the region for years before his career took him to more exotic climes. He knew the area like the back of his hand. Though that meant it held little surprise, it also lent him superior knowledge of where to acquire the best footage of the river and the wildlife that inhabited its waters and banks. After leaving his Manhattan apartment before dawn, he had just stopped near such a vantage point.

Billings looked upwards to gauge the light. It was a bright day, but moderate cloud cover meant that the excesses of direct sunlight were diffused enough to make his life a lot easier. He had already spent the past year up and down the Valley, gathering specific footage of the various creatures required for his project. Now all he needed was some basic shots of the river flowing, trees swaying in the breeze, and so on. He could then complete a rough cut and shop it around the nature channels.

He cricked his neck, opened the rear passenger door, and pulled out his equipment bag and tripod. Most people unfamiliar with his craft often expected him to produce a sizable camera like they had on Hollywood film sets. However, in his world, bigger didn't always equal better. He had seen friends produce professional-quality material using just their smartphones, so his shoebox-sized camera was exactly what he needed. More importantly, due to the environments he often found himself in, it was also robust and light.

He closed the door, locked the SUV, and stepped off into the undergrowth, which began as grass and soon gave way to a thicket of bushes and trees. The parking area was meant for visitors to nearby picnic tables overlooking the river, but Billings knew a prime spot off the beaten track where he could work in peace. Though it was only about a hundred yards, the trek through the bushes and low trees with their scratching branches meant it was not a convenient walk, but the pay-off was worth it.

Billings emerged out of the thicket not far from the riverbank and spotted what he had been heading for. It was a collection of various branches, fallen tree trunks, and other river debris built up over time. At first, they had piled up against a part of the bank that jutted out into the river, gradually adding more pieces as they floated down and randomly drifted towards the side. Silt, mud, and rotting biomass had acted as natural mortar over the years. It had bound all the loose debris together into what was, effectively, a short pier that nature had accidentally constructed.

While it was only a few meters long, with the camera perched upon it, it would allow Billings to get closer to the river's surface and point his camera directly upstream rather than from a slightly sideways angle. He had tested it before while taking still photographs and knew the debris pile would take his weight.

Billings stopped and assembled his equipment. He tentatively prodded the pile with his foot to make sure it hadn't loosened since his last visit, but it held firm.

While it was not perfectly flat, there was more than enough surface for his boots to get a grip, and he slowly made his way to the midpoint and set up his camera.

He crouched low and checked the image through the viewfinder, adjusting the angle and settings until he was happy. The wide flowing river dominated the bottom third of the frame. The remainder showed the Saratoga Bridge about two miles upstream, with the Catskill Mountains' misty outline in the very far distance. If he had swung the camera 180 degrees, he would have seen Independence town some two miles away in the opposite direction.

Content, Billings started recording and eased his backside down onto a log that ran along the pile's length. He would often let the camera run for a few minutes to have plenty of footage and long recordings of ambient sounds. He felt his stomach rumble and heard it too. He had skipped breakfast to try and make good time but had wrapped up a bagel to take with him.

He fished it out of his pocket and peeled away the cellophane. He took a bite, paused, then sniffed the remaining three quarters. The cream cheese was off. He had been rushing to leave and so had just smothered it on without checking the use-by date. He sighed and casually tossed the bagel forwards into the water. At least the fish wouldn't be so discerning.

The bagel rested on the surface of the water, not that this was unusual. But the way it rested gradually caught Billings's attention. The bagel simply sat there, unmoving, neither spinning nor drifting off. He carefully rose and leaned forwards. He hadn't noticed it before, hadn't thought to look, what with his attention on the horizon, but there was something just below the waterline, something the bagel rested on, something dark and solid that he couldn't quite make out.

Billings looked around and spotted a large floating branch bobbing up against the edge of the pile. He reached out and grabbed it, and then turned his attention back to the mysterious sub-surface object. He flicked the bagel away with the tip of the branch and then poked it into the water. It instantly touched something firm, but there was a tiny amount of give. Whatever it was had a degree of buoyancy, but was probably stuck or caught on something below.

Billings dunked the branch at various spots until it went deeper than in other areas. He had found the edge of the object. He lowered the branch a couple of feet down and pulled it back against the debris pile, using it as a lever. He grabbed the end with both hands and pulled. After a few seconds of sustained effort, he felt the object give. Now loose, it continued to rise until it broke the surface. Billings leaned in for a closer look and instantly started to feel his stomach knot. It was soaked through and dirty, but with a belt around the waist, it was obviously the back of a long coat. Someone was still wearing it.

CHAPTER FIVE

After leaving home, Amanda had decided to take the social route through Independence town center. It was 'social' because she would invariably be spotted in her patrol cruiser by a range of townspeople. From retired folks walking their dogs to those heading for work, to the owners of the brown-brick boutiques, craft shops, delis, and coffee houses along the clean-swept and tree-lined Main Street, most would wave or nod in her direction, and she would return the gesture.

Even rush-hour in Independence was a leisurely affair during the week, with the stream of tourists often at its height on weekends. They came searching for a taste of quaint, small-town life with its white-picket-fence fantasy that local traders were all too happy to indulge.

Halfway down Main Street, the road ran parallel to the main town square, a two-acre park of green grass crisscrossed by walking paths and enhanced by benches, small fountains, and multi-colored flower beds. At the far end was the town hall, which hosted the mayor's office, the councilors, and the various departments responsible for keeping the town and county running.

To the left of the park, the sheriff's department and fire station buildings stood adjacent to each other. The courthouse and neighboring library were on the right side, with the small-but-proud local museum located on the latter's top floor. It was here that Maggie now spent many of her days as president of the Independence Historical Society. When the volunteer position had become vacant, Amanda had prodded her recently-retired mother to apply for it, not that Maggie had needed much convincing. Only a few months after leaving her classroom, she had thirsted for a new challenge.

Located at the center of the park was a memorial, a polished marble obelisk. At its base, a brass plaque listed the war dead of Independence, from the Revolutionary War to the present day. Amanda remembered visiting the memorial every so often with her father when she was a child, and in recent years with Glenn during their walking patrols. Both men were Vietnam veterans, and she'd seen their attention drift for a few moments when they had spotted a familiar name from that conflict.

Amanda had been too young to quite grasp why such a reaction was stirred in her father. However, she had looked on at Glenn with complete understanding during his moments. Her own memories and experiences of the first Gulf War had given her the necessary perspective. She often found her own mind drifting when she gazed at the roll-call of history's dead, even though she was not intimately familiar with any of the names.

Nevertheless, honoring a sense of history and community was as important to her personally as it was to the town, as befitted a settlement founded in the early 1700s. Even the municipal buildings retained their original colonial feel, despite being repeatedly renovated over the years. Amanda always looked forward to the July 4th fireworks and the fairground atmosphere that the town square played host to, right outside her office window.

She had been daydreaming about the previous year's festivities when her drive had been interrupted with a crackle of static. The call came through over her radio that a body had been found near the picnic spot on Riverside Road, a couple of miles out of town. Wayne Sexton, the sheriff's department administrator, dispatcher, and all-around Mister Fix-It, had told Amanda that one of her deputies, Jake Murrow, had been close by on patrol. He had headed over to the site and was waiting with the man who had found the body.

Amanda had been within a minute of arriving at Glenn's place for her second breakfast, but immediately turned around and headed back through the town center. She pulled out her phone and tapped out [Body Found] in a text message and sent it to Glenn. He would immediately know that breakfast was canceled, just as he himself had missed numerous engagements during his time as sheriff.

Amanda drove down Main Street at a steady pace. There was no reason to rattle the pubic by switching on the sirens and screeching her tires just to reach the body five minutes faster. If Jake was already at the scene, she had every confidence that he was already doing what needed to be done.

Jake had been with her department for almost two years, though she had known of him eight years before that. Back then, he had been a prominent member of the local high school football team, the Independence Rebels, which Max Sr. had coached before dropping dead on the touchline. Though the North East of the United States was not as mad about football as, say,

Texas, the town had a habit of upping its usual level of interest in the Rebels whenever the team was doing well.

During her years as a deputy under Glenn, Amanda had often accompanied him in policing some of the busier games. Despite her mixed feelings about the sport, she had still admired Jake's prowess on the field as a wide receiver. Though Amanda had heard rumors that scouts had been paying attention to Jake and the team quarterback, Rick Norris, for some reason, Jake had elected not to attend college. He had instead signed up with the Marine Corps after graduating. Eight years and several foreign tours later, he had left the Corps and returned to Independence.

For several months she had spotted him propping up bars around town, often nursing the same drink for hours on end, a haunted look in his eyes. Amanda had recognized the same potentially deadly cocktail of a lack of purpose and emotional demons in several of her old comrades. She had even taken a few sips from the glass herself.

She had only recently won the election to take over from Glenn. Most of his staff had also decided that the change in sheriff was a good time to finally make a move to Florida, or devote more time to fishing. She had needed to rebuild, put her own stamp on the department, and approached Jake to ask him to consider applying.

It was seemingly the spur he had needed, and gradually she saw the old spark he had possessed during his football days return. As veterans who had both seen combat, they shared an instinctive understanding. Still, Amanda had not let this influence her assessment of him or cause her to play favorites. Since being deputized, Jake had worked hard and had proven himself capable and intelligent, though he still had a few rough edges. Not unlike the ones she had possessed when Glenn had given her a chance, Amanda thought.

Once she had reached the outskirts of town, Amanda turned onto Riverside Road and sped up, the Hudson River to her left. It was not long until she passed the proposed site for a new suburban development, not that anyone would have known it. The only indicator was a large, slightly worn sign erected in front of acres of roadside scrub and trees. It displayed faded concept art for what looked like an idealized slice of the American property dream. The washed-out look was perhaps an apt metaphor for how parts of the country had seen that dream gradually fade away.

The sign's age also hinted at how long the project had been gestating. It was trapped in planning committee hell as a political tug of war took place between conservationist and development-minded interest groups and councilors. Amanda was torn on the issue. She was keen to see Independence's future made more secure through growth, but was wary of surrendering it to rolling hills of identical, soulless housing. Some things were best left to the politicians to work out.

Amanda carried on down Riverside Road and reached the picnic area parking space five minutes later. She instantly spotted Jake's patrol car parked next to an SUV, pulled up next to her car's twin, and stepped out. She heard some quiet conversation from the other side of the SUV and walked towards it.

She passed the rear and saw Jake standing near the front passenger door. Despite a few tiny shrapnel scars on his brow, he still retained a clean-shaven youthful look. It was complemented by a neatly cut head of mousy brown hair and a cheery smile he would deploy when in the right mood. He was certainly more physically imposing than he had been during his high school days. He had height back then, but after years in the Marines, he had since added lean, well-sculpted muscle, which he had maintained well.

Amanda saw that Jake was talking with a man who sat in the passenger seat sideways, his legs hanging out. In both hands, he nursed what looked like a cup that unscrewed from the top of a thermos flask, half-filled with coffee. The man looked a little pale and was staring into space, only semi-engaged in the conversation with Jake. This was obviously the poor soul who had found the body. Jake looked up.

'Ah, Amanda. This is Mr. Keith Billings. He called in the body about thirty minutes ago. Mr. Billings, this is the sheriff, Amanda Northstar.'

Billings glanced over and nodded in acknowledgment. Amanda stepped over but was careful to leave some space between them. She didn't want Billings to feel like she and Jake were crowding him, physically or psychologically.

'Mr. Billings, I'm sure it's been a difficult experience, but if I could just ask you to repeat to me what you've told Deputy Murrow, I'd appreciate it.'

'Well, there's not much to it, really,' said Billings with a sigh. 'I'm up here from Manhattan making a wildlife documentary. I knew there was a great spot just by the river over there where I could set up my camera. Over the years, driftwood has just piled up depending on how the river flows, and that's where I found the body. She must have drifted in and snagged on something underneath the waterline.'

'She?' Amanda asked.

'Yeah, it's definitely a woman. I didn't know at the time it was a body, but as soon as I freed it, it floated right up, and I could tell it was a lady. I don't know if I should have, but I dragged her onto the bank. I didn't want to risk her floating away or something. Then I grabbed my equipment and came back here to make the call. When your man showed up, I took him to the body right away. We'd just returned when you drove up. I didn't really want to wait around on the bank, you know? The only dead bodies I tend to see are the wildlife being eaten by lions or wolves.'

Amanda faked a smile to reassure Billings's nerves and nodded.

'Thank you, Mr. Billings, that's all really useful. Would you mind waiting here while we go take a look?'

Billings nodded and took a sip of coffee from his flask cup. Amanda beckoned to Jake to follow her back to her car. She opened the trunk and pulled out two pairs of white rubber gloves from the equipment box she kept in there. She tossed one pair to Jake as she pulled on her own.

'How's it look?' she asked.

'His story seems to check out,' replied Jake as he stretched his gloves out and inserted his fingers. 'Told you the same as he told me, no deviations. He took me through his actions, pointed out the branch he'd used to dislodge the body, and where he pulled her onto the bank.'

'So it's definitely a woman?'

'From what I could see. I was about to go in for a closer look, but Billings looked like he was about to pop, so I thought it best to bring him back and settle him down. While he was pouring himself a coffee, I called Ruth Chalmers, then you showed up a minute later.'

Amanda nodded. Ruth Chalmers was the county medical examiner and had displayed a dogged efficiency for as long as Amanda had known her. Whatever the circumstances behind the body appearing, Ruth would quickly provide useful information. Amanda retrieved some plastic sheeting and a digital camera from the trunk, handed Jake the latter, and closed the lid.

'You remember the way?'

'Yep,' he nodded. 'We have to crawl through a little jungle, but it's not too far.'

'Lead on,' said Amanda with a twirl of her hand.

She followed Jake into the undergrowth and then into a mass of scratching, tangled branches. They quickly emerged out of the thicket and found themselves on the river bank. They pivoted left, and after a few dozen yards, Amanda clearly saw the substantial pile of driftwood that jutted out into the water.

Not far from that was a woman's body, the head closer to the tree line and the feet a few inches away from the water. Despite their drenched state, the cashmere coat and skinny jeans she wore suggested the sex, and the long hair and slender frame sealed the deal. What immediately stood out to Amanda was that the right foot was missing its shoe.

She and Jake advanced cautiously. He led a few steps in front. Every few seconds, he would pause and snap away on the camera. He then circled the body and repeated the procedure. Eventually, he was satisfied he had captured all the relevant angles and nodded to Amanda.

She laid out one of the plastic sheets to the side of the body so that when she pulled it over, its back would rest on the sheet. She looked up at Jake, who was standing by with the camera.

'Ready?'

Jake nodded. Amanda grabbed the right side of the body and heaved it from being face down to flat on its back. Amanda stood up with a sharp intake of breath. Jake lowered the camera as if he needed to make sure the digital eye he looked through wasn't playing a trick on his real ones.

'It's Judy Sterling,' Amanda said.

Her skin may have been pale and slightly wrinkled after being submerged in the Hudson's cool waters, but Amanda definitely recognized the face, having seen Judy around Independence for years.

'I thought I recognized her,' said Jake.

'As well you should,' replied Amanda. 'She's been a county councilor for seven years.'

Jake shook his head.

'I don't mean it that way. About two weeks ago, I responded to a domestic disturbance call. It was getting late, and the neighbors could hear a pretty loud argument going on. When I knocked on the door, a guy answered, but I saw Judy here standing in the hallway behind him. She looked like she'd been crying, but I couldn't see any signs of violence against her.'

Amanda considered Jake's words for a moment.

'What did the guy look like?' she asked.

Jake pursed his lips.

'About six feet, mid-forties, thinning hair, glasses. He looked like he was stacked in his prime but had eaten about half a million cheeseburgers since.'

'That'll be her husband, Ray Sterling,' Amanda said, nodding. 'He's a lawyer, often represents some of the richer kids we bust for reckless driving or possession. Any idea what they were arguing about?'

'No,' replied Jake, shaking his head. 'He just said it was a private matter and that they apologized for disturbing anyone. After that, it was quiet, with no more complaints.'

'I'll need to see Ray to inform him, ask him to make a formal identification,' said Amanda. 'Couples fight. It might not mean anything, but still, it's something to think about.'

'So, what are we thinking?' prodded Jake as he recommenced taking photos.

Amanda crouched down and leaned in for a closer look.

'I doubt it was a car accident. If it was, she would have sunk to the bottom of the river along with her vehicle. If she'd been thrown clear, there would be some physical sign, either traumatic or something small, like blood or fragments of glass, and I don't see anything obvious.'

Jake finished taking snaps and crouched down opposite Amanda.

'So she could have either jumped or fallen. Intentional or accidental.'

'Maybe,' mumbled Amanda.

'You think door number three? Pushed?' asked Jake, his eyebrow raised.

'All three doors could be viable until we get the autopsy results,' replied Amanda.

'We have a missing shoe,' said Jake as he pointed to the exposed wet and muddied sock on Judy Sterling's right foot.

'It could have come off in the river,' suggested Amanda. She tugged at the left shoe but found it firmly secured. 'That said, this one isn't loose enough to just slip off, even if she was knocked around under the water.'

Amanda proceeded to check what easy-to-reach areas she could, from Judy's wrists to her scalp, by way of her midriff, throat, and neck. No traumatic injuries stood out, no bullet holes, stab wounds, cuts, or signs of blunt force trauma. However, two things caught her attention.

First, the rings around Judy's eyes were unusually dark. Amanda had had enough continuous late nights in her life to know that raccoon eyes were the inevitable cost, but these struck her as excessive. Secondly, there were small patches of dark purplish-red discolorations just behind and below each of Judy's ears. However, their exact distributions didn't indicate a blow to the head, unless from some unlikely two-pronged instrument struck with uncanny precision.

After a moment of thought, Amanda checked Judy's left hand and noticed a pale band of skin where her wedding ring should have been. She gently patted down Judy's body and checked her coat pockets, finding nothing.

'No wedding ring, purse, phone, keys. They may have fallen out in the river, may have been taken, though I don't see any injuries that indicate assault.'

Jake pointed towards Judy's fingernails.

'She's got something under her nails. Scratched an attacker fighting them off, maybe?'

Amanda gently picked up Judy's right hand and examined her fingernails. Underneath them was a blackish-brown substance, but it was hard to guess what it could be. It was the same for the nails of her left hand.

'It doesn't look like blood, but let's wait and see what Ruth comes up with.'

Amanda's radio crackled, and she gently lowered Judy's hand.

'Come in, Amanda, over.'

Amanda immediately recognized the voice of her other deputy, Casey Norris. She stood, unclipped the radio from her belt, and brought it up to her mouth.

'Amanda here. G o on Casey, over.'

'I'm at the Saratoga Bridge and... well, I think you'd better get over here.'

CHAPTER SIX

Amanda left Jake to watch over Judy Sterling's body until Ruth Chalmers arrived at the scene and made her way back through the thicket to her patrol car. She found Billings still staring into space, his cup now emptied of coffee. She handed him her card and told him he was free to go, but that if he remembered anything else of relevance to get in touch.

She then hopped into her car and drove back out onto Riverside Road, continuing in the northerly direction she had been heading in before reaching the picnic parking ground. This time she drove with a greater sense of urgency and applied more pressure on the accelerator.

Casey had followed up her opening radio comment by describing the scene she found herself at, highlighting a seemingly abandoned vehicle left unlocked. Casey had heard about the discovery of a body by the river over her radio. With the Saratoga Bridge only two miles upstream from where Judy Sterling had washed up, she had reasoned that it could somehow be connected.

Amanda had agreed and had asked Casey to preserve the scene. Five minutes after pulling out of the picnic area parking ground, Amanda parked up next to Casey's patrol vehicle on the western side of the bridge, a dozen yards from the abandoned car, a ruby-red Lexus.

She got out and approached Casey, who was leaning against the side of her car, waiting. The clouds had thinned, and the sun had become stronger, and so Casey wore a pair of shades to shield her eyes. A stiff breeze still blew, and so, like Amanda, she had retained her jacket over her standard deputy's uniform. It clung to the lean, athletic figure that befitted a champion cheerleader, even if Casey had hung up the pompoms almost a decade previously. Her hat covered her light blonde hair, which had been tied back into a short ponytail.

Her natural good looks, athleticism, and cheerleader history would have perhaps given any casual observer the notion of dismissing Casey as a typical bubblegum blonde. Her cheerful, upbeat personality also risked her being regarded as vacuous. Still, even if Casey could be a little naïve at times, Amanda knew better. Behind the looks and sunny disposition, Casey Norris possessed a keen analytical mind.

In high school, Casey had been head of the cheerleader squad but had also maintained a healthy grade-point average, despite a difficult home life. She had scored well enough in her SATs to attend many reputable colleges around the country.

As it was, she had been in a relationship with Rick Norris, the star quarterback of the Rebels football team at the same time Jake had been playing. The quarterback-cheerleader partnership may have been a cliché in-keeping with high school's established social norms, but their relationship had been genuine. So, she had followed him to the same college where he had been offered a football scholarship. The same scholarship had been withdrawn three years later after Rick's lower right leg had been snapped in two by a horrendous tackle.

Never the most academically gifted in the first place, Rick had quit college and returned to Independence, eventually finding work in the lumber mill. By this time, he and Casey had become engaged. Though she had been keen to finish her degree in criminology, a mixture of emotional pressure on his part and misplaced guilt on hers saw her join him not long after his return.

They eventually married, and for several years she had managed to find work as an assistant librarian at the Independence town library. There, she continued to read and expand her mind as best she could, dreaming of a wider world her narrowed circumstances prohibited her from experiencing.

It had been at the library that Casey had met Maggie Northstar, who based herself at the town museum on the building's top floor. They had formed a fast friendship over numerous coffees. Amanda had first met Casey when she had visited her mother one cold December lunchtime almost two years previously, bearing a flask of clam chowder and a freshly baked baguette.

Maggie had invited Casey to literally break bread with them. As the trio chatted, Amanda was struck by how fascinated Casey was with law enforcement. It was to be the first of many such encounters. Amanda had quickly come to appreciate the scale of Casey's general knowledge, everything from drug trafficking to cybercrime, built up over several years of textbook consumption and internet research.

When the last of Glenn's deputies had retired, Amanda had decided to roll the dice and ask Casey if she would be interested in the position. Jake had already started some months before, and Amanda could tell he would make for a reliable right-hand man in the field. However, she also recognized that she needed someone who was research savvy, who could eagerly track down facts and spot details. The young woman seemed like an encouraging prospect, someone who could flourish if given a chance to realize such unfulfilled potential.

Casey had been flattered at the offer and clearly excited, though was unsure how her husband would react. Amanda had encountered Rick Norris numerous times since his fall from grace. She had often been called upon to help break up bar fights or petty squabbles he had instigated thanks to a potent mixture of alcohol, ego, and self-loathing.

In short, Amanda regarded Rick Norris as a first-class asshole, with honors. He was someone who carried the bitterness of having once been the king of the castle, but who found the only thing he lorded over now was a molehill. However, it wasn't her place to speak of Rick that way. If Casey had remained with him, then at least it confirmed to Amanda that his wife possessed some sense of loyalty and patience.

Surprisingly Rick had enthusiastically agreed to the proposition. However, Amanda thought it more likely that Casey's increased pay-packet had swung him, more than any warm-hearted support for his wife satisfying her aspirations. Upon finding out that Casey would be joining their small team, Jake had initially seemed unsure, which surprised Amanda.

She knew they had been close friends when he had been on the football team, and Casey had cheered them on. After a short time, Jake had warmed to the idea, and Amanda thought nothing more of it. That had been almost a year and a half ago. As Amanda approached Casey in her uniform, she was reminded of how far the young woman had come in such a short time.

'So what do we have?' asked Amanda as she reached Casey, who pulled off her shades, exposing crystal-blue eyes.

'I was just finishing my shift when I heard from Wayne on the radio that you and Jake were with a body washed up downriver. Then I was crossing the bridge to head home when I spotted this vehicle. Now I know there's a walking trail right by here, so nothing unusual in a parked car, but I thought I'd check it anyway. Come see.'

Casey nodded towards the abandoned car, and the pair walked towards it. Taking the time to study it, Amanda realized that she recognized the vehicle, having seen Judy Sterling drive off in something similar after numerous council meetings and public engagements. Based on that observation alone, the odds were increasingly stacked in favor of a connection between the car and Judy's body. Still, Amanda knew Casey wouldn't have recommended she drive out to the scene simply based on a hunch like that. They stopped with Casey beside the driver's door. She pulled on the handle and opened it.

'Maybe you go walking and forget to lock your door. Sure. But leaving your keys in the ignition?'

Casey shook her head and nodded down to the set of keys dangling down just behind the wheel.

'Did you find anything else?' asked Amanda.

'Sure did,' replied Casey.

She leaned inside and opened the glove compartment. Inside was a purse, phone, and an envelope with the words *Jason and Raymond* written neatly on the front. All three items had been carefully arranged, not merely tossed in as with most glove compartment contents. The find confirmed it in Amanda's mind.

'Soon as I saw them, I got onto the radio to you,' said Casey. 'Who'd you find anyhow?'

'Judy Sterling,' answered Amanda. 'Not official yet, but I know it's her.'

Casey raised a surprised eyebrow.

'The councilor? Jesus. Why would she want to go and do such a thing? She always seemed so happy whenever I saw her around town.'

'You never know what goes through people's minds sometimes,' said Amanda as she reached in and gently retrieved the envelope. 'Maybe this will tell us.'

She opened the envelope and drew out the folded sheet of paper, a small one of high quality, clearly used for writing special letters. At the bottom of the envelope, she saw a ring, likely Judy's absent wedding band. Between that and the intact phone and purse, robbery could be ruled out, though the note would have done that by itself.

My dearest Jason and Raymond,

I know this must be a difficult time for you both. I know you may never understand what I have done. You may both hate me for it, and that's fine. I'm not sure that I fully understand it myself, but all I know is that for the longest time, I have felt trapped. Trapped by my job, trapped by my life, and trapped by the way I feel. It's no one's fault. It's just how it is. I can't remember the last time I was truly happy, and that's just no way to live. I was too weak to seek help when it might have made a difference, but it's too late now. So with the strength I had left, I made a choice to help myself in the only way that was left to me, by freeing myself from my traps. I hope with time that you can both forgive me.

All my love forever, Judy

The text was written in clear and flowing handwriting, with Judy's name signed at the end. Amanda finished reading and looked behind her shoulder to find Casey mouthing the words silently to herself. She frowned, saddened.

'That poor woman. I guess having the car, the house, and the money isn't worth anything if you feel like that every day.'

Amanda said nothing and simply nodded. She refolded the paper and slid it tidily back into the envelope with the ring. She turned to Casey, stared past her a moment, and then walked towards the bridge. She kept a swift pace and eventually stopped at the halfway point on the bridge walkway, Casey quietly following a few paces behind.

Amanda peered over the walkway barrier and down towards the flowing Hudson. It was a drop of a couple of hundred feet at least. Death would not have been absolutely certain, but still more than likely.

'You think she jumped here?' asked Casey.

'A short walk from her car, then a long drop into the river,' nodded Amanda. 'It would make sense to do it here. No point complicating things if you're determined.'

Amanda stepped away and started back towards Judy's car. She looked at Casey as they walked.

'Give Jethro a call and get his tow truck out here. Take the car to the impound lot, but try to be discreet. I don't want anyone spotting that it's Judy's and setting the rumor machine off. We'll keep a hold of it for a few days until we're sure everything's been worked through.'

'It looks like a clear suicide to me, Amanda,' said Casey, slightly puzzled that anything actually remained to be worked through.

'You're probably right,' Amanda conceded. 'But something feels a little off. I can't say why, just a gut feeling.'

When they reached the car, Amanda leaned in, retrieved Judy's purse and phone, and handed them to Casey.

'Before you head home, bag these up and secure them at the office. They may be worth looking at, but even if they're not, I'd still rather keep them out of Jethro's line of sight. Loose change tends to magically vanish in some of the vehicles he tows.'

Casey nodded.

'What are you going to do now?' she asked.

Amanda sighed.

'Someone has to deliver her final letter.'

CHAPTER SEVEN

Amanda left Casey and headed back into town. She took out her phone and dialed the number for Raymond Sterling's office. After a few rings, his receptionist answered and said that Ray had not come in and had decided to work from home. Amanda thanked the receptionist and hung up. She hadn't needed to ask where Ray lived.

During her campaign for sheriff, Amanda had canvassed enough homes around Independence to know where most of the county's more prominent citizens lived. Those she hadn't met had invited her around for coffee or dinner soon enough after winning the election. Securing power, influence, or a position of responsibility often acted as a social lubricant, regardless of the prior status of the newly crowned. Amanda had been no different. The plucky, attractive deputy, so often seen in peripheral vision when accompanying Glenn Shepard at public events in years past, was now sheriff, placed at the front of the stage.

Amanda drove to the north-west of the town, which had acquired the nickname of The Hamptons on account of the expensive homes that occupied the area, with well-tended gardens and luxury cars in their driveways, each separated by high hedgerows. To say that the houses of Independence's great and good were palatial would have been stretching the truth, but they were all grand and finely built. Most of them were decades old, sturdy and ornate, painted white or other inoffensive, conformist colors.

Amanda soon spotted the entrance to the Sterling property's driveway, turned in, and gently pulled to a stop behind Ray's black Lexus. Its red twin, Judy's car, would shortly be on its way to the impound lot, while its owner, Judy herself, would likely now be en route to Ruth Chalmers's examination table at the Independence Community Hospital morgue. A macabre race to their respective holding areas.

Amanda got out of the car, adjusted her hat, and approached the front door, stepping up onto the porch. There were a couple of fine wooden rocking chairs to her left, no doubt handcrafted at great expense, positioned next to each another. Next to the nearest chair rested a small ashtray full of bent, extinguished cigarette butts.

Amanda had met people without a worry in the world who still chain-smoked, but it had been her general observation that tearing through at least one pack of cigarettes over several hours was not the behavior of a calm soul. Amanda suspected that the ashtray had been filled throughout the previous night, as she doubted that anything so unsightly would simply be left around for more than a day, cheapening the carefully maintained visage. Not in The Hamptons.

In her mind's eye, Amanda saw Ray Sterling, his shirt sleeves rolled up, his tie loosened at the collar, rocking back and forth on the chair, sweating as he extinguished one cigarette and lit up another, his eyes trained on the entrance to the driveway, waiting in the dark. But waiting for what? His wife to return and end his growing worry as to her whereabouts, or for a sheriff's cruiser to pull up and deliver grim news?

If the first, then he was a poor widower, unaware of his wife's anguish, or at least complacent about it, living in the hope that she would somehow fix herself. If the second option, then why would Ray expect the worst? Had another screaming row, similar to what Jake had interrupted a few weeks prior, finally tipped the scales and sent Judy on a path that led to the Saratoga Bridge and the dark waters below? Had Ray suspected the worst had happened?

There were many questions, most of them speculative. Amanda recognized that each could spin off into several others, constructing a web of conspiracy as intricate as any spider's and just as delicate, easily pulled apart. Nevertheless, it was her nature to consider things from every angle, especially when death was involved. She did not dismiss such questions from her thoughts but mentally shelved them. They would either be brought back down for further consideration or left to harmlessly gather dust.

Either way, she instinctively felt that Ray Sterling had known his wife had been missing throughout the night. He had not gone in to work due to tiredness or a willingness to hold out a little longer in case Judy stepped through the front door.

Amanda rang the doorbell and waited. Whatever truth lay behind Judy's actions, a family was about to find out that a loved one was gone, leaving a gap that could never be filled. That alone merited sympathy. Amanda hated the duty of informing relatives, but it came with the job. She had done it several times since her election, and many times before that with Glenn. Most incidents were due to accidents, some down to foul play. Each and every time, she would have a small knot in the pit of her stomach.

It was not only because of the nature of the task itself but also because it always reminded Amanda of when she had opened her own front door seventeen years ago. She had found a saddened Glenn standing there, weighing up how best to break the news that her fiancé had dropped dead on the football field. Not that Glenn had needed to say anything. There were only a few reasons why a cop with a sympathetic expression turned up at your door, and none of them were good. As Amanda heard the lock turning on the other side of Ray Sterling's door, she knew he would be having exactly the same thought.

Sure enough, when Ray caught sight of Amanda standing in his doorway, her uniform instantly did the talking, despite her attempts at a poker face. Ray's initially welcoming smile dropped. He took a step back, as if putting some physical distance between himself and Amanda would somehow dampen the news to come.

'Morning Ray,' Amanda said, raising a slight smile.

'Sheriff,' replied Ray flatly, swallowing hard.

'I wonder if I might come in a moment?' asked Amanda gently, though it wasn't really a request but a statement of intent dressed up as one.

Ray nodded and opened the door fully, stepping aside to allow Amanda through. She removed her hat and walked into the hall, where directly in front of her a grand polished wooden staircase led to the house's upper levels. To her left was the dining room, with its long, thick glass table and black wooden chairs. To her right was the main sitting room, a combination of cream rugs and white leather sofas and armchairs, a huge high-definition television fixed to the wall.

Everything about the decor of the house screamed new and clean, sterile even. It was a stark contrast to Amanda's own home, with her artwork hanging on the walls, small antiques resting on shelves and side tables, and hand-made quilts thrown over the cracked leather of her own furniture, kept not for their looks but because they were still comfortable.

Ray closed the door and turned to Amanda, though his eyes didn't quite meet her own, focusing just off hers. Sweat was already beginning to bead on his balding head and brow, and patches were starting to spread under the arms and back of his shirt, which was pulled tight over his still considerable frame. Ray had put on the pounds since his days as a high school athlete, but a solid musculature still remained underneath.

'Would you like something to drink, Sheriff? Coffee, water?' he asked, nervously.

'No thanks, I'm fine,' said Amanda, with a shake of her head.

It was a question she was regularly asked in these situations, but she always declined. She knew that people were just being polite. What they really wanted was to be told the news and told it now. She nodded towards the sitting area.

'Let's sit down for a minute Ray. I'm afraid I have some bad news.'

Ray dropped his gaze towards the floor and slowly walked into the lounge, where he eased himself onto one of the sofas. Amanda sat on an armchair opposite. She placed her hat upon a nearby side table and leaned forward slightly. Ray stared at her, his fingertips pressed against each other into a pyramid shape beneath his nose.

'It's about Judy, isn't it? Something's happened.'

'I'm afraid so, Ray. I'm sorry to have to tell you this, but her body was found on the river bank a couple of hours ago.'

Ray closed his eyes and raised his hands to cover his face.

'Oh, Jesus. Sweet Jesus. What happened?'

'At the moment, it looks like she took her own life. She's currently with the medical examiner, so we should have a report by tomorrow. But that's the way it looks. She left this in her car by the Saratoga Bridge. That's where we think she jumped.'

Amanda reached into her jacket pocket and fished out the envelope that contained Judy's letter and wedding ring. She passed it to Ray and waited patiently for a few minutes while he slowly read what Judy had written. His facial expression morphed from pained to confused, showing hints of anger as he progressed through the text. Eventually, he folded the letter and placed it on the coffee table in front of him.

'Could I just confirm that it's her handwriting?' asked Amanda gently.

Ray nodded absently, then tipped the wedding ring out of the envelope into the palm of his hand and stared blankly at it.

'I'm sorry to have to ask,' Amanda prodded. 'But did anything happen recently that might have caused Judy to do what she did?'

'You mean our fighting, don't you?' asked Ray as he placed the ring next to the letter.

Amanda was about to respond when Ray raised his hand.

'It's okay. Remember, I've been a lawyer for some time, I know how these things work. I'm sure as soon as you recognized her, that deputy of yours told you he'd been here recently. It was nothing, just a usual lovers tiff, but I appreciate why you'd bring it up given the circumstances. But it wasn't the first argument we'd had, and it wasn't the last. It was just the loudest.'

'She seemed to be a very troubled woman. Was she seeing someone, taking anything for it?' Amanda asked.

'A shrink and pills?' said Ray, an eyebrow raised. He shook his head. 'No, nothing like that. Not that I knew anyway. Our marriage had issues, Sheriff, I won't lie about that, but she never struck me as someone with mental health problems. And if she had them, then she was a pro at keeping them hidden.'

Ray stood up and walked over to the corner of the room, his hands in his pockets.

'Even when we fought, whoever walked out first always came back after letting off steam. I knew something was wrong when she didn't come home last night. Seeing you in the doorway just now confirmed it.'

He stood staring at what seemed to be a shrine erected in honor of the Sterling men's sporting achievements. Above a collection of polished trophies and medals that rested on a shelf, hung slightly faded color photographs of Ray in his prime as a high school athlete. Next to them in crisper, higher definition were images of a young man in similar action poses. Bridging the two sets was a single large framed portrait of Judy and Ray standing next to the young man in his football jersey, smiles all round.

'This is going to crush Jason,' said Ray, absently.

Amanda stood and walked over to join him. She scanned the images of the young man. He was tall and handsome, with short cut brown hair, dark eyes, and a charming smile, a college football recruiter's dream made real.

She worked her way up from the lowest photo to the highest. Each one was taken in consecutive years, so that the most recent was from the previous football season. A space above it indicated that a defining image from the season just about to begin would soon join the others, the final one before Jason presumably left for college.

In all the photos, Jason was tall and muscular. Still, Amanda noticed a distinct difference in the one taken of him with his parents. He seemed bulkier all round, even more so than before. Someone had undoubtedly been pumping serious iron. She nodded towards the family portrait.

'Do you mind if I ask when this was taken, Ray?'

'About a month ago, give or take. It was the last family photo we had done. Look at her, Sheriff,' said Ray as he pointed at Judy, beaming proudly, her hands resting on Jason's shoulders. 'Does that look like a woman in deep pain and despair? Doesn't make any sense, none at all. And to do it just as Jason's senior year starts. He's got college scouts onto him, you know? What's this going to do for his concentration? Poor kid's been at the gym all through the summer, sometimes twice a day. And now he has this crap to deal with.'

Amanda said nothing. Ray seemed almost to be talking to himself as much as to her. She could sense that anger was mixed in with grief, and she wasn't sure which would bubble up and erupt first once reality had sunk in. She certainly hadn't expected Ray to burst into tears in front of her. He simply wasn't that kind of man. His grieving process would have to be his own. If diverting his own personal hurt into concern for his son's well-being suited him at present, then that was his choice.

People grieved in different ways, some not at all, depending on how they felt about the deceased. Amanda could tell that Ray felt betrayed more than anything. Considering his genuine surprise at seeing her on his doorstep, Amanda suspected Ray had not known about Judy's death until a few minutes previously, whatever his worries throughout the night. If he had known, then he was as good an actor as he claimed Judy had been in concealing her depression from him.

'I'm sorry Ray, I know this is a lot to deal with, but I'm going to have to ask you to come down to the hospital in a little while and make a formal identification. We know it's her, but procedure has to be followed.'

'I understand,' he said with a nod. 'When?'

'Judy should be there right now. We'll give it an hour or so for Dr. Chalmers to make her ready, then we'll go down. What do you want to do about Jason?'

'I don't want him to know just yet,' said Ray immediately. 'He's got practice this afternoon. I just want him to have one last session without the stress or the pain. Let him be carefree a little longer.'

'I understand,' said Amanda. 'I'm going to go wait outside a while, give you some time. I'll knock when we're ready to go.'

'Thank you, Sheriff, that would be good,' replied Ray, though he didn't look at her as he spoke.

Ray concentrated on the images of sporting prowess on the wall, just as a man on a slowly sinking ship would focus on an island ahead of him, prioritizing the positive thoughts of being anywhere else except the dire situation he found himself in.

Amanda retrieved her hat, quietly made her way back outside, and gently pulled the front door behind her. She left it open an inch to allow her back inside when she needed to collect Ray. Amanda sat on the porch steps, took out her phone, and sent a text to Max, telling him to meet her at Glenn's place after school. She could catch up with her old mentor and treat her son to a stack of Glenn's famous ribs at the same time. Frankly, Max could order whatever he wanted. She just didn't want to be alone in the house come evening.

Chapter Eight

Max finished clipping in the strap of his football helmet and gave it a brief shake to make sure it was on securely, but not too tight. The fit wasn't perfect, but acceptable. Truth be told, most of his kit wasn't great, comprised as it was of second-hand leftovers from the equipment locker, but then he hadn't expected much just for a tryout session. In fact, he had been surprised that the team was even offering tryouts so close to the start of the season. However, he'd heard that several players had already been injured on the practice field. They needed more bodies, for appearances if nothing else.

Max had hesitated to join in at the start of the school year, knowing his mother would be less than happy. He didn't feel comfortable not telling her about his plans at breakfast that morning. He hadn't technically lied but had certainly omitted the truth, which was pretty much the same thing according to her moral code. But he'd known what kind of reaction he would have received, and it wouldn't have featured hugs and warm words of support.

He couldn't blame his mother. It wasn't so much the sport that she had an issue with, though, like most parents, she would be less than keen to see her child pummeled in various acrobatic ways. Instead, it was the negative emotional connection she had, not just to the game but to the very field that Max stepped onto as he walked out of the locker room.

He'd have been lying if he had said he didn't feel a slight shiver every time he approached the spot where his father had died. But that was why Max had finally decided to take the plunge and try for a place on the team. What was a negative memory for his mother was his primary emotional connection to his father, a man he only knew from pictures and diary entries. Max had always enjoyed football as a spectator. While he had no illusions about how hard actually playing would be, if he could feel the way his father had out on the field, even fleetingly, it was worth taking a few hits.

But first, he had to make the team, which was not a foregone conclusion and another reason he had decided to keep his mother in the dark. If he failed, she would be none the wiser. He had felt regret when he believed the final tryouts had passed him by and so was determined to seize the opportunity now presented to him.

He certainly wasn't going to be blocking or forcing his way past some of the big guys, not with his tall, lean frame. But speed was his friend, honed during several years on the running track. If he could marry that up with making some decent catches, then he stood a reasonable chance of making the cut, which was all he hoped for at this stage.

He checked his watch. The school day had ended, and a few minutes remained until the official start of practice. Players had already started drifting onto the field, chatting and laughing. It was easy to spot others like him, newbies, standing tentatively on the sidelines, waiting for direction.

Max glanced over to the stands and saw his friend Chelsea Bannerman sitting on the first row. She eyed him up in his kit with a mixture of bemusement and her usual cool stoicism. Max had been friends with Chelsea since their days at elementary school. While romantic feelings had come and gone with the ebb and flow of their teenage hormones, their relationship had remained platonic. In many ways, they were opposites, with Max's optimistic view on life contrasting with Chelsea's more cynical interpretation. Still, as a result, they complemented and balanced each other out.

Max also had a happy-go-lucky approach to life, keenly aware that you had to make things happen for yourself, but that it was useless trying to conform to some kind of masterplan, a roadmap laid out for the coming years. The twists and turns of his mother's life had taught him that lesson well enough.

Chelsea, on the other hand, had a plan. It was to leave Independence as soon as graduation and financial circumstances allowed, head to a liberal arts college as far away as feasible, and study something she deemed as non-blue collar as possible.

It seemed to Max that Chelsea was determined to avoid repeating the life pattern of the women in her family, whether it was her mother or her sister, Casey Norris. In other words, dropping out of college, staying in Independence, and marrying the wrong man. It amused Max that, barring their age gaps, all three women looked strikingly similar to each other and that Chelsea perhaps represented 'third time lucky'.

In contrast to her mother and sister, Chelsea had never taken the girly-girl route. She retained her femininity but did not emphasize it, keeping her hair cut short or to neck-length at maximum, her makeup light, and her legs covered by dark jeans. Currently accompanying those jeans was a white short-sleeved shirt with the logo for Glenn Shepard's bar and grill sewn onto the left breast.

'Heading to work?' asked Max as he walked over to meet her, his head tilted upwards towards her elevated position on the stand.

She looked down upon him from her seat.

'In a minute. Just thought I'd be supportive. Though you realize you're going to get your ass handed to you, gift-wrapped in a blood-stained bow, right?'

'Thanks,' he replied with a raised eyebrow. 'Supportive, as you said.'

'You know I'm kidding,' Chelsea said, grinning. 'Only not really. These guys don't hold back. More fool them and their joints in twenty years.'

'I'm sure it'll hurt. But only if they catch me,' said Max with a wink.

Chelsea rolled her eyes.

'What are you trying out for anyway? And keep it simple, you know I know nothing about this sport.'

'It's called the wide receiver. Basically, I run as fast as I can, avoid the opposition, try and catch the ball the quarterback throws, then haul ass to the end zone to score.'

'Sounds simple enough.'

'Yeah, everything does on paper.'

Max saw Chelsea's attention focus on the field and turned to see the head coach, Henry Booth, walk out, flanked by his leading players CJ Townsend and Jason Sterling. Booth was a tall, reedy man with greying hair and thick-rimmed glasses. His appearance befitted a mild-mannered librarian rather than a high school football coach. However, those who had been unfortunate enough to feel his wrath at practices or Friday night games could testify that appearances could be deceiving.

Carter Townsend Junior, or CJ as he was commonly known, was the team quarterback and de facto leader. A handsome face, strong jawline, and shiny hair made him a player straight out of central casting. Max was surprised not to see several smitten cheerleaders throwing rose petals in front of him. He possessed a magnetic smile that would surely see him well one day in business or politics, which Max thought would have been appropriate given that his father, Carter Townsend Senior, was one of Independence's most prominent businessmen and head of the council.

'Jesus,' said Chelsea. 'What's with the man-mountain over there?'

She was indicating Jason Sterling. Max hadn't seen much of him over the summer, but he had since grown and then some, his musculature far more defined than at the close of the previous season. Max's mind's eye conjured up a montage of Jason embarking on a series of ridiculously intense exercises worthy of any inspirational Hollywood sports movie.

It certainly made sense for Jason to bulk up, given that, as running back, it was often his task to smash through the opposition with the ball and charge for the touchdown. Max was just glad that, if things worked out, he would be part of the offensive line of players and so wouldn't have to experience Jason barging into him at practice.

'Jason Sterling,' Max explained to Chelsea. 'He's senior year, like us. CJ Townsend too. I'm pretty sure they'll have to put on a show for the college scouts.'

'And you're supposed to be their supporting act?' she asked.

'Something like that.'

'Well, just make sure you're not their water-boy or something.'

'Don't worry, I'm just here to have fun,' he said.

Max turned back to the field as Booth emptied his lungs at the highest volume.

'Alright, newbies, get your asses over here! Let's see if you're worthy of even cleaning this team's boots, never mind a place on it!'

'You better go have some fun then,' said Chelsea, using her fingers to air-quote the word 'fun'.

'I'll see you at Glenn's later,' said Max, as he started jogging out onto the field towards the gathering group of players. 'I'm meeting my mom for dinner.'

'Just don't end up on the menu yourself!' shouted Chelsea after him.

***

An hour later, and Max was in pain. He had known it would be in the mail but hadn't expected such a swift delivery. His arms ached, his right ankle was sore, and he was sure he had stretched his groin a little too far. A hot bath and some painkillers were the order of the day when he got back home. However, he would have to grin and bear it during dinner with his mother, doing his best not to signpost discomfort and prompt equally uncomfortable questions.

Whether the whole experience had been worth it, Max couldn't tell. He thought he had done reasonably well, making some decent catches that first an assistant coach had thrown, and then CJ Townsend, presumably to test him further.

However, for all the good catches Max had made, he had missed as many. He also needed to gain awareness of what was around him. Initially, he had made a catch only to have what felt like a freight truck hit him as he was tackled from the side by one of the defensive players.

Max had quickly learned to dodge or sprint faster, if nothing else, to avoid the unescapable dose of pain that came with tackles. He'd spotted Coach Booth raising an eyebrow several times. Still, the man's expressions rarely gave anything away, so stony were his looks they could have been chiseled from granite.

Even if Max did make the team, he doubted he would see much action. During quiet moments he had observed the team practicing Booth's playbook. It was clear that most of that book was filled with plays that made maximum use of the Townsend-Sterling partnership.

Max had looked on with a mixture of awe and unease as Jason, seemingly a man possessed, had received the ball from CJ and steamrollered his way through the defensive opposition time and again. On occasions, he had let out a war cry worthy of an ancient warrior unleashing himself upon a battlefield.

While Booth had no doubt approved, the glimmer of a smile cracking the surface of his face, he had still sent Jason for several timeouts to calm down, lest his spirited drives to the end zone ended up breaking the limbs of several teammates. Throughout the session, Jason had been unsmiling, his temper fierce, and on a hair-trigger.

At the close, it didn't seem that the past hour's exertions had soothed his mood any, as Max watched everyone except CJ keep their distance as the team headed back to the locker room.

'What's your name, son?' Max heard Booth call over from a few yards away.

Max stopped, unclipped and removed his helmet, and turned towards Booth, who stood next to a couple of assistant coaches holding clipboards.

'Northstar, sir,' Max replied.

'Yeah, I thought so. Recognized you from the track team. Well, you weren't completely useless out there today. You need some polishing for sure, but at least that means you're not a turd, otherwise I wouldn't waste time on you. You're playing for me now, got that.'

It was a statement, not a question.

'Uh, yes, coach,' said Max trying and failing to conceal a satisfied smile.

'Damn right. You can tell your mother the good news.'

Booth nodded in the direction behind Max. He turned, and his smile instantly evaporated as he saw his mother standing near the playing field entrance, with whom he recognized as Jason Sterling's father next to her. She stood straight, arms crossed, and her focus directed at Max. Her face was a blank, her eyes concealed by shades, but Max could tell she was pissed. She directed her attention towards Booth.

'Coach Booth?' she called out. 'Could we see you and Jason, please?'

Booth nodded and started in her direction, while Jason froze at the mention of his name. He turned to CJ, who simply shrugged. Booth pivoted towards Jason and patted him on the back as he walked by. Jason followed Booth towards his father and Amanda. She took the coach to one side while Ray placed a hand on his son's shoulder and started talking. After a moment, Jason bowed his head and dropped his helmet to the ground.

Max prayed for a sinkhole to open up and swallow him whole. When none appeared, he turned and walked back to the locker room, which was filled with questions and gossip about why the sheriff and Ray Sterling were talking with Jason. Amanda was clearly here on business, and so Max knew to stay away until he saw her later at Glenn's, when she was out of uniform and just his mother again. Perhaps that would soften the verbal lashing he was bound to receive, but he doubted it.

Prior to the tryout, Max had heard Chelsea warn him about appearing on the menu, and he had managed to avoid doing so. Leaping from the frying pan and into the fire of Amanda Northstar's temper was another matter altogether.

CHAPTER NINE

Amanda sat on one of Glenn's barstools and waited to catch his attention. She rarely drank on a weeknight, but between an increasingly humid evening and catching Max on the playing field, she could excuse herself one cold beer. Glenn's place was getting busy, with lone patrons, couples, and families gradually streaming in for drinks or food, a reward for the end of a busy work or school day.

Glenn prided himself on running an establishment that was welcoming to all. It was well-lit and decorated with dark red leathers and light wood, with wall-mounted screens that displayed various sports on mute. Sporting memorabilia hung from free spaces, while soft rock music filled the air from an old-style jukebox in the corner.

Amanda had spotted Casey sitting in one of the booths with her husband, Rick. He looked slightly disheveled after his shift at the lumber mill, in contrast to Casey, who looked bright and refreshed after taking the day off to recharge after covering the weekend night shifts. Casey had spotted Amanda in return and waved with a smile. Amanda had waved back but without much energy. It had been an emotionally draining day.

Amanda's visit to Ray to deliver the bad news had stirred up unpleasant memories. Following the formal identification of Judy's body at the hospital, they had left Ruth Chalmers to conduct the autopsy and headed to the high school sports field. Amanda led the way in her patrol car while Ray followed. Butterflies had started flitting around in her stomach, as they always did when she had to visit that place. They had quickly vanished when she arrived at the side of the field and saw Max conversing with Coach Booth.

In retrospect, Amanda felt it had been for the best that she had worn her shades, lest Max or anyone around him had seen the dagger stare she had aimed in his direction. She had quickly shelved her emotional shock to concentrate on the job, calling over Booth and Jason.

While she left Ray some privacy to explain to his son what had happened to Judy, she had done the same with Booth, telling him only what he needed to know and nothing more. Despite his reputation as an uncompromising hardass, Booth had been sympathetic. However, Amanda was sure his thoughts had quickly turned to calculating how the news would impact his preparations for the season.

After watching Ray take Jason home, Amanda had returned to the sheriff's office to complete some paperwork and change clothes. She always stored spares and a travel bag in her office and quickly slipped into some blue jeans and a white blouse before finishing the day's report. She filed it away and said goodbye to Wayne as they locked up for the evening.

Except for emergencies or holding perps in the cells, the sheriff's department was always closed for the night during the quiet weekdays, with either Amanda, Jake, or Casey on call at home should anything require the involvement of the law. The busy weekend period saw the office open throughout the night and day to deal with the usual frictions that could result when alcohol, tourists, and certain awkward locals mixed together. Still, the income generated for the town coffers from the weekend commerce made it worth Amanda allocating overtime.

After throwing her uniform into the trunk, Amanda had decided to take a walk around the town square park and let her thoughts drift before heading to Glenn's. She had known something had been a little off with Max that morning, and now she had an explanation why. He knew full well how she felt about football, or more specifically about that football field. Which was why he hadn't told her, of course.

After the initial flush of anger had subsided, it had given way to more of a sense of disappointment. She had always felt that Max could come to her with anything on his mind, but increasingly it wasn't happening. Her mother was right. He was almost a man now and entitled to his own secrets.

But why did it even have to be a secret? He was joining a sports team, not a cult. Most parents would have been delighted to see him participating, instead of being locked away in his room, glued to a computer. Hadn't she also kept her own parents in the dark about enlisting in the army until she was sure she had been accepted? Max may have concealed the truth, but she recognized her growing hypocrisy enough to realize that his was the lesser of the two evils.

Amanda had finished her walk and driven to Glenn's, where she had parked up front and chatted with some of the patrons, briefly putting her public engagement election pledge into action before Sheriff Northstar punched out and Amanda signed in.

She was weighing up what food to order for later when an open bottle of beer was placed down in front of her. She looked up from the menu to see Glenn considering her with his usual studious eyes. A tall man built like a bear, and just as hairy, he towered over Amanda even when they were standing, let alone with her now sitting.

Amanda still couldn't get used to seeing him out of uniform, his sheriff's outfit replaced by black pants and the white shirt that bore his business logo on the left breast. He had started shaving his head to fully embrace his receding hairline. A previously grey mustache had been grown out into a silver, neatly trimmed beard.

'Amanda Jean,' he finally said, playfully adding her middle name as he occasionally did. 'You're ten hours late.'

'I hope you kept the coffee warm,' she replied with a smile.

'Black as tar and just as thick by now.'

'The way I like it, then.'

'Well, you'll have to settle for this beer. Compliments of the house,' said Glenn. 'Just the one mind you. The sheriff has to set an example.'

'And all those six packs I used to see you put away?' Amanda scoffed.

'That's the point, Amanda,' said Glenn as he leaned in a little. 'You're the only one who saw me.' He grinned and pulled back. 'And always off-duty, mind you. You are allowed to let your hair down from time to time, as I recall trying to teach you. Nice to see you were paying attention.'

'I'm sorry,' she said, underlined with a sigh. 'It's been a busy day.'

'Well, it would have to be to miss my bacon and pancakes. So, a body?'

Amanda leaned forward slightly and lowered her voice.

'Judy Sterling.'

Glenn raised an eyebrow, but otherwise betrayed little surprise should anyone have been watching them. Amanda continued.

'We kept it quiet at first so that Ray Sterling had time to tell his son, but I've put a press release out, so it'll be in the Star tomorrow,' said Amanda, referring to the town's long-established newspaper, The Independence Star. 'Ruth performed an autopsy, so we should have results by morning. But it looks like a suicide. A note in her handwriting, troubled marriage, an abandoned car, and a clear drop off the Saratoga Bridge.'

'Case closed,' said Glenn.

'Yeah, like I said, it certainly looks that way.'

Glenn scratched his beard a few times.

'But not in the mind of Sheriff Northstar?' he probed.

'I don't know,' replied Amanda with a shrug. 'Something just doesn't feel right. A gut instinct, I can't put it any better than that. Nobody saw it coming, not even a hint that she had problems, let alone that she'd do something like that to solve them. It's all so... neat.'

'Well, not every case has to be messy. Cars will crash without scvered brake lines, often the guy standing over the body with a knife is the one who did it, and people decide to end their lives, for many reasons or none at all.'

'There's no such thing as a clean death. However it happens, there's always a mess left behind,' said Amanda.

She picked up her beer and took a swig.

'You know Amanda, I'm pretty sure there's a party somewhere out there that needs the life sucked out of it,' remarked Glenn, drolly.

Amanda smiled slightly, conceding the point.

'It's not just that. I caught Max at football tryouts earlier.'

'And?' said Glenn with an unconcerned shrug.

'Well, you know I get a little uncomfortable about it.'

'And?' he repeated in the same tone.

'What do you mean 'and'?'

'How is that Max's problem? If the kid wants to play, let him play.'

'His playing isn't the issue, it's that he kept what he was doing from me.'

'Well, suck it up and give him some support. You ride his ass on this, he'll keep far more important stuff from you in the future, like when he knocks up his college sweetheart.'

'Jesus, Glenn,' said Amanda, frowning at the thought.

'Ah, you know I jest. The kid's just like you, so damned honorable he'd probably ask permission to put a condom on. Did he make the team at least?'

'Coach Booth is giving him a chance,' Amanda said with a nod.

'Well then, my prescription for tonight is for a full rack of ribs. Put some meat on the boy.' Glenn nodded past Amanda's shoulder. 'And maybe an icepack.'

Amanda turned around to see Max enter. He was washed and changed, his school bag slung over his shoulder. She glanced back at Glenn, puzzled.

'I don't see him limping.'

'I didn't say it was for his leg.'

Amanda looked back towards Max and saw him try to discreetly adjust the area around his groin, wincing slightly. She turned back to Glenn and matched his grin.

Max sheepishly approached the bar and quietly took the free stool next to Amanda. Glenn opened a bottle of soda and placed it down in front of Max, who nodded in thanks.

'I'll get started on that order,' said Glenn, winking at Max as he disappeared into the kitchen at the rear.

Max took a sip, as both he and Amanda stared ahead.

'Look, Mom, I'm-'

'Congratulations,' said Amanda.

She raised her beer. Max took a moment to register the gesture then smiled. He picked up his bottle and clinked it against hers.

'Your father would be proud,' she said, patting him gently on the shoulder. 'And I am too. There's no need to hide what makes you happy. I'll support you whatever you decide to do, now and in the future.'

'Thanks, that means a lot.'

'But I do expect to see some spectacular touchdowns in return.'

'Yes, Ma'am,' said Max, raising a playful salute.

They smiled at each other and returned to sipping their drinks, their thoughts their own in the contented silence.

CHAPTER TEN

For the second time that day, Ray Sterling heard a knock on the front door and instinctively knew he wouldn't want to see who was on the other side. It had started off as the worst day of his life and had gone downhill from there, if such a thing was possible. Now all he wanted to do was numb his emotions with copious amounts of alcohol. His new visitors were disturbing his progress towards that sweet oblivion.

He placed his tumbler of whiskey upon the coffee table, stood, and headed for the door. He opened it to find Gary Brennan, the mayor of Independence, standing slightly to the side. A thin man with a slight potbelly, short cut brown hair, and the pale skin of a plucked chicken, Gary seemed an unlikely public figure. However, a genial manner, underestimated cunning, and a reputation for organizational skill had seen him twice elected to the highest office in the county.

He planned to run for a third term the next year, but, like a growing number of people, Ray sensed that Gary's political career was circling the drain, however desperate he was to hang on. That desperation formed one of several reasons why Ray found himself in Gary's company, along with the third member of the porch club, Carter Townsend.

Carter exuded a potent combination of confidence, charm, and intimidation, deploying each as required to advance his agenda. Ray knew that Carter always had an agenda, not to mention a finger in every pie and a shovel in many a grave. Ray may have been thinking metaphorically about the last point, but nor would he have been shocked if it ever transpired to be true.

Carter's devilish qualities were complemented by his appearance. A black-but-greying goatee matched the color of his luscious hair, swept back to the base of his neck like some 18th Century romantic rogue. His body was well-toned for his age, a testament to his iron self-discipline. In his large, leather-gloved hands, he held a bouquet of flowers. He nodded respectfully.

'Good evening Ray. I'm so sorry for your loss.'

'Thank you, Carter, I appreciate it,' Ray replied, nodding in return, his tone neutral.

'We brought flowers, Ray, you know, as a token,' Gary chipped in, seemingly eager to become part of the conversation in any way. Carter and Ray were the only two who mattered in this exchange, though, and everyone knew it.

'Would you mind if we came in?' asked Carter.

Ray stepped back and opened the door wide, the invitation silent but clear. Carter and Gary walked through, and Ray closed the door. He extended an arm towards the lounge and led the way, keen to return to his whiskey. Ray took his seat, as Carter and Gary moved towards the sofa opposite.

Carter noticed that the glass of the wall-mounted television had shattered in the middle of the screen, sending out a spiderweb of cracks. Something had clearly impacted, hard.

'Accident?' enquired Carter as he pointed at it.

'Something like that,' replied Ray dismissively, disinclined to discuss it further.

Carter and Gary sat down, the flowers put aside and quickly forgotten.

'Is Jason around?' Carter inquired, glancing around the room.

'No, he's out with friends,' Ray lied, ignorant about where his son had gone after storming out. 'Better he let off some steam his way than mope at home with his father.'

'Good, that's good,' said Carter, nodding. 'A young man needs his friends, especially in times like these. But then so too do old men.'

'My wife's resting on a slab tonight, Carter. Get to the damn point,' said Ray impatiently.

Normally Ray wouldn't have dared use such a tone in Carter's presence. However, melancholy and ample whiskey had dampened his discretion and stoked his courage.

'That *is* the point, Ray,' Carter responded without missing a beat. 'However it happen-'

'It was a suicide,' interrupted Ray.

'However it happened,' continued Carter. 'Frankly, there's a silver lining to this cloud.'

'That's cold, Carter, even for you,' said Ray, shaking his head as he stood up.

He walked over to the photographic shrine to his and Jason's sporting prowess.

'Maybe it is,' continued Carter. 'But the fact remains that a significant roadblock to progress in this town has been removed, and with progress comes great rewards.

But you know that and, frankly, were pretty much banking on it, right?'

Ray could only sigh at Carter's brutal but correct logic.

'What do you want me to do?' he asked.

Carter leaned back in his chair.

'Exactly what's been called for, as agreed from the beginning. I'm genuinely sorry about Judy, I am. But frankly, the world keeps turning, and Gary and I needed to make sure you were still on board now that the train finally looks like it's leaving the station.'

Ray cast a long look over the photos, resting on a well-captured shot of Jason barging his way through opposing football players. He downed the remnants of whiskey and ran his tongue over his teeth.

'Yeah, I'm still on board. It isn't like I have a choice, is it?'

'There's always a choice, Ray,' said Carter, as he raised an unsettling smile. 'I'm just glad you're making the right one.'

CHAPTER ELEVEN

After helping to deliver Judy Sterling's body to the hospital morgue, Jake had stayed until Amanda had arrived with Ray and then returned to his regular shift duties. It had been a quiet afternoon, and after clocking off, he had returned home and changed straight into his running gear. Jake had then circled the entire town, a route that took two hours. He had left his phone and music behind, content for nature to be his soundtrack, left alone to his thoughts.

It could either be a good idea or a bad one depending on Jake's mindset. Despite the transformative effect that taking the deputy's job had had on his mental state, Jake was still prone to bouts of crippling self-doubt. He sometimes felt he was undeserving of everything, sometimes even having lived when dear friends had not. There was no rhyme or reason to it, no logical foundation for why he should feel that way. Yet he did, and so every day, he ran and felt better.

The endorphins from the exercise no doubt helped, but the running reminded him of happier times when he had caught a football and sprinted for the touchline, the only thing required of him to receive adulation. Most other times, he knew that he was simply outrunning the black dog, but that it would eventually pick up his scent, and then the chase, and his escape, would commence once again.

After his run, Jake returned home, warmed up some chili cooked up over the weekend, and quickly devoured it. After a brief shower, he threw on some jeans, boots, a t-shirt, and a leather jacket. Even when he was in a moderately good mood, Jake still preferred the company of others. He grabbed his helmet, hopped onto his vintage motorcycle, and headed to Glenn's, where he usually allowed himself one beer only and, if the company was right, ample conversation.

Unfortunately, it seemed that the choice of company at Glenn's that night was somewhat limited as Jake saw patrons leaving just as he arrived. He came across Amanda and Max on their way out and briefly made small talk about the latter gaining a place on the Rebels team. Jake was genuinely pleased to hear it and offered to help Max out with any pointers if he thought it would be useful, an offer that Max had keenly accepted.

After saying their goodbyes, Jake entered Glenn's to find the place sparser than he had expected, though night had pretty much fallen and so he shouldn't have been too surprised. He took a stool at the bar and flagged down Glenn.

'Evening Jake, just the one?' asked the old man.

'As usual,' Jake nodded in response.

Glenn didn't even have to ask what Jake wanted. He always ordered the same thing, a craft beer brewed and bottled in a microbrewery located in the cellar underneath the bar, yet another retirement hobby Glenn indulged in. Glenn set the bottle down in front of Jake, along with a small bowl of peanuts.

'I'll be with you soon, son, just closing the kitchen down.'

Jake nodded, took a sip, and cast his eye around the establishment. He quickly settled on a small party of four congregating around the pool table towards the rear. From what he could make out, Casey and Rick were teamed up as a pair opposing two other men he vaguely recognized as workers at the lumber mill.

The group laughed, cheered, or gently booed as they potted balls, missed them, or executed deliberate or fluke trick shots. After a moment, Casey glanced over and caught Jake looking at them. She smiled and waved. Jake returned the smile and raised his bottle in her direction.

'You still got it bad for her, don't you?'

Jake turned around to see Chelsea standing behind him, leaning against the bar and looking towards her big sister. She switched her gaze from the group to Jake and raised an eyebrow, daring him to confirm or deny. Jake noticed the backpack she carried and chose to take the middle road and ignore her question entirely.

'Heading home?'

'Yeah, kitchen's closed, and my work here is done, serving the good people of our fine town the best artery cloggers that money can buy. Every shift I work, I wonder if I should go vegan. But it'll never happen. Damn Glenn and his secret sauce. But don't change the subject.'

'And what subject would that be?'

'Don't play dumb, Jake. You may have been a jarhead by name, but not by nature. You still carry a torch for my sister. Hell, I could see it when our mom dragged me to football games, and you had the puppy dog eyes for Casey in her cheerleader outfit. But then, which guy didn't? Well, apart from Callum Janey, but I hear he's nicely settled with his boyfriend now.'

Jake raised a wry smile but kept his tone dry and noncommittal.

'You amuse me, Chelsea, always have.'

'Well, that's encouraging to know if I'm ever called on to entertain the troops abroad, but for now, Jake, I'd settle on you growing a pair and telling Casey how you feel.'

'Even if you were right, it'd probably be a little tricky given that she's married.'

'To Rick. Yeah, he treats her okay, but he's still a bum, just like our dad was before he walked out. I know she sees it too, but she's like you. Too proud to admit the truth. God help them if she ever gets knocked up.'

'Weren't you heading home?' asked Jake, his impatience starting to rise.

'I'm going, I'm going,' replied Chelsea, aware she had probed the limits of the conversation. She nodded over towards the pool table. 'Anyway, why settle for the junior version when you can have the real thing.'

Chelsea smiled and took her leave, as Jake turned back to see Casey finish whispering in Rick's ear and head towards the bar, his hand gently brushing her rear as she passed him. Jake debated whether it was worth returning his attention to his beer, but knew it would seem strange to fake nonchalance when he had so obviously noticed Casey.

It was foolish of him to feel nervous around her. He saw her almost every day, after all. But that was on the job, in uniform, in a different context. He could compartmentalize his feelings, prioritizing friendly professionalism and comradeship over the romantic attraction Chelsea had correctly identified. He settled on a slightly awkward smile as she reached the bar and took the stool next to him.

'Hey Jake,' she said breezily. 'Long day, huh? Amanda told me you were delivering the package to Ruth.'

Casey was deliberately vague in case any curious ears were within range. Still, Jake knew that the news about Judy Sterling would have already spread halfway around town before becoming official in the next morning's paper.

'Definitely a one beer kind of day,' he replied, tapping the neck of his bottle. 'Can I get you one?'

'No thanks, just a coke or juice for me, at least for a while.'

'Oh? Turning over a healthy new leaf or something?'

'Yeah,' said Casey, smiling. 'Something like that.'

'So how's Rick?' asked Jake. 'I haven't seen you two out together in a while.'

Casey glanced away slightly and rubbed the back of her neck.

'Yeah, well, we deserve a little celebration.'

'Oh?' queried Jake.

Casey sighed.

'I know I can tell you this because we're close, that you'd keep it to yourself, but things haven't been so good on the money side lately. Rick was on reduced hours, and even with my salary, we were starting to worry about the mortgage payments. But a few weeks back, he said a contract had come in to supply a new development, that he'd been offered more hours and more money.'

Jake listened attentively, a slight unease growing in his stomach as he took in the news of Casey's financial worries. It should have subsided when she spoke of the positive outcome, but it remained. Jake knew it was because Rick's salvation meant that Casey would be more enamored with him than ever, the hard-working husband coming through despite most people's low opinion of him. It was envy, pure and simple. Jake didn't like himself for it, but nor could he resist it.

'Well, that's good news,' he said, feigning an upbeat attitude.

'Definitely. We decided we should let our hair down. This was the first night in a long time we could do it.'

Jake looked past Casey to see Rick approaching with a cocksure swagger. He stood between them both and slapped Jake hard on the shoulder.

'Murrow! Long time partner, how you doin'?' said Rick with a slight but noticeable slur.

'Good, thanks,' replied Jake neutrally with a nod.

'Why are you sitting here like some lonely, miserable bastard?' poked Rick. 'Come join us over at the pool table, show us some of those hustler moves you used to have.'

'Thanks, but I'm just here for a quick beer then a long motorcycle ride,' lied Jake, suddenly keen to escape and head home.

'Next time then Murrow, next time,' said Rick, nodding in acknowledgment that he had been thwarted.

He finally directed his attention towards Casey, who had seemed an afterthought since his intrusion. 'Babe, get us a couple of pitchers. I'm just heading out for a smoke.'

He pulled a crumpled-up batch of bills from his pocket, tossed them on the bar, and kissed her heavily on the forehead. Within seconds he was gone.

'Still Rick, huh,' said Jake, stating not questioning, as he finished his beer.

'Yeah,' conceded Casey with a slight smile. 'Still a man-child. I know you guys haven't properly spoken since we finished high school. It's not my place to ask why, but for all his immature moments, he has just as many kind ones.'

Jake stood and adjusted his jacket.

'I'd best head off. Please tell Glenn I'll catch him soon. I'll see you tomorrow but have a good night. Sounds like it's been needed.'

'You too,' said Casey.

She rubbed his arm briefly but tenderly as he passed her.

Jake exited and headed down the wooden steps to the parking area. Apart from his motorcycle and a few scattered cars, it was quiet. He took a moment to breathe in the evening air. He glanced towards the outside smoking area, a small open-air hut with tree stumps for seats. He expected to see Rick sitting, puffing away, but all the seats were unoccupied. Jake looked around but saw no obvious evidence of Rick's presence. Apart from the muffled music coming from inside Glenn's, it was eerily quiet.

Jake looked at the ground and tilted his head, attempting to focus his hearing. After a moment, he thought he caught a brief sound of chatter coming from his right, around the far corner of the building, towards where the trash cans were stored.

Jake quietly made his way towards the garbage area, hugging the exterior wall until he was able to peek around the corner. He discreetly advanced his head forwards and instantly spotted Rick standing a dozen yards away, his back gently illuminated by the small security light on the wall above the trash cans. He was talking to another man standing just on the tree line and who was fully cloaked in shadow.

Whatever conversation they were having had clearly wrapped up, as they shook hands and made to part ways. Rick began to turn and Jake instantly pulled back. He back-stepped several yards as quickly and quietly as he could, stopped, and advanced again. Rick emerged from around the corner, his expression of surprise indicating that he assumed Jake was approaching that way for the first time, just as Jake had hoped.

'What's up, Murrow?' asked Rick calmly as if nothing was out of place.

'Just thought I heard some noises back there. Didn't want raccoons making trouble in Glenn's trash,' Jake responded, equally calmly.

'Well, look at you, always out to bust the big crimes,' said Rick without even attempting to conceal his sarcasm.

'What were you doing back there, anyway?' asked Jake.

'Needed to take a leak.'

'Outside?'

'When you gotta go, you gotta go, you know?' said Rick with a shrug. He patted Jake on the shoulder as he walked by. 'I didn't see any raccoons back there, but better put out an APB on them to be on the safe side, huh?'

Jake silently watched Rick head back to the entrance and ascend the stairs. Once he was inside, Jake swiftly headed back and peered around the corner. The man in shadow was gone.

CHAPTER TWELVE

The next morning Amanda had followed her usual routine and had made bacon and eggs for Max. If he was indeed set on a place on the Rebels team, he would need plenty of protein in his system over the following months. While she left him to ready himself, she had showered and changed and set out to the sheriff's department early, keen to start.

She entered the reception area to find Wayne already at his desk. She sometimes wondered whether he ever slept. Despite being in his seventies, when most people would be enjoying their retirement, the white-haired, bespectacled, and slightly turkey-necked Wayne prided himself on his punctuality and work ethic and showed no signs of stopping.

A widower with family a distant drive away, Wayne insisted that his three joys in life were his work, his cat, and his church, and he wouldn't be giving them up anytime soon. With such energy and determination, Amanda hadn't even considered replacing Wayne when she had taken over from Glenn. His years of experience and institutional knowledge of the department made him even more of an asset.

'Morning, Amanda,' said Wayne cheerfully. 'Well done on Max making the team.'

'Thank you, Wayne,' she replied, genuinely feeling some pride. 'I see good news travels fast. How about the bad?'

Wayne nodded, knowing what she was referring to. He held up a fresh copy of The Independence Star for Amanda to study the front page. The headline was big and bold: COUNCILWOMAN STERLING FOUND DEAD ON BANK OF HUDSON. It was accompanied by a photograph of a smiling Judy taken from the council website.

Amanda quickly scanned the first few paragraphs of the story. She was glad to see that ambiguity remained as to cause of death. The Star didn't go in for sensationalism. It had stuck to the facts presented in a press release Wayne had drafted after Amanda had briefed him over the phone.

The only nod to speculation was a collection of comments from townspeople and Judy's council colleagues, offering their sympathies and questioning what reasons lay behind her death. Amanda was just as keen on finding out herself and headed through a nearby archway into the main office.

It was a large room, with filing cabinets lining one of the walls and a series of cork boards on the other, with various information sheets pinned to them. Two large maps were also stuck up, one for Independence town, the other of the county, with thick red marker lines representing the jurisdictional boundaries. In the middle of the room were four desks, separated into two pairs, their backs to each other. The couple to the right were vacant, ready to accommodate any visiting law enforcement personnel, whether state or federal. However, Casey often used one as a research desk for her laptop and copious notes.

The desks to the left were occupied by Jake and Casey and were the closest to Amanda's office, which was divided from the main area by a door of frosted glass. At the end of the main area, to the far right, was the entrance to the cellblock and interview room. The building had a second floor, but it was essentially one huge space, an attic in all but name, where files were archived away in hundreds of cardboard boxes.

Jake and Casey were at their desks, sipping morning coffee. Amanda removed her hat and jacket and hung them up on hooks next to those belonging to her deputies.

'Morning, kids,' she said as she walked over to the coffee maker in the nearby corner and poured herself a cup. 'Have we heard anything from Ruth yet?'

'Should be any minute now,' answered Jake.

Right on cue, the phone on his desk rang. He picked it up and identified himself, listened a moment, thanked the caller, and placed the phone back down.

'She's ready to see us.'

Amanda glanced down at her cup, sighed, and took a brief sip before setting it down. She unhooked her hat and jacket and turned to Jake and Casey in turn.

'Jake, with me. Casey, I'd like you to head back out to the Saratoga Bridge.'

Casey nodded in acknowledgment, but her expression still hinted at confusion.

'Sure thing, but what am I looking for?'

'Nothing specific, but take a walk around, really study the area, try and put yourself in Judy's shoes. We didn't have the time yesterday, but I just want to be sure we haven't missed anything, no matter how small. I know it sounds odd, but indulge me.'

Amanda put on her hat and jacket and headed out the front entrance, quickly followed by Jake. She nodded towards her parked cruiser, indicating her intention to take only one vehicle to the hospital. Jake walked around to the passenger side but paused before opening the door.

'Something's bugging you, isn't it?' he prodded. 'Something small, but it's there. Otherwise, why send Casey out?'

Amanda opened the driver's door and paused.

'Glenn told me that most of the time things are just as simple as they look. He's usually right, but I still have this feeling that we're missing something.'

'Well, if we have, then Ruth's often the one to find it,' said Jake with a shrug.

'We'll see,' said Amanda as she took the driver's seat. 'Maybe Judy's body can answer more questions than her letter did.'

CHAPTER THIRTEEN

Amanda parked at the rear of the Independence Community Hospital, where the morgue had an additional entrance that didn't involve walking through the main building lobby. She and Jake quickly made their way through the white, brightly-lit corridors and entered the examination room. They found Ruth Chalmers standing over Judy's pale body, scribbling notes on a clipboard.

Short and stocky with brown crew-cut hair, Ruth's appearance and professional manner gave her a rather butch quality. However, Amanda knew for a fact that she was married, with four children in college. A white sheet was pulled up to Judy's chest, concealing her bosom, but was low enough to expose the incision marks where Ruth had cut to examine the internal organs. Amanda thought it eerie how the corpses she had seen on that table always seemed as if they were sleeping temporarily rather than eternally.

'Morning, Ruth,' said Amanda.

Ruth peered over the top of her half-moon spectacles.

'Good morning, Sheriff, Deputy,' Ruth responded in a formal but not unfriendly tone.

'So, what do we have?' asked Amanda.

She knew from experience that Ruth was not one for small talk and, in any case, was impatient to discover the findings of the autopsy, to either help dismiss her niggling doubts or confirm them. Ruth didn't disappoint and immediately began.

'Death was by drowning, which you would expect from a river plunge. It can depend on the height of the bridge from the water, angle of impact, and so on. However, when someone usually hits the surface, they're knocked unconscious and take water into the lungs. As for the time of death, the Hudson's temperature this time of year could throw it off, but I'd still say it was within twelve hours or so before she was found. We're looking at the previous night at the earliest, or the early hours of that morning at the latest.'

'What about the raccoon eyes and discolorations behind her ears?' asked Amanda, indicating the areas with a nod in their direction.

'Those are the result of a basilar skull fracture, which is to say at the base of the cranium. I imagine it happened when Judy hit the water headfirst, the pressure causing the sphenoid, temporal, and occipital bones to fracture,' replied Ruth.

As she mentioned each bone, she placed a finger on either side of her own face, beginning with the areas just behind her eye sockets, moving to her temples, and then to the rear base of her skull. She then pointed to Judy's darkened eyes and continued.

'The raccoon eyes are caused by a rupture of the internal carotid artery within the cavernous sinus. It's basically a large collection of thin-walled veins that create a cavity, and this borders the sphenoid and temporal bones I spoke of. In a nutshell, if those bones are damaged, it's likely the cavernous sinus will be too. If that ruptures, then any excess blood will be forced into the orbits around the eyes.'

'And what about behind the ears?' probed Jake. 'Same kind of thing?'

'In a way,' said Ruth. 'Sections of your temporal bone are hollowed out. We call these mastoid cells, and they can vary in size and number, but a lot have air in them. If you want a very basic visual idea, think of a bath sponge. When these fracture, blood pools in the remaining space just below the skin, hence the discoloration. If the water hadn't washed it away, you'd likely also see blood seeping from her ears and nose as a result of these injuries.'

Amanda looked on, her arms crossed, biting gently on a knuckle, deep in thought.

'So piecing this all together, you'd say that Judy hit the water headfirst. This caused the fractures and the skin discolorations and knocked her unconscious, with drowning the result?'

'That sounds logical to me,' replied Ruth with a nod.

'And no sign of any blunt force trauma that could have caused these fractures?' asked Amanda, just to be sure.

Ruth shook her head.

'If you're asking me whether she was struck on the head, the answer is no. Nothing I can see points to that. There is one thing I need to mention, something that seemed strange, though I can't see it relating to cause of death.'

'Oh?' said Amanda, her ears pricking up.

Ruth retrieved Judy's nearby autopsy file, opened it, and produced a color photograph, which she handed to Amanda.

'All the photographs and details are in the report, but this one struck me as a little odd, with no explanation,' said Ruth.

Amanda examined the image. It appeared to show a completely straight line of gentle bruising running along Judy's lower back, about five inches above her buttocks. The bruising itself was not very wide, perhaps less than an inch thick. She looked up to Ruth.

'Could this be a sign of someone striking her from behind?'

'I doubt it,' said Ruth. 'You can see the bruising is straight and constant across the skin, and I'm not sure of what object would leave such a mark. Not a baseball bat, nor a crowbar. A plank of wood perhaps, but you can see for yourself that the mark isn't very wide. Therefore the plank, or whatever instrument it was, would have met her side on rather than flat. It's not really a practical way to strike a blow. In any case, while the bruising is perhaps gentler than it would have been had it had time to mature before her death, there are no signs of fracture on the vertebrae in that area. You would expect there to be something in the way of damage if an object had been brought down with enough force to leave such a consistent mark.'

Amanda handed the photograph back to Ruth to deposit with the others in the file. The mark on Judy's back had raised another question, but the fundamental one was seemingly closer to being answered. All the medical findings complemented the physical evidence, principally that Judy's car had been parked a short walk from the Saratoga Bridge, a suicide note in her handwriting left inside. All that had been left to do was jump.

But why had that jump been headfirst instead of simply leaping off as most jumpers tended to do? Had it been some kind of macabre swan-dive into oblivion? Whatever the reason, Judy Sterling had hit the water pointing downwards, the pressure of impact fracturing her skull and sending her straight into unconsciousness, unable to feel her lungs fill up with water. It was a cold, dark way to go, Amanda thought.

She had checked most of the questions for Ruth off her mental list, but one remained.

'Last thing, Ruth, but any idea what the substance under her fingernails was?'

'I placed a sample I'd retrieved under the microscope,' replied Ruth. 'I'd say it's mostly mud. It likely got under her nails when she washed up close to the river bank. There was something else mixed in with the mud, though, some small black flakes. They were a lot deeper under the nails. I can't say what they are with certainty. I've sent a sample off to the lab in New York in case it's relevant, but results could be a day or two in coming.'

'Thanks, Ruth, we appreciate your efforts,' said Amanda with a nod.

'Any time, Sheriff,' said Ruth. 'Though not too often, nor too soon, I hope.'

***

Amanda and Jake returned to her cruiser and sat in silence. Jake knew that it was best to leave Amanda alone to collect her thoughts until she was ready to speak. Eventually, after a few moments, she did.

'Seems pretty cut and dry,' she said, staring ahead rather than looking at Jake, as if she was thinking aloud rather than directing the comment at him.

'Maybe,' said Jake, raising an eyebrow. 'Or you're just saying it to convince yourself. Keep repeating, and it might stick, doubts or not.'

'What about the mark on her back?'

'I'll admit it's a wrinkle in what would be a smooth solution,' Jake acknowledged. 'But Ruth did say it was unlikely to be caused by a blow. It could have been an accident of some kind. I've got a nice, fat bruise on my shin after I tripped jogging last week. But to someone who didn't know that, it could seem like I was kicked.'

'So you think I'm looking for something that isn't there?'

'It's not what I think, Amanda. You're the boss, it's your call. From my viewpoint, it looks and walks like a duck. Just because you haven't heard it quack yet, doesn't mean it isn't so. But then if you have doubts, I've known you long enough now that there's a reason that they're there.'

Amanda mulled a moment more. She sighed and turned the keys in the ignition.

CHAPTER FOURTEEN

Amanda pulled to a stop beside Casey's cruiser. Both were parked near the walking trail entrance close to where Judy Sterling had left her car two nights previously. She stepped out with Jake and spotted Casey halfway across the Saratoga Bridge, crouching down and casting her eyes over the road's surface, glancing back occasionally to check for traffic.

Amanda led Jake towards the bridge, casting a quick glance towards Judy's last parking space as they passed. There were no markers to indicate potential evidence, therefore Casey had not spotted anything of note.

As Amanda continued walking, Casey looked up, acknowledged them with a raised hand, and lowered her gaze back down to the asphalt. Amanda saw Casey take out her phone and hold it a few feet above the ground. She tapped the screen, changed the angle, and tapped it again. She was taking photographs. Clearly, Casey had spotted something or at least thought she had. She stood when Amanda and Jake reached her.

'I might have something, but then it might be nothing,' she said.

'Go on,' said Amanda encouragingly.

'Look here,' said Casey, as she pointed down at the road surface.

Amanda instantly spotted what she was indicating. Two dark tire skid marks were apparent on the grey asphalt. They were initially straight and then curved to the right, crossing the painted line that separated both lanes.

'Someone stopped here, fast,' ventured Casey.

'Too fast,' added Jake. 'This wasn't a controlled deceleration. They slammed on the brakes, hard, almost losing the front end.'

'Exactly,' continued Casey. 'Not only that, but these marks stop around where Judy may have jumped.'

Amanda turned around, away from the road and towards the walkway that ran along the side of the bridge. The three of them indeed stood at the center, only a few paces from the walkway barrier where it made sense for Judy to throw herself off to guarantee the desired result.

'Whoever it was could have braked to avoid an animal,' suggested Jake, assuming the role of devil's advocate.

'True,' conceded Casey, 'but the nearest trees are back where we parked, so I can't see any animal venturing out this far. Plus, if it was night, the bridge lights would help someone spot something on the road and slow down. Finally, these tire marks are relatively fresh. It rained heavily three nights ago, a day before Judy died. These must have been made since then. Otherwise, they would have been washed away or faded.'

Jake pursed his lips, impressed at the fullness of her answer. She seemingly had every base covered. Amanda allowed herself a small smile. This was Casey's analytical mind showing what it could do.

'Okay, let's play this out,' said Jake. 'Whatever happened, it's a safe bet that whoever slammed on the brakes was going at a hell of a speed. If we think this has something to do with Judy, that leaves two possibilities. One, someone was driving along, saw Judy jump and stopped hard, first in shock and then to see if there was anything they could do.'

'But then they would have called us, and no one did,' countered Casey.

'Exactly,' said Jake, raising two fingers to make his next point. 'That leaves us with our second possibility, that the driver was going so fast because he or she knew that Judy was going to be here and wanted to get to her. They see her on the walkway and hit the brakes.'

'They get out, go to her, but she still ends up dead,' continued Casey. 'Or, based on option one, they just missed her and saw her jump, but didn't call it in. Either way, something isn't right.'

'Maybe so,' said Jake after a moment's thought. 'But this is still all supposition. We could be looking at a suspect, a witness, avoiding hitting an animal, and everything in between. I'll admit, Casey, you've given us something to think about, but the basic facts haven't changed since Amanda and I left the morgue. There's nothing on Judy's body that indicates foul play. Unless we're still missing something here?'

He looked towards Amanda, who had been patiently observing her deputies exchanging their thoughts while keeping her own open. She felt it was good for them to exercise their own deductive reasoning, to make them better investigators, but she also found it useful to step away sometimes and consider what interpretations other people brought to a situation.

Casey had argued her case well, especially about the tire marks being close to Judy's potential jump point. Amanda walked over to the barrier and peered over the side again, as she had done the day before. The view was the same, a high drop into the waters below. She turned around to face her deputies and leaned back on the barrier.

It was then she felt it. The railing that ran along the top of the barrier was square. Its corners were slightly rounded, not sharp right angles, but she still felt the inside upper corner through the back of her jacket, a few inches above her waist. Amanda stood straight and turned her head slightly so that her body mainly faced forward, but she had eyes on the railing.

She then let herself fall back slightly, letting gravity control her, not her leg muscles. It was only a foot or so, but she still winced as her lower back hit the railing's upper edge, and it dug into her. She felt the metal in a narrow band that stretched all the way along the width of her back.

Amanda remained in place. The pieces were starting to fall into place, and finally, she could begin to see the image the puzzle revealed. It was of Judy Sterling being pushed into the barrier with force, her back hitting the railing, its rounded corner digging into her flesh and promising a nasty bruise that had only half-formed before death had halted the process.

Amanda closed her eyes and tried to mentally put herself in that position. She had been pushed, she had hit the barrier, but surely such force might have caused her to keep going and pivot over the edge. What did someone do when they felt the sensation of falling, of losing balance? They lashed out with their hands and arms, searching for anything to grab, hold onto, and pull back on. Both Amanda's hands found the railings and attempted to grip, but it was smooth. She clawed her fingers across the flat top of the metal, trying to gain purchase but finding nothing.

Amanda opened her eyes and brought her hands up to her face. She examined her nails, under which had collected compressed flakes of a black-colored substance. She looked down at the railing where her hands had been and found scratch marks where she had scraped off the black paint with her nails, exposing the grey metal underneath. She looked up to Jake and Casey, who were watching her curiously.

'Whatever exactly happened that night, I'm thinking this much,' said Amanda. 'Judy Sterling didn't jump. She was pushed.'

CHAPTER FIFTEEN

Amanda stood in the main office of the sheriff's department, sipping a fresh cup of coffee from the maker. She started to gently pace up and down in front of Jake and Casey, who sat at their desks, watching. Amanda often moved around when her mind was racing. She simply couldn't sit still and needed to do something physical as well as mental. She had known something had not been quite right with Judy Sterling's death. Her gut instinct had told her so, but it had still needed some basic facts to encourage her suspicions.

Even before discovering the bruising on Judy's lower back and the connection between that and the railing on the bridge barrier, tiny things had played on Amanda's mind. The lack of any signs of mental illness that even hinted that Judy possessed an inclination towards suicide was one factor. The black material buried deep under her fingernails, far deeper than simply brushing them along the muddy riverbank would have infused, was another relevant point.

Her missing shoe was the most significant question mark hovering over Amanda's head, however. If her left one had been secure and tight enough to stay on, what had been so different with the absent right one in exactly the same environment and circumstances? That annoying detail would have to be shelved for the time being.

There was enough physical evidence to strongly suppose that Judy had been pushed and so a murder had taken place. Amanda was inclined to run with it until she had cause to either pause or stop. Now that murder seemed to be the most probable cause, the questions had changed along with the facts. The why of the matter still loomed large, but the who had now seen Judy replaced with 'unknown suspect'.

'So what are you thinking?' asked Jake as he leaned back slightly in his chair, receptive to an answer. Amanda stopped pacing and faced him.

'The line of bruising across Judy's back was from the impact of the railing on the bridge. She was pushed into it, hard, and it tipped her over the edge. That's probably why her injuries are consistent with hitting the water headfirst, because she fell that way. I'll also bet that when the lab results come back, we'll find those dark flecks under her nails is paint from the railing. You don't scrape and claw for your life if you're intent on jumping.'

'But the note she left was real,' said Casey, confusion evident on her face. 'It's in Judy's handwriting explaining why she's taking her own life. Plus, she left her possessions in the car, like she'd never need them again. It doesn't make any sense.'

'But this leads us to the main question,' interjected Jake. 'Why would someone looking to commit suicide be murdered?'

'Unless she wasn't looking to kill herself,' said Amanda.

Jake and Casey exchanged glances across their desks, trying to see if the other had grasped what Amanda was reaching for. Amanda sipped her coffee and stared at the far wall of the office as she continued to explore her thoughts out loud.

'Think about it. If she really intended to kill herself, then why would someone go to the bother of beating her to it? If you wanted Judy Sterling dead and she really was going to jump, then you'd just look on and let her leap.'

'But what if she still intended to jump and someone got to her before she did it?' suggested Casey.

'Then it's still murder,' replied Amanda. 'Whether she meant to end her life that night or not, someone did it for her.'

'Okay,' said Jake as he patted the arms of his desk chair. 'So our assumed killer races to the bridge, stops on a dime, gets out and confronts Judy. There's a struggle, she's pushed, she hits the railing and topples over the side. Correct?'

'Seems a good fit,' nodded Amanda.

Casey leaned forward to contribute.

'Like you said before, though, they could have let her get on with jumping and kept their hands clean, assuming she was going to jump. If they'd done that, it would indicate some planning, some calculation. But the fact they raced in there shows a lack of planning, of acting in the heat of the moment. A crime of passion?'

'Very good,' said Amanda, raising a slight smile. 'And what usually solicits a crime of passion?'

Casey stroked her cheek a moment. Amanda had already started forming possibilities in her mind. Still, she wanted to test her deputies, to encourage independent thought and deduction as Glenn had done in her.

'Well, what motivates most murders?' responded Casey. 'Money, love, revenge. That's the usual unholy trinity, right? So whoever killed her either stood to make a few dollars or hated her enough to push her off a bridge.'

'What about Ray Sterling?' ventured Jake. 'We know that he and Judy had been arguing a lot, and family often benefits from life insurance.'

'Life insurance still has a premeditated quality to it, though,' said Amanda. 'Still, we need to be thorough. Casey, can you investigate Judy's policy, please?

'Sure, I'll get right on it,' nodded Casey.

'What about me?' asked Jake.

'If Casey's dealing with the money, you can look into the possible love motivation. Check Judy's phone and the GPS in her car. Hopefully, one or both may tell us more about who she'd been talking to and where she'd been recently.'

'You think she was having an affair?'

'I wouldn't rule it out. Perhaps Ray and Judy were arguing about bigger things than the usual marriage issues on the night you saw them. Also, if you're potentially going to fake your own death, then you're either doing it to escape from someone, or to be with someone.'

'And what about you, Amanda? Where are you headed to?' asked Jake.

Amanda finished her coffee, turned, and grabbed her hat and jacket from the nearby hooks.

'I'll take motive number three. Revenge, or resentment. However you want to term good old-fashioned malice.'

'Whoever'd hate Judy that much? She seemed such a sweetheart,' said Casey.

Amanda paused at the entrance archway and turned, her eyebrow raised.

'Have you ever seen local politics in action?'

CHAPTER SIXTEEN

Amanda walked out of the sheriff's department and headed across the park to the town hall. It took her a few minutes to reach its brown-brick and white-wood paneled Colonial-era facade. Well-trimmed hedges ringed the exterior walls, and a giant American flag fluttered gently from a pole above the main entrance. She took the stone steps one at a time, keeping as considered a pace as her walk over had been.

Amanda had formed a plan of action. First, she would investigate Judy's political activities and then consult the mayor, Gary Brennan. He kept a keen eye on all the councilors, not least his own wife, Mary Brennan. If there was reliable information, gossip, or rumor floating around local government, Gary would usually be the one to grab them like nuts and squirrel them away for future advantage.

Gary always gave the impression of someone better suited to being the sidekick than the hero. Still, Amanda had known him a while, if only as an acquaintance involving town and county business, rather than as a friend. She had quickly picked up on how Gary, once a councilor himself, had used his organizational skills, institutional knowledge, and no-small-dose of discreet cunning to aid people with all manner of problems.

From helping to secure planning permission to small business promotion, he had scratched many backs. In doing so, he had built up enough credit for when he had campaigned for mayor and won, to the surprise of many. Amanda had enjoyed a functional relationship with Gary since winning her own election to the sheriff's office. She had made sure to keep a certain distance though, diplomatically turning down social invitations where it promised to be just the two of them.

Amanda had a feeling that any such meeting would see Gary attempt to solicit her political support in some way. However, she was determined to remain neutral in such matters, backing only those she deemed the best qualified for any elected position. Though she doubted Gary was involved in anything illegal, he still reminded her of a small town Richard Nixon, rising above natural limitations to realize his ambitions.

Like Nixon, though, Amanda wondered how many dirty hands Gary had shaken along the way, and she had no desire to see any dirt on his palms rub off on hers.

Independence was a world away from the machine politics of big cities. Still, Amanda was an honest campaigner and had not struck deals or made promises to gain any advantage. She would rather lose honorably.

Just as Gary had cultivated friends, one way or another, it was not inconceivable that Judy had made some enemies of her own during her time on the council. Amanda knew that Judy had not worked a main job like most of her peers, who undertook council business as a part-time occupation. There was no need for her to work, given that Ray provided a good standard of living for the Sterling family. As a result, Judy had spent far more time on her council activities than most, gradually increasing her knowledge and influence and with them, power.

Like moths to a flame, power attracted envy and resentment from those who had lost it or had never wielded it in the first place. Perhaps any political ire Judy had attracted would not have been enough to encourage such a step as murder. However, while Jake and Casey dealt with their tasks, Amanda wanted to be proactive. She felt nothing would be lost by considering all the angles.

Amanda walked through the large glass doors and entered the main lobby. It was a large room, big enough to allow a hundred seated persons, with a polished marble floor and a white-painted wooden dome at the ceiling's center. The lobby itself had once represented the entirety of the town hall, built in the mid-1700s, and large enough to host most of the population of the time. As requirements grew, the building had expanded over the centuries, with extensions added to the rear and sides and then a second floor.

In its current arrangement, the council occupied the ground level, with a central debating chamber ringed by a few small committee rooms and the multiple shared offices of the councilors. There were 35 of them in all, with a third comprised of Republicans and Democrats, with the remaining two-thirds made up of Independents. Independence town and county was not just a name, but a motto, with local politics preferring to take its own route and bypass the partisan feuding of the two main national parties.

The floor above was reserved for the office of the mayor and other departments essential to the smooth running of the area, such as sanitation, public works, education, and the like.

Amanda walked up to the main reception desk, behind which sat a young woman who quickly put her smartphone down and pretended to be interested in some documents next to her.

'Afternoon, Sheriff,' said the receptionist. 'How can I help you?'

'Is Shelly Goodwin in today?' asked Amanda. 'I'd like to see her if she has the time?'

'I'll just check,' replied the receptionist. She picked up a desk phone, tapped in a short internal number, and waited a moment. It didn't take long.

'Hi Shelly, I've got Sheriff Northstar up at reception. She was wondering if she could come down and see you?'

The receptionist nodded and said thank you, then put the phone back down.

'That's fine. Would you like me to show you the way?'

'I'm fine, thanks,' replied Amanda. 'One more thing, though. Could you check with Mayor Brennan's office what time he'll be here until?'

'Sure thing,' said the receptionist as she picked up her desk phone once again and repeated her inquiry procedure. She put the phone back down and looked up to Amanda.

'The mayor's secretary says he's here until closing, at five o'clock.'

'Great, thanks,' said Amanda. 'I'd better let you get back to work.'

Amanda nodded goodbye and headed towards a set of doors to the right of the reception desk, which led to the council section of the building. Amanda peered back over her shoulder as she opened the doors, spotting the receptionist discreetly scan the lobby and return to the fun and games of her personal phone.

Amanda found herself in a short corridor. Straight ahead was another set of double doors that led to the debating chamber, committee rooms, and the councilor offices. Halfway down the corridor and to the left was another door, just a single one this time, which led down to the basement. A sign above said 'Council Clerk and Archives'. Amanda walked through the door and descended an old fashioned spiral staircase.

The stairs were painted a soft white, like the walls around it, and benefitted from sufficient lighting. This was no grimy basement where records went to die, and staff were forgotten. It was simply a matter of using the space available. Just as the sheriff department's attic fulfilled an archiving role, so did the town hall basement. That said, there was no one like Shelly Goodwin anywhere near Amanda's building, let alone attic.

Amanda stepped off the staircase and, after a few paces, found herself outside Shelly's office, a small cube in the corner of the basement, opposite which were several computer desks and terminals. The rest of the vast floor space was devoted to rows of library stacks, which were mounted on rails and required handles to be turned to move the shelves horizontally to make space to walk between them.

Shelly's door was ajar, but Amanda still knocked out of politeness. She immediately heard a slightly shrill, cheerful response.

'Come in, Sheriff!'

Amanda opened the door and stepped through. Shelly was sat behind her desk. She was a large girl in her early thirties, more curvy than overweight. She wore a red dress and a white cardigan. With a bun of dark blonde hair, thick-rimmed glasses, and ruby-red lipstick, taken together, her appearance echoed a 1950s teenager waiting for some handsome, leather-jacketed greaser to whisk her away to the school dance.

Shelly's office was small, but she had personalized it with posters of planets and nebulas to make up for lack of a window. Various comic book and fantasy action figures struck poses upon her desk and flat surfaces around the room. Shelly raised a perfect pearly smile as Amanda walked in and invited her to take the seat opposite the tiny desk.

'Good afternoon, Sheriff, so nice to see you! I don't think I've seen you down these parts before, with us mole people. Can I help you with anything?'

Amanda picked up the stack of files atop the spare seat, placed them on the ground, and sat down.

'I hope so, Shelly. I'd like to find out as much as I can about what Judy Sterling did on the council.'

'Oh, I saw the paper this morning. Such a shame, poor dear,' said Shelly, frowning. Suddenly she raised an eyebrow. 'What? D'you think something she'd done here might have gotten her killed? Oh my!'

'No, no, Shelly, calm down. Nothing like that,' replied Amanda, raising her hand into a 'slow down' gesture, even though Shelly wasn't that far from accurately guessing Amanda's line of inquiry.

As pleasant as she was, Shelly was well known to have an overactive imagination, which she nurtured with amateur dramatics and an enthusiastic following of all things fantasy, science-fiction, and comic book in nature. The worst thing Amanda could have done was to encourage such dramatic leaps. What she now needed from Shelly was a clear head and her expertise as the council clerk.

Shelly was responsible for recording and archiving council business, from the minutes of various meetings, annual reports, votes taken, and everything in-between. With any luck, Shelly would be able to gather a decent amount of information on Judy's activities in a timely and efficient manner, allowing Amanda to look for anything that struck her as noteworthy or suspicious.

'We're still looking into the exact circumstances of what happened to Judy,' said Amanda, truthfully, if vaguely. 'I just wanted to get a better sense of what she did here, in case it might help in some way. I did see her at various meetings and social gatherings, but I never knew much about her role in detail. Think you could pull something together out of your records that relate to her and help me out?'

'Oh yes, absolutely!' responded Shelly enthusiastically. 'I keep very meticulous records, you know. I'm very proud of it. Would you like just the computerized records, or the paper files as well?'

'What's the difference?' asked Amanda.

'Well, the paper files go all the way back to when she started as a councilor seven years ago. In fact, that goes for all the councilors elected in the election before last. It also applies for the first year after the last election, which was three years ago come November. Two years ago, though, we had some money come through for a modernization drive to help computerize a lot of the council services and internal business. So everything for the past two years exists digitally. Understand?'

Amanda nodded a little absently in the affirmative, despite Shelly racing through her explanation as if she had challenged herself to accomplish it in one breath.

'So what you're saying is that I can go through five years of paper records and then the two most recent years are electronic?'

Shelly nodded excitedly.

'Yep. I can get started now if you'd like? It shouldn't take too long to gather all the boxes. There are only ten or so, I think.'

Shelly made to stand. Amanda raised her hand again.

'That's okay, Shelly, could I just take a look at the last two years please, on the computer? I'm assuming it's all categorized and searchable?'

'Of course,' replied Shelly with a hint of disquiet, as if the thought that her system would be anything other than perfectly ordered bordered on blasphemy.

She stood and beckoned Amanda to follow her. They stepped out of the office and walked over to the computer research area opposite. Shelly took a seat in front of one of the terminals, booted it up, and started the search process for Judy Sterling.

Within seconds several clickable files appeared on the screen in different rows. Each row corresponded to meetings, votes, expenses claims, and various other types of documents where Judy appeared in the text. Shelly stood and offered the chair to Amanda.

'There you go, Sheriff, everything that featured Judy's official duties. The only thing we don't have available are emails. You'd have to get a court order to examine those, or at least the ones we have on our server.'

'Thanks, Shelly, I really appreciate it,' said Amanda as she removed her jacket and hung it on the back of the chair. She sat down and placed her hat next to the mousepad as she scanned what was available on the screen. She glanced at her watch. It was three o'clock, and the town hall closed in two hours. She looked up at Shelly, who was still hovering to the side.

'I take it there's no problem with me printing certain documents if I need to take them away for reading?'

'No, no problem,' said Shelly, shaking her head. 'It's on the public record. We're hoping to make it all available online early next year, before the mayoral and council elections in November. Let the voters see what their representatives have been doing in their name. We've wanted to do it for so long, but you know…'

'Budget,' nodded Amanda. 'I know that very well, Shelly.'

'Well, I'll, uh, let you get on then. Do call if you need anything. I'll be right there like any good sidekick!' Shelly giggled nervously.

'Will do,' said Amanda, raising a polite smile.

She deliberately left silence in the air. After a moment, Shelly bowed a little and glided back into her office, her sparkling red high-heels click-clacking on the wooden floor. Amanda returned her attention to the computer screen and studied what was on offer.

She didn't see it as an issue that the computerized records only covered the previous two years. If anything relating to Judy's work had been a factor in her death, then it most likely would have been recent, occurring within the past few weeks or months. In any event, if Amanda needed to go further back, then she could. Still, until it was necessary, there was no point in making extra work for herself.

After discounting copies of official press releases and articles from the council newsletter and website, Amanda narrowed down her search to Judy's monthly expense claims, the minutes of full council debates and committee meetings, and the results of committee and council votes.

Amanda opened each expense claim in turn, but found nothing out of the ordinary, mainly costs relating to local or regional travel, food, hotel accommodation, and other minor claims. Each expense had been receipted and approved by the auditor, and in any case, were few and far between.

Unless Judy had been involved in a conspiracy to defraud the local treasury of a few hundred dollars, there was no apparent financial irregularity that could have come into play when considering her death. Just to be safe, Amanda printed off the expense claims from a printer at the corner of her desk. She then turned her attention to the minutes of the various meetings Judy had attended.

Amanda decided to focus only on the meetings since January rather than the whole two years available. She clicked open several files and quickly noted the page counts of each. Many of the documents were dozens of pages long. She scanned through them and was able to pick out Judy's specific contributions among all the speakers, but it would still take hours to get through. Again, she set each document to print, deciding she would read through them later that evening with a red marker pen to underline anything of interest.

While the minutes were printing out, Amanda opened Judy's voting records. There were only a few in comparison to the large number of minuted meetings. Clearly, local government was little different from its higher cousins regarding the ratio of talk to action.

A few of the voting records were related to budgetary measures and infrastructure initiatives that had been up before the council as a whole in the main chamber. However, most of them seemed to apply to Judy's position on the Planning and Environment Committee. She was one of eight members of one of the more influential committees, since it had the power to approve or deny major planning applications and environmental initiatives before the measures were sent up to the main council chamber for debate and final voting.

There had been five committee votes since January, two of them in that particular month. The first had concerned the demolition of several houses deemed too old and unstable to be redeveloped, with a children's playground and garden proposed to take their place. The vote had gone 5-3 in favor of the park, with Judy voting against.

The second January vote related to the Riverside Road development, by far the most significant building project that Independence had seen in years. That is if it had gone ahead and not been gridlocked by endless reviews and debate for what seemed like forever. The voting record that Amanda viewed on the screen summed up the situation perfectly. The vote had been a 4-4 tie, with Judy voting in favor. The approval or decline of the development would have to be delayed yet again pending further consideration.

The third vote of the calendar year had been in March, with the committee deciding on the merits of extending the walking trail that began near the Saratoga Bridge all the way into town, in doing so potentially attracting more tourist dollars. The extension gained approval on a 6-2 majority, with Judy again voting in favor.

The fourth vote had been in June, with planning permission granted for a small apartment complex for retirees. However, this time the vote had tightened to 5-3, the same as with the playground proposal. Amanda was unsurprised to see that Judy had voted in favor of the development. A pattern was emerging where she placed priority on projects with an economic return, above any concerns about potential environmental impact.

Amanda clicked open the fifth and final voting record, which was dated September, the month that was about to end. Amanda immediately saw that it was a re-run of the Riverside Road vote. Once again, it had resulted in a 4-4 tie. Amanda read through the voting list, expecting to see Judy's name in favor. Instead, she was surprised to find that Judy had voted against the development.

This action not only broke the chain of how Judy had behaved in the previous votes, where she had prioritized economic benefits. It was the complete opposite of how she had voted on the exact same issue the first time around. Amanda noted the date of the vote. It had been held on September 15th, exactly two weeks previously. She remembered something that Jake had told her on the riverbank the day before.

Amanda pulled out her phone and quickly typed a text message to Jake, asking him the date he had been called out to intervene in Ray and Judy's domestic disturbance. A reply came swiftly, asking her to wait a minute while he checked his records. A minute later, a ping indicated that he had an answer. Jake had been called out late on the evening of September 15th.

Amanda did not dismiss that genuine coincidence was possible, if rare, but this alignment was far too neat. Judy had seemingly voted against her usual pattern and had argued fiercely with her husband later that same day. One of them had clearly disapproved of her actions, and logically that person was Ray.

But why would he have taken issue with what she had done? He was a lawyer, not a construction contractor or property developer. That particular job description, she knew, applied to Carter Townsend, the head of the council. However, he had been allowed nowhere near the Planning and Environment Committee due to the conflict of interest it would have created.

Amanda glanced at her watch. An hour had raced by, and it was already a little after four o'clock. She needed to leave herself enough time to visit Gary Brennan. However, instead of the basic list of queries she'd had lined up regarding his recent observations and impressions of Judy, Amanda now had a genuinely intriguing question to ask of him. When it came to the future of the biggest development Independence had seen in years, why had Judy Sterling reversed her vote against all expectations?

CHAPTER SEVENTEEN

Jake texted his reply to Amanda, slipped his phone back into his pocket, and turned his attention to the one upon his desk. Judy Sterling's phone had been retrieved from the evidence locker soon after Amanda had left for the town hall. Jake had hoped to find some kind of clue that would shed light on the mystery that now consumed the activities of all three officers of the Independence sheriff's department.

He had been disappointed. Upon activating the phone, a start-up screen had immediately appeared, requesting the user input all manner of new data. A quick internet search had determined that this meant the device had been restored to its factory setting before Judy had abandoned it. All the information on the phone had been wiped.

The opportunity to attempt to reconstruct Judy's last days through her calls and texts had been lost, at least for the immediate future. From prior investigations, Jake knew that cell phone companies kept call records for up to a year. A subpoena would only allow access to basic information on the phone's owner, such as name, address, and credit card details, which Jake had no use for. A court order would be required to view the calls and texts Judy had sent and received.

Jake questioned if anything noteworthy would turn up on her personal number. Had Judy been involved in anything she wished to keep quiet, whether an affair or something else nefarious, it would have made more sense for her to have used a completely separate, unknown phone, probably a prepaid one. Nevertheless, it was an avenue of inquiry worth pursuing. So Jake had put in a call to Judge Hawkins's office to get the ball rolling on obtaining a court order the following day. All he could do was wait.

Jake sighed and looked across his desk towards Casey, who had just put her phone down after conversing with the Sterling family's life insurance provider.

'Anything?' he queried.

'It's getting too late today,' she replied. 'But they assured me that I'd have Judy's policy details emailed through first thing tomorrow. Was that text from Amanda?'

'Yep, she wanted to know when exactly I was called out to the Sterling house a couple of weeks back. I'm sure we'll find out why tomorrow.'

'Again with tomorrow. Is there anything we can actually get done today?' asked Casey, half in query, half in encouragement of taking action.

'Well, I still need to check the GPS in Judy's car,' said Jake, as he retrieved the keys to the vehicle from the zip-locked evidence bag atop his desk. 'Though, if she was careful enough to wipe her phone clean, then I wouldn't put money on us finding out much about her recent travels. But it's worth a try.'

They stood up and took the department's rear exit located at the end of the cellblock area. Immediately outside was the small impound lot surrounded by an eight-foot chain-link fence. Sandwiched between two old unclaimed vehicles was Judy's red Lexus. Jake took out his keys, unlocked the padlock to the gate, and walked through with Casey close behind. As they strolled towards the Lexus, Jake decided it was time to gently probe what, if anything, Casey knew about what he had witnessed regarding Rick the previous evening.

'So when did you and Rick end up calling it?'

'A little after eleven.'

'On a school night?' Jake tutted in teasing disapproval.

'Glenn was closing by then anyway. So we went to an illegal barn dance until three in the morning.'

'Plenty of drugs and moonshine on offer?'

'Of course. Why else even go?'

They looked at each other for a moment in mock-seriousness before breaking into broad smiles.

'Actually, we were in bed a half-hour after leaving Glenn's. Rick had to get up early, he's got a full shift today.'

'How sore was his head? He seemed to be making good progress through those pitchers.'

'His head was fine, just his pride took a dent. We lost at pool to his workmates. But even that was good fun and we did need it. That's why I let him out for a smoke when he saw you. Normally I'd kick his ass, but it was a night off for the both of us.'

Jake had replayed the previous night's events in his mind. At no time had he smelt anything that indicated Rick had been smoking before they had encountered each other outside. The meeting with the man in shadow had been the primary motive of Rick's supposed cigarette break, not to answer any nicotine cravings.

He was sure any deal had been less than honest. Otherwise, why meet where no eyes were likely to spot them? Yet, Jake had seen nothing change hands. Could it have been a preliminary meeting to set up something more significant, best discussed in person than over the phone or email? He put aside such thoughts as they reached Judy's car.

Jake pressed the unlock button on the key fob, and the door locks opened with an audible click. He took the driver seat while Casey opened the passenger side. Jake inserted the key into the ignition and turned it slightly for the electronics to come on, if not the engine. The GPS touchscreen in the center of the dashboard lit up. Jake navigated through the various options on the screen until he came to 'Previous Destinations'. He tapped it and was unsurprised to find a blank screen. Judy had obviously pressed the 'Clear History' option visible at the bottom of the screen.

'Figures,' he said with a sigh.

'Wait, give me a second,' said Casey as she pulled her phone out of her pocket.

He watched her a moment as she tapped at the phone's screen.

'Care to fill me in?' he asked.

'I bet that a lot of people accidentally clear their journey history, just like you might delete an email by mistake or something.'

'You don't think she accidentally covered her tracks, do you?'

'No, I'm sure it was deliberate. But, like most people, maybe Judy assumed that once she'd cleared her journeys, they were gone. There may be a way of retrieving the data that she didn't know about. Yep, here we are.'

Casey switched her focus between her phone screen and the GPS as she followed the steps she had found on an advice website. She entered into the 'Settings' section and several further submenus until she found a button labeled 'Restore Data'. She tapped it and then swiftly backed up until she had returned to the 'Previous Destinations' screen. This time it was full of addresses. Jake smiled.

'Well, would you look at that. I'm impressed.'

'I'm not just good at choreographed backflips, you know.'

Jake started scrolling through the list of addresses Judy had previously typed in. Unsurprisingly most of them were unfamiliar destinations outside of the county, presumably work-related or personal leisure trips. Judy would not have needed to frequently use the GPS as a guide to Independence, given that she had lived there for years and would have easily known her way around. Jake stopped when he spotted a familiar local zip code, which stood out against all the strangers. He glanced at Casey.

'Search for this place, would you? I don't remember any buildings around there.'

Casey opened a map app on her phone and leaned towards the screen.

'Dry Lake Road. That's pretty out of the way.'

She typed in the address, and the map quickly zoomed in on the navigation pointer centered on a road on the county's margins. It was deep in the forested area to the northwest of Independence, beyond which lay the gentle foothills that were the beginnings of the Catskills. The road itself was a white-colored artery on the map, with small, grey capillaries representing dirt trails that led off into the forest at various points. Casey tilted her phone towards Jake to allow him to see the search result.

'Well, you were right,' she said. 'There's nothing out there, of any interest anyway.'

'Wrong,' said Jake, shaking his head. 'If Judy visited there, whatever her reasons, then it's of interest to us.'

'You want to check it out?'

'No, better wait for Amanda. Let's see if she's managed to turn up anything. Then we can add it to this and hopefully your life insurance findings in the morning.'

'Okay, then. Anything else?'

'No, I think we're good,' said Jake. 'I'll close up here.'

Casey nodded and stepped out of the car. She was about to close the door when Jake leaned towards it to catch her attention.

'Wait a sec. What are you and Rick up to tonight?'

'Well, tonight's my gym night. Pilates and then a half-hour on the treadmill.'

'First no beer and now this? You taking part in any triathlons you want to tell me about?'

'A woman's got to keep herself in shape for her man now, doesn't she?'

'Well, speaking of your man…' Jake pressed.

'After his Tuesday shift, Rick just tends to watch whatever sports are on TV,' she responded. 'Why do you ask?'

'Just curious, I guess,' replied Jake with a shrug, though he knew full well the real intent of his question. 'You know you can always join me for a run sometime if you get bored with the treadmill.'

Casey gave him a skeptical look.

'Thanks, but I've seen how fast you run on the football field and how long you can keep it up for after the Marines. Combine the two, and I'd be a mess before you even broke a sweat.'

'Well, you never know until you try. If you give it a go, then maybe I can be persuaded to attempt some of those choreographed backflips.'

'You're on, Mister,' said Casey.

She winked and closed the passenger door.

Jake watched her head back inside the station through the rearview mirror. He took out his phone and searched online for the office number of Townsend Lumber, the mill Rick worked at. He dialed, and a receptionist answered within a few seconds.

'Hi, I was wondering if I could possibly speak to Rick Norris? I believe he's on the floor today.'

'One moment please,' the receptionist replied. 'I'll just check with the floor manager if he's available.'

Jake was put on hold and forced to listen to tinny elevator music. If Rick was available, he'd make some excuse to hang up quickly, but something in Jake's gut told him he wouldn't need to think that fast. The music ended, and the receptionist came back on.

'I'm sorry, but the floor manager says that Rick wasn't due in today or tomorrow. Can I take a message?'

'No, that's fine, I'll catch him another time. Thanks again.'

Jake hung up. So much for Rick working a full day's shift. Either Casey was lying to him, or Rick was lying to her. Jake knew which he thought more likely. Rick's absence suggested that he'd been deceitful for far longer than just today, principally about all the supposed additional work hours he'd been offered.

If the mill wasn't providing him with extra wages, then the money he'd been flashing at Glenn's the previous night had come from somewhere. Jake doubted it was a legitimate source. Rick had always been more of an asshole than a criminal. Still, financial troubles could make that line all the easier to cross, and Casey had spoken of times being tough.

Jake decided that he would have to pay closer attention to his former teammate. He had prepared the ground with his earlier question to Casey about her and Rick's movements that coming evening. For a moment, Jake felt a twinge of guilt, perhaps even shame. Was he almost willing Rick to be up to no good so that he could tear him down with glee in front of Casey and the entire town? No, irrespective of who he was married to, if Rick was engaged in criminal activities, he had to be held accountable.

Jake realized that he had started to feel something he had not experienced since his time with the Reconnaissance Marines in Afghanistan, surveilling Taliban compounds for commanders on his unit's target list. It was a subtle feeling, but definitely there. He was feeling the thrill. The thrill of the hunt.

CHAPTER EIGHTEEN

Amanda finished up in the town hall archives, gathered her printouts into a neat pile, tucked them under her arm, and thanked an ever-keen Shelly for her time. She ascended the spiral staircase and exited into the main corridor. Instead of taking a right turn back into the lobby, Amanda took a left. She headed towards the council section, which held the main debating chamber, committee rooms, and shared offices. It was a decision she had taken on a whim, curious to see Judy's office for herself since she was so close. There was still enough time to sate her curiosity and pay a visit to Gary before the day was up.

Amanda walked through a set of double doors and was faced with a long corridor, either side of which were the councilors' offices. Had she turned left, another shorter passage would have led her to the council chamber and the handful of committee meeting rooms.

Amanda stepped forwards and slowly made her way along the corridor, turning her gaze from left to right and back again as she scanned the brass nameplates next to each office door. Each displayed two names, indicating the occupiers. The only one she could see that had a single name engraved on it belonged to the office at the very end of the corridor. It was occupied by Carter Townsend, the head of the council. Amanda was surprised to see no red carpet leading to the door.

About halfway along, Amanda stopped in front of Judy Sterling's office. According to the nameplate, Judy shared it with Mary Brennan, who Amanda had met casually during events and festivities, but had no active social relationship with. The door was open with space for Amanda to poke her head through. It was an open invitation, though she still knocked before entering.

'Hello?' she asked the room.

Amanda opened the door fully and took in the office, a medium-sized space with enough room for two large desks and a small seating area for visitors. Bookcases lined the walls, filled with texts on politics, history, and local governance. A large central window looked out upon the park outside. Sitting at the desk furthest from the door was Mary Brennan. She was a short woman but had a lean elegance, complemented by a well-fitting pantsuit and a cream silk scarf wrapped around her neck.

In her late-forties, Mary was naturally pretty. She wore gentle makeup, and her black hair was styled into a bob, with occasional grey strands apparent but not numerous. She had been gazing absent-mindedly out of the window and looked at Amanda as she entered. Mary's eyes were slightly reddened and puffy. She had been crying recently and not just a few tears.

'Good afternoon, Sheriff,' said Mary, attempting a sincere smile and failing.

It was not a rude tone, Amanda sensed. It felt more like Mary wanted to be welcoming, but simply couldn't summon the emotional energy to follow through. She touched her hair briefly, checking she looked presentable.

'I wasn't expecting you, I'm sorry,' she said.

'Not at all,' replied Amanda reassuringly. 'I didn't expect to visit here myself, but I've been down in the archives looking through some documents, so just thought I'd explore a little. I didn't realize Judy shared an office with you.'

'Yes, I moved in at the start of the year. I was on the other side of the corridor, without a window. I was finally at the end of my tether. Judy's former office mate is standing down next year and kindly offered to swap with me for the duration of his term.'

'So you and Judy got on well then?' asked Amanda.

Mary scoffed a brief laugh and quickly reigned it back in. She pointed at her eyes.

'These aren't crocodile tears, Sheriff. Judy and I were close friends. It's funny, really, we were elected at the same time but rarely spoke until we both found ourselves on the Planning and Environment Committee. A seed of friendship was planted then, but only bloomed properly when I took this desk.'

Mary's lips started to quiver slightly, and she sniffed back the tears that threatened to appear. She shook her head a little and looked to Amanda.

'I'm sorry, that all sounded very flowery, literally. I'm still having trouble processing what she did to herself. I guess it's proof that you can't ever truly know someone like you think you do.'

'How did you know Judy killed herself?' asked Amanda, her attention raised. 'It wasn't made clear in the press.'

'Oh, I spoke to Raymond,' Mary quickly offered by way of explanation. 'When I called to offer him my condolences.'

'I see,' said Amanda neutrally.

She glanced towards Judy's desk. It was clear and uncluttered and looked like it was empty and waiting for an occupant. Either Judy really was as environmentally conscious as her final vote had indicated, and refused to use much paper, or she had meticulously cleared the desk, knowing that she'd never use it after leaving the office a final time.

Again the most puzzling aspect of her death was highlighted. Here was a woman who, one way or another, had intended to leave Independence, but had seemingly been killed before she'd had a chance to do so. Amanda looked down at the stack of printouts under her arm.

'A quick question. I was looking through Judy's committee voting records for this year. In each one, she seems to have voted for the option with the bigger economic boost, including the first Riverside Road vote in January. Then, at the second vote two weeks ago, she did a complete one-eighty. I mean, whichever way you slice it, a green light for that development would have brought in dollars and jobs. But she voted against it. Any idea why?'

Mary thought for a moment and sighed.

'I would say you'd have to ask her yourself, Sheriff. But that's not possible, unfortunately. Perhaps you should read the transcript of the meeting and her explanation.'

'Thank you, I will,' said Amanda. 'Though I noted that you voted against the development as well, both times. Surely you discussed it with each other if you were both voting the same way?'

'What can I say, Sheriff? I'm an environmentalist, as my own voting record shows. Maybe sharing an office with me broadened Judy's horizons?'

Mary raised her eyebrows, questioning what more she could offer. A moment of awkward silence followed, and Amanda decided that she had mined all she could out of the conversation. She slowly moved back towards the door.

'Well, I had better be off. I'd like to speak to Gary before you both leave for the day.'

'Oh, we won't be leaving together,' said Mary coolly. It was a statement and one which did not invite any follow-up questions. Mary turned her attention back to the window and the park outside.

'Well, take care,' said Amanda with a nod. 'And I'm sorry about Judy.'

She retreated through the doorway and gently pulled the door behind her, leaving it as open as it had been before. As she turned to make her way back to the lobby, Amanda was sure she heard some tearful whimpering before it was muffled.

**

Amanda returned to the lobby and headed up the staircase that led to the mayor's office and other public service departments. She walked past a small outer room, where Gary's secretary smiled and nodded her through.

Amanda entered the mayor's office, a large room with a conference table to the left, a semi-circle of leather armchairs near a fireplace to the right, and a large varnished wooden desk towards the back of the room.

Behind the desk was a semicircular window that afforded a view of most of the town square park, a mixture of buildings and church spires beyond that, and the forested hills even further out.

Gary sat at the mayor's desk. Its surface was covered by a computer, phone, and framed photographs of himself standing next to various minor celebrities and figures from state politics, with the occasional Congressman adding a dose of Washington glamour.

'Sheriff, good to see you,' said Gary cheerfully as he rose from his desk and extended a hand.

Amanda approached and shook his hand. He indicated the seating area.

'You're lucky you caught me today. I won't be around tomorrow, got some business away that needs taking care of.'

They both sat down. Amanda half-disappeared into the soft leather chair, clearly not a cheap purchase. She scooted forward slightly and perched on the edge.

'Can I get you a coffee? Something stronger for the afternoon?' Gary asked, indicating a drinks tray atop the mantelpiece of the fireplace.

Amanda raised an eyebrow.

'No thanks to the first, and I'm on duty for the second.'

'I know, just teasing. The ever incorruptible Sheriff Northstar,' replied Gary with a chuckle. However, Amanda suspected he wouldn't have batted an eyelid if she had accepted a shot of bourbon, like many of his visitors surely had. There was a reason the bottle upon the tray was half empty.

'So, what can I do for you, Amanda?' asked Gary.

Amanda didn't mind when people used her first name and never insisted on being addressed by her title, even though most people did as a mark of respect. As two leading members of the community, Gary and Amanda would sometimes trade official pleasantries, but would quickly revert to informal conversation. The most important thing was to get things done, and Amanda hoped that this meeting would be fruitful. Whatever Gary's faults, he could usually be counted on to talk straight.

'I'll get to the point, Gary. I'm here about Judy Sterling,' she replied.

'Oh?' said Gary as he shifted slightly in his chair. 'Damn awful thing. Bad for the family. I'm not sure how I can help, though.'

'Did you notice anything different in her behavior lately, any signs of anger, frustration, depression, things like that?'

'Not that I saw, but then I hadn't seen much of Judy lately.'

'She shared an office with your wife. Didn't you see her when you visited Mary?'

'You're assuming I visit Mary,' he replied, flatly. 'We try and keep out of each other's way here, to maintain a line between work and life, you know?'

Amanda nodded. She had wanted to ask a couple of obvious questions to warm Gary up. Now she lined up the one which had attracted most of her attention since her visit to the archives.

'It's fair to say you're pretty plugged into what's going on around here, politically.'

'Well, it *is* my job,' he said with a chuckle.

'So nothing gets by you?'

'I'd be a pretty poor political operator if it did, Amanda, just like you'd be a poor sheriff if you let crimes regularly slip by.'

Amanda drew out the voting record document from her printouts and held it up.

'So maybe you can explain to me why Judy voted in favor of the Riverside Road development in January, but then opposed the exact same thing eight months later?'

Gary stared blankly at her a moment, then at the paper. He shrugged.

'I really wish I knew. I thought it'd be a tight vote, but I'll admit I was surprised when Judy switched and caused a tie. As to why, I can't say. It was her prerogative. Now, I'll make no secret that I approve of the development. It'll bring new residents to Independence, improve infrastructure, increase the tax base. Sure, we'll lose a few hundred acres of land, but the rodents and birds can go elsewhere. It's not like we're lacking for natural habitats in this county.'

'Sounds like those rodents and birds had strong support on the committee,' said Amanda. 'Including Mary.'

'That's another reason why my wife and I try not to mix too much politics with the personal. Sure, we agree on a lot, while still not exactly seeing eye to eye on some things. But then she's never had to sit in my chair and look at the big picture. Conserving nature is all very well, and I'm all for it, but not when it gets in the way of progress.'

'And would you say that Judy made some people unhappy in stopping that progress, especially when it looked like it was finally going ahead?'

'Where are you heading with this?' asked Gary cautiously, raising an eyebrow.

Amanda held her hands up slightly.

'I'm just covering all the bases, Gary. As you say, if I let anything slip by me, I wouldn't be a very good sheriff now, would I?'

'Kind of sounds like you're looking for some Watergate-style conspiracy.'

'And where am I going to meet Deep Throat? At Glenn's place? Come on, Gary, hardly. But doesn't it strike you as the least bit strange that Judy suddenly went against months of consistent voting?'

'No, Amanda, it doesn't. It's called politics. People have a right to change their minds, including politicians. We're still people after all.'

'Okay, so tell me what happens now.'

'In what way?'

'I'm guessing the wheels need to keep turning. Judy will have to be replaced, both on the council and on the committee.'

'That's true,' nodded Gary. 'Just as when someone in office dies or resigns unexpectedly, there'll be a special election next month in her old ward for a replacement. Regarding the committee, one of the existing councilors will be assigned her vacant seat, and normal business can go on.'

'And that normal business could include a new vote on the Riverside Road development?' asked Amanda.

'There's no reason it couldn't. The new member of the committee will have his or her own opinion to bring to the debate. It could finally break the tie, one way or another.'

'And who assigns a replacement member to the committee?'

'The head of the council, of course. Carter Townsend.'

Amanda stroked her fingers along her cheek a moment, processing her thoughts. She had started the day with the feeling that a jigsaw puzzle needed to be solved but had no idea what the image was or what pieces constituted it. Now, she still couldn't quite see the final image, but at least she had started to generate some of the pieces.

There were signs of murder, an unexpected vote that had derailed a major project, and the ability for interested parties to take advantage of Judy's death to get their cherished development back on track. On their own, these pieces of the puzzle were evidence of nothing, merely conjecture. However, if she could collect yet more, Amanda could begin to assemble them and see what secrets the unknown image revealed.

She snapped out of her musing when Gary coughed politely.

'I'm sorry, Amanda, but I'm leaving soon and still need to finish off a few things.'

'No, I'm sorry Gary, I was in the clouds for a minute there. It's been a long day. I'll leave you to it.'

They both stood and shook hands in parting.

'Don't work too hard now,' said Gary in a jovial tone, trying to lighten the slightly tense mood that had descended during their conversation.

'I'd like to follow your advice,' replied Amanda as she opened the main door to exit. 'But I've got some reading to do tonight.'

She held up her printouts, smiled, and exited.

Gary's own smile dropped instantly. He quickly walked over to his desk, picked up his cordless phone, and dialed. He started pacing back and forth as the phone rang. He stopped when it was answered.

'Carter, it's Gary. We may have a problem.'

CHAPTER NINETEEN

Max wrote his surname on a piece of silver masking tape and stuck it on one of the distant lockers in the Rebels changing room. It was tucked far enough away from the main assembly area where the team sat for Booth's speeches. Max was just pleased to have a locker of his own alongside a few of the new recruits. He appreciated there was a certain hierarchy to the team, and with seniority came privileges, such as proximity to the coach's office and the showers.

Nevertheless, he was still a member of the team and had earned a spot on merit. He would be nobody's whipping boy, nor some sheepish newbie. This was his senior year, and he intended to end it with his head held high, not bowed low. If the application guide he had just received was any indication, he would need to make a positive impression if his tentative future plans were to be realized. The nature of the institution he was considering applying for was yet another secret he held from his mother, but this was normal among teenagers everywhere figuring out what they wanted from life, weighting their options until they were sure.

Max stripped off his equipment, stored the protective gear in his locker, and threw the soiled blue and white uniform into the nearby laundry basket. He stood in his underwear and admired a whole new set of fresh bruising he had acquired during the practice session that had just finished. He had joined the rest of the team in regular drills after school and then stayed behind for an extra half-hour for more practice catches with one of the assistant coaches.

It was an instinctive skill beyond simple repetition. Still, the more running catches Max caught, the more fluidly he grabbed the ball and ran with it, sometimes so perfectly that he barely had to slow his sprint to receive it. Max had quickly realized that praise from Coach Booth was a precious commodity, even for the team's stars, but that his assistants were slightly softer and more supportive. Whether it was a deliberate 'good cop-bad cop' arrangement, Max couldn't tell. Either way, he was satisfied that the assistants seemed pleased with his ability and were genuinely surprised that a rookie was performing so well.

Max wrapped a towel around his waist and headed for the showers. It was so quiet that he had assumed he was the last one remaining and so was startled when he turned a corner and saw Jason Sterling sat on a bench by himself. Jason was still in his playing gear and was keenly focused on a copy of the playbook that rested open upon his lap. He looked up as he heard Max gasp.

'Hey,' he said casually.

'Hey,' replied Max, shaking off his momentary scare. 'I thought I was the only one here.'

'Nah, I wanted to get some quiet time in to study the plays,' said Jason.

Max considered it strange that Jason seemed so remarkably calm. He thought it even more bizarre that he should be at training in the first place instead of emotionally recuperating at home. But then he'd heard his mother tell a few war stories about what shock could do to people and how they all dealt differently with grief and trauma. Perhaps smashing through the opposition on the football field was just Jason's way of dealing with things.

'You're one of the new guys, right? Northstar?'

'That's me. Call me, Max.'

'I saw some of your catches. Looking good for a newbie. Shame you won't get much time on the field, but it's all good memories.'

'Just happy to be a part of it,' said Max. 'Speaking of being a part of it, I didn't think we'd see you today. Since you weren't at classes, I mean.'

'No way is my head in the right place for geometry right now,' Jason said with a dismissive wave of his hand. He tapped the playbook with a gloved finger. 'But this is my kind of education. Out on the field today, I had a clear mind, clear goals. I could forget about what happened, put it to the back of my mind, just for a second. I felt free. I think the coach could see that.'

From what he had seen of Coach Booth's competitive intensity so far, Max suspected that allowing Jason to play had more to do with preserving a tried and tested winning strategy, rather than any kind of grief therapy. Still, if it provided Jason some comfort, then who was he to argue?

'Yeah, about what happened with your mom. I know I'm probably the hundredth person to say it, so you're probably sick of hearing it, but I'm sorry for your loss.'

'Well, we've all got something to be sorry about,' said Jason, a melancholy tone creeping into his voice. 'But thanks anyway. I appreciate it, especially coming from you.'

'How do you mean?' asked a puzzled Max.

'I live and breathe football, Max. I'm a Rebel, like hundreds of guys before me, my Dad included. I've watched old tapes and DVDs from the archive. I saw Coach Northstar doing his thing on the sidelines, helping us win State back in Ninety-Six. My point is, at least I had time with my mom. You never even met your father.'

Jason's comments ignited realization in Max that he would now have access to old videos of his father, ones he had never seen due to his mother's sensitivities. What Jason had said was meant in sympathy but had, in fact, generated mild excitement in Max. He suppressed a smile, though Jason raised a small one, reflective of his serene mood.

Max couldn't believe the contrast in the person before him, so calm and stoic, whereas the day before, Max would not have been surprised to see Jason tearing limbs off his opponents. He wondered if the wounded young man had been given some kind of medication to help him cope. Or perhaps it really was as Jason said, that playing out on the field had given him some temporary respite from traumas that still probably hadn't fully inflicted the mental damage to come.

'Well, I'd better clean up,' said Max, deciding not to stretch the conversation too long. 'My grandma's making spaghetti and meatballs for me and my mom tonight, so I don't want to be late. You gonna be okay?'

'I'll be fine,' said Jason. 'I want to get at least some of these new plays solid in my head.'

Jason pulled off his right-hand glove, revealing tightly bandaged fingers. Max took notice and nodded towards them in concern.

'You okay?'

'These? No problem,' replied Jason as he gently flexed his fingers. 'Just a little accident at home last night. I was emotional, got a little clumsy. Cut my fingers, but nothing a first aid kit couldn't handle. I don't let the little things stop me.'

'You're aiming for the pros, aren't you,' said Max, a statement not a question and one made with a mixture of bemusement and wonderment at the single-mindedness on display.

Jason refocused his attention on the playbook.

'That's the plan, Max. Always has been, always will be. Whatever it takes.'

CHAPTER TWENTY

Jake sat in his personal vehicle, an old-style military surplus jeep he had salvaged from a wreckers yard and restored over several months. It was what he used when the motorcycle wouldn't suffice, such as for grocery shopping or camping trips. He had replaced almost everything inside and out, to the extent that the only thing that could be said to still be original was the body.

It had become his little project shortly after leaving the Marines, but before Amanda had approached him with her job offer. It had been an effective way of giving his life purpose and mind something to focus on other than dark thoughts. As the jeep had come together, from the mechanical and electrical insides to the exterior looks, from the new paint job to alloy wheels and canvass roof, Jake had felt himself be renewed along with it. Both were no longer decaying as they had once been.

Now he was parked a little down the street from Casey's house, deliberately placing himself between two street lights so that neither cast their full glare upon him. Jake had waited until darkness had fallen and pulled up close enough to monitor the Norris residence, but not so close that he would have been easily spotted.

He pulled out some miniature binoculars from his jacket pocket and scanned the house, not for Casey, but for Rick. His former teammate would either sit in and watch sports as Casey had said, or he would make some kind of move. If the latter transpired, then Jake was there to discover what that move was and whether it involved any illegality.

Through the binoculars, he spotted Casey exit the front door. She wore sneakers, lycra pants, and a hooded running top. A small backpack was flung over her shoulder. She inserted some earphones and started bobbing her head to the rhythm of whatever it was she was listening to on her phone. Casey began jogging in the opposite direction to Jake, heading towards the sports center.

Jake lowered the binoculars and checked his watch. It would probably take Casey fifteen minutes to jog to the center, forty-five minutes for a pilates class, say a half-hour on the treadmill, and then fifteen minutes to run back. That meant an absence of an hour and forty-five minutes if she stuck to her routine. If she decided to ditch the treadmill and suffice with the run home, that meant an hour and a quarter. Either way that didn't leave Rick much time if he was going to take advantage of the window of opportunity.

Jake sat and waited. Sure enough, after five minutes, Rick appeared out of the front door and hopped into his car parked in the driveway. He started it up, backed out, and headed off in the opposite direction to Jake. Jake started his jeep but kept his beams on low. He set off and quickly caught up with Rick, but kept a decent distance so as not to arouse suspicion.

They headed out of the neighborhood. Within minutes they were on one of the main roads heading south from town, away from the forested foothills of the northern part of the county and towards the flatter farming country.

If other vehicles pulled out onto the road in front of Jake, he let them, while still keeping Rick's car in his line of sight. If he needed to, he would overtake slower vehicles, but this would also have been construed as everyday driving. Jake's aim was to do nothing to attract Rick's attention, though he doubted Rick would have been particularly on edge or looking out for a tail. He didn't know that Jake was onto his suspicious activity. If Rick was anything like he was at high school - and indeed he was - then his cocksure attitude probably made him think he was untouchable anyway.

After fifteen minutes, they had well and truly entered the rural part of the county, with no lighting on the road other than from their headlights and the moon above. As a result of heading further out from town and even beyond the scattering of hamlets on the outskirts, it had become more difficult for Jake to blend in with other traffic, mainly because there was none. He had to keep further back than he would have wished, but just about managed to keep Rick in view. The latter rounded a tight corner, and Jake lost sight of him. When Jake emerged from the corner himself, the road ahead was completely dark, with no red taillights in view. Rick was gone.

Jake slowed and whipped his head from side to side, desperately trying to find some kind of road that Rick may have disappeared down. He suddenly spotted one to the left, an unsigned dirt trail that led off into darkness through thick bushes. Jake carried on, not wishing to make an obvious stop at the mouth of the road and not so foolhardy as to head straight down it.

He pulled over to a grass bank on the side of the road and killed the engine. He reached over to the back seat, opened a small protective case, and pulled out an old pair of night-vision goggles. It was a useful piece of equipment he had picked up in Afghanistan and had 'forgotten' to return. Independence was not the kind of place where counterinsurgency equipment was usually required. Still, on occasions, Jake had found that a little hi-tech kit had its uses, such as scoping out illegal raves before raids or monitoring public areas at night during bouts of drunken-teen-inspired vandalism.

Jake reached into the glove compartment and pulled out his sidearm, a 9mm semiautomatic pistol. He ejected the clip, checked it, inserted it back in, and chambered a round. He slid it into the shoulder holster underneath his jacket and zipped up halfway. Jake did not anticipate the need to draw his weapon, let alone use it. Still, he was heading into the unknown in pursuit of Rick, so it was better to be cautious. As he had learned from both real life and the movies, it was better to have a weapon and not need it, than to desperately need one and be empty-handed.

He hopped out of the jeep, checked both directions, and crossed the road. He jogged to the entrance of the side road, put on his goggles, and activated them. The world suddenly turned from gently moonlit silhouettes to sharper shapes of greens and blacks. The road ahead of him became clear and visible, and he carefully made his way down it. Through his boots, he felt the occasional squelch of soft mud or the sharpness of small stones.

For a hundred yards, the road zig-zagged slightly. Though Jake would have preferred to stick to the sides in case Rick headed back to the main road, the overgrown bushes and brambles meant that a route through the center presented the least resistance. Jake intended to find out what was at the end, what Rick's destination had been, and wanted to do so quickly to avoid potentially missing anything.

Finally, the road opened up. In the middle-distance, Jake spotted a rickety-looking farmhouse. A dilapidated barn and tool shed were nearby. The rusting remains of various agricultural vehicles and equipment were scattered around. The several hundred acres of surrounding fields were overgrown, left to nature to reclaim. The darkness, absence of any sign next to the entrance road, and the state of the long-unmaintained trail itself had all thrown Jake off. However, seeing the buildings helped him to realize that he had ventured onto the old Moorcock farm.

The owner of the land had been a crusty old goat on his last legs even when Jake had been in high school, content to farm only as much as he needed to provide for himself, which was minimal. Since returning to Independence, Jake had heard that Old Man Moorcock had passed away. His only living relatives, who had inherited the land, lived in Virginia and thus never visited.

No doubt they were waiting for the day when the farm would fetch a reasonable price for property development, but as it had yet to do so, they were content to keep a hold of the deeds and do little else. The long-abandoned buildings invited squatting, while the distance from any population center made it an ideal place to conduct criminal activities out of sight and thus out of mind.

Jake quickly assumed that squatting was taking place, at least, given that Rick's car was parked next to a pickup truck. However, the truck itself was so old and rusted that it could have easily blended in with the rest of the decrepit farm machinery. Though attempts had been made to cover up some of the larger farmhouse windows, slivers of light still made it through, and some of the smaller windows were cracked open, presumably for ventilation.

Jake crouched down and swiftly advanced. He kept low and ducked behind a rusted tractor with tattered tires. He was about a dozen yards away from the main farmhouse but thought better of getting too close. If he was spotted, then there were presumably at least two people in the house who could take him on, possibly more. Jake had intended this to be a reconnaissance mission only and was not equipped to mount any kind of raid.

As Jake leaned his head towards the house to try and hear as best he could, the front door burst open, and he quickly pulled back. He heard the stomping of boots on the porch and the exchange of two heated voices, one of which was Rick's. The other belonged to a Southern-accented man.

'Goddammit Keats!' yelled Rick. 'I paid you in full last night, so I expect a full batch, not half. I got guys expecting this stuff!'

'Then just tell half of 'em that they're gonna have to wait a while!' replied the man called Keats in a similarly heated tone.

'You know that isn't how it works,' said Rick. 'I don't know them by name, and they don't know me. It's safer that way. I leave the stuff, they take what they've ordered and leave the money. What d'you expect me to do for the ones that go empty-handed? Send them an IOU?'

'Your customer service issues ain't my problem, Rick.'

'I didn't have any issues until you threw a damn wrench in the machine!'

Jake peeked his head around the rear of the tractor as much as he dared. He could tell which one was Rick by his build. Still, even with his night-vision goggles, it was difficult to discern the features of Keats's face, just that he looked far smaller and weedier than his partner. He raised a finger, a clear signal for Rick to shut up, which he duly did, swiftly and compliantly.

In any other circumstances, it would have been logical to suppose that Rick would have dominated the conversation by virtue of his size alone. Yet Jake had the impression that Keats was in control. Rick was prepared to display frustration but never risk showing disrespect, even to a little man he towered over. It was potentially a mark of just how dangerous Keats was.

'I never guaranteed consistent supply!' Keats hissed. 'Besides, you ain't the only client for my wares. Count yourself lucky I'm still bothering to cook up the stuff you want. The profit margin don't really make it worth it compared to the real-deal product my boys in the Bronx want.'

'You know I won't touch that crap. It's far too hot for this part of the world,' said Rick, his voice quietening, a sign of submission to Keats.

'Your loss, I guess,' said Keats with a shrug. 'Never mind, I'll still cook the boosters up for you, even if it is a pain in my ass. For old time's sake. Call me sentimental.'

Jake gauged that the argument had dissipated, the initial anger on both sides having evaporated. Keats had reaffirmed his supremacy, which was enough.

'Look, thanks, I appreciate it,' said Rick. 'Can you give me what you've got, at least?'

'Yeah, okay,' replied Keats. 'I'll do my best to fix up the rest for you. I'll need to head out tomorrow to pick up some supplies. Hopefully, I'll square you away by tomorrow. Day after, at the latest. Come on, it's in the barn.'

'What, that's your new lab now?' asked Rick.

'Hell yes,' answered Keats, as if it were obvious. 'You don't expect me to sleep in the same house as the stuff that could poison me or blow the hell up, d'ya?'

Jake carefully watched the two men walk towards the barn. Keats opened a padlock on the main entrance, and both men entered, closing the doors behind them. A light immediately popped on inside. Like the farmhouse, efforts had been made to block larger gaps in the structure to stop light from slipping through. However, it was an impossible task to completely seal off such a large, rickety old building.

It didn't take a genius to realize that Keats was some kind of drug manufacturer, and Rick was a distributor for one of his products. He most likely cooked up drugs during the day, when light-leakage would not have been an issue. Of course, the Moorcock farm was isolated enough that it was unlikely any nighttime activities would have been noticed anyhow.

Jake was now sure that Rick's recent influx of cash was in no way related to extra work hours or anything so reputable. The secrecy involved in their manufacture could only mean that he was distributing illicit drugs. The cautious nature of how product and payment were exchanged between Rick and his clients could also mean that they were local. In Independence, it was generally easy to run into familiar faces on the street, none of whom would have wished to be recognized and potentially exposed. The blanket of anonymity kept all under it warm and safe.

Jake now had confirmation of his suspicions, but he needed to compartmentalize. It looked like Keats wasn't going anywhere, at least in the immediate future. Jake could return to investigate the farm further, backed up with a search warrant and his colleagues, fresh off an official confession from Rick about his supplier's identity and location. Right now, though, Rick was the priority.

He had clearly visited Keats to collect some of the product for his clients and would likely be taking it to the drop-off location. All Jake had to do was follow

Rick. It would present a prime opportunity to catch him red-handed, recover the product to analyze exactly what it was, and deny his clients their fix. No doubt Jake would be asked why he was following Rick in the first place, but he would cross that bridge and form that answer when it came to it.

Jake turned and headed back to the farm's entrance road, keeping as low as he could just in case. He figured it would only take a few minutes for Rick to obtain his supply and hop back into his car. Jake needed to be ready to tail him again when he appeared back on the main road. When Jake was confident he was far enough away from the farm buildings, he rose and sprinted down the entrance road.

Within a couple of minutes, he had opened his jeep door, tossed his goggles onto the back seat, and sat down, his fingers ready to turn the ignition key. He kept a keen eye on the rearview mirror, waiting to see the first trace of Rick's headlight beams emerge from the farm road. He did not wait for long.

CHAPTER TWENTY-ONE

Amanda sat at her kitchen table, the printouts from the town hall archives spread out across the surface, a red marker pen in one hand and a glass of wine in the other. Maggie was busy at the stove, boiling spaghetti, frying meatballs, and stirring her homemade sauce. Boomer snoozed in the far corner, occasionally twitching in response to something he was dreaming about.

Amanda looked up to her mother and smiled as she flashed back to the same room some thirty-years previously, as her teenage self tried to complete her English homework before dinner, while Maggie cooked, and her father sat in the lounge watching the evening news.

The older Amanda had swapped the shorts and vest top of her youth for a pair of sweatpants and a t-shirt, though in both cases, she had loosened her bun and let her hair down. Like her past self, though, she also expected to be told to clear the table at any minute. The present-day Maggie soon obliged.

'Come on dear, Max will be home soon, let's set the table. Besides, you've been going through those ever since you got home. Pour yourself another glass of the red stuff and take it easy.'

'I'm almost done,' said Amanda with a weary sigh. 'But it still doesn't make sense to me.'

'What doesn't?' asked Maggie as she started to cut a fresh baguette into slices to pile atop a plate.

'I've read through all of Judy's transcripts before each planning committee vote this year. In the first four, especially the first Riverside Road vote, she's clearly for development, even if the environment takes a hit. She talks about inward investment, growth opportunities for the town and county, that we have to respect the environment without letting ourselves be constrained by it, stuff like that.'

'I'm guessing there's an exception coming up?'

'You got that right. Like a bolt from the blue. In the second Riverside Road vote, which was two weeks ago, she talks about how, after further consideration, she simply can't support the development given the impact it would have on local wildlife, as well as the natural beauty of the area.'

'Since when did that bother her?' asked Maggie as she set the plate of bread down upon the table.

'Exactly,' said Amanda. 'But it's only when you start digging deeper into how the other members of the committee voted that the plot thickens. Most of the other seven councilors generally stick to their principles while leaving room to be pragmatic. It seems that their definition of the environmental interest isn't just conserving nature, but also what makes Independence a nice place to live, to help it keep its character. You know, that 'great place to raise a family, where everybody knows your name' feeling.'

'Well, is that such a bad thing? It's why our family has lived here since its founding,' said Maggie as she drained the spaghetti.

'So,' continued Amanda, 'if you can have the economic benefit without too much impact on the environment, then they'll vote for it, like with the extension of the walking trail. If the environmental cost is too high, like sacrificing a children's garden in favor of more housing in an already built-up area, they'll vote against. Some, like Mary Brennan, will vote for the environmental side of the argument consistently.'

'What's your point, dear?' probed Maggie as she poured the sauce onto the meatballs.

'There's one member, Will Richardson, who seems to fit the pragmatist mold. He votes against Riverside Road in January. He goes one way or the other on the following votes. However, come the second attempt at Riverside Road, he's completely switched sides and votes in favor. His statement almost reads like Judy's first one, explaining how, after due consideration, he can't ignore the positive case for jobs and economic development. With both Judy and Richardson suddenly changing their votes, they effectively swapped with each other and created another tie.'

'And stopped the development going ahead once again,' concluded Maggie as she ignored Amanda's raised eyebrow and cleared away the archive printouts. 'I'm sure that wasn't part of anyone's plan.'

'I'd say not,' said Amanda. 'Judy had been so consistent in her voting that I'll bet everyone thought she was a shoo-in to offer another thumbs-up for the development. All that was needed was to switch one of the pragmatists, like Richardson, from a no to a yes, and it would have been a 5-3 majority for Riverside Road to get the green light.'

Maggie plated three lots of spaghetti and spooned the accompanying meatballs and sauce upon them.

'So whoever convinced Richardson to switch must have assumed Judy was already in the bag and didn't see another 4-4 split coming,' she said, recognizing Amanda's train of thought. 'She was clearly set on causing some mischief.'

'The question is why,' said Amanda as she twirled a finger through her hair in thought.

As Maggie placed the three plates on the table along with the necessary cutlery, they both heard the front door open and close. A moment later, Max stepped through into the kitchen, his eyes lighting up at the sight of Maggie's culinary efforts and that he wouldn't need to wait to sample it.

'Looking good as ever, Grandma,' he said as he took his chair next to Amanda.

'Well, thank you,' Maggie responded with a smile.

'How do you always time these things so well?' Amanda asked of her mother as the three of them began eating.

'Forty-five years of mental arithmetic, dear. If I could sense when you needed raising from your crib for feeding, I can work out how long it takes Max here to get himself back from school. I assume you walked?'

'I did,' Max nodded. 'Chelsea was working, and I had practice, so no ride.'

'Very good of that girl to pick you up so often. You should invite her round for dinner sometime.'

'And I'm sure you'd provide the candlelit setup, right Grandma?'

'You can't blame me for being a romantic now, dear,' said Maggie, with her customary wink.

'How was practice anyway?' asked Amanda. 'Still have all your ribs intact?' It was a gently teasing tone.

'It was good,' replied Max. 'It's coming together well considering how quickly things have happened, but I'm not expecting much action. I'm a rookie and a back-up for the wide receiver, so I'm realistic. The coach has built his strategy around CJ and Jason, everyone accepts that. Can't say I blame Booth after seeing how determined Jason is.'

'You saw him today?' asked Amanda, surprised.

'Yeah, he was at practice. Not in class during the day, but I think they gave him a pass to join the team. They can see how much it means to him. He says he'd rather be out on the field than miserable at home.'

'You spoke with Jason?'

'Just before I showered and came home. He was still staring at the playbook as I was leaving.'

'How did he seem to you?' probed Amanda.

'Calm, I guess,' replied Max with a shrug. 'Maybe it's still sinking in, what happened to his mom. You know, like denial, or something. Or maybe he just let enough anger out on the field. He was totally different talking to me than he was playing. I think he actually scares some people when he gets going. The coaches have to calm him down sometimes. But when he is calm, he's kind of sad. Not depressed, just… morose. But then that's not surprising given what he's dealing with.'

Amanda listened keenly. From what Max said, it seemed as if Jason found the football field almost a kind of refuge from his troubles. When she had visited Ray to inform him of Judy's death, he had indicated that they were having marital problems. While Jason wasn't a child, he was still a young man in need of stability at a crucial time in his life. The simple dichotomy of victory and defeat, plus the close bond of teammates, perhaps provided him with an escape from a troubled household.

Amanda cast her mind back two weeks and to the night following the second Riverside Road vote, the night Ray and Judy Sterling had argued loud enough to concern the neighbors. Amanda was convinced that there was a connection, that Judy's vote was the spark that had ignited the underlying tensions. Perhaps that fateful fight had turned their marriage into a furnace from which she had to escape by faking her own death.

Thinking about Ray Sterling, Amanda's initial gut reaction was that he had genuinely been surprised to hear of Judy's death. But as new facts emerged, she was less sure that his hands were completely clean. For whatever reason, Ray seemingly had an interest in Judy voting in favor of Riverside Road and had exploded when she had not done so. Coupled with underlying marital issues, had it been enough to push him over the edge? Someone capable of such premeditation could easily prepare themselves to simulate a convincingly pained reaction to news of his wife's death.

Whatever the reasons for Ray's displeasure with Judy's vote, it was doubtful he was the only one left frustrated. For some people, there had been a lot riding on the approval of the Riverside Road development. Gary Brennan had openly told Amanda that he was supportive. The economic benefits of the construction phase would start to be felt by the following year's mayoral election, which Gary was not the favorite for. Had he felt that an opportunity, no matter how slim, to revive his electoral prospects had been denied him?

On the matter of the Brennans, it was apparent to Amanda that Gary and Mary's marriage was not a ship sailing on calm waters. The frostiness between them had been evident, which was quite something when they hadn't even been in the same room as each other. Gary and Mary's political priorities - his economic and hers environmental - were opposed to each other. Could Mary have used her friendship to convince Judy to switch votes and help her get one over on her husband, to damage his prospects or, at the very least, spite him? If that was the case, surely Gary was guilty of something that Mary felt demanded such a response.

Then there was Carter Townsend, the unseen hand. Amanda couldn't shake the feeling that he hovered like a storm cloud over proceedings, withholding the thunder and lightning he could no doubt unleash if so inclined, yet still blocking out the sun. As the primary contractor, the Townsend Group, his company, had stood to gain directly from the Riverside Road development. However, this was not a crime in itself. It was not uncommon in a small community that successful local businessmen and politicians would be one and the same.

Carter had been kept at arm's length from any form of decision making, but that didn't mean that he hadn't been able to use his position of influence. No doubt, some favors had been traded with Will Richardson to change his vote. It had all looked to be going so smoothly until Judy sprang her Damascene conversion on everyone. How had that derailed Carter's plans? Enough for him to take revenge and, as a positive bonus, open up a place on the committee that could be taken by a more pliable councilor?

Once again, Amanda was wary of spinning too many webs out of theories. However, the evidence gathered since her initial weaving gave her confidence that some of those possibilities were not entirely without merit. Nevertheless, as Amanda sat and enjoyed dinner in the company of her family, the primary questions still nagged at her. Why had Judy Sterling decided to vote the 'wrong' way two weeks ago, and had doing so ultimately gotten her killed?

CHAPTER TWENTY-TWO

It had taken Jake fifteen minutes to tail Rick to the drop-off site. There was not much time left if Rick wanted to get back home in good order to make it seem to Casey like he had been watching sports all evening. Right now, though, Rick's timekeeping was the least of Jake's concerns.

He had followed Rick back into town and pulled his jeep to the side just as he had seen his quarry turn down a short side road. Jake had left his vehicle and quickly but quietly made his way down the road, finding a seemingly abandoned concrete maintenance shed at the end of it.

The shed was adjacent to a chainlink fence. Beyond that fence was a sight that made Jake's heart sink, whereas, for years before, it had made his spirit soar. It was the Independence High School football field and running track, with the gymnasium, swimming pool, and the other smaller sports buildings just beyond. There could be no coincidence in the location of Rick's drop-off site. Whatever he was supplying was right on the doorstep of dozens of young athletes.

In Jake's head, the pieces suddenly started falling into place. During the exchange between Rick and Keats, he had overheard the word 'booster' in association with whatever it was that had been cooked up. With such a convenient drop-off point for potential clients in the student athletic body, Jake assumed that such boosters could be performance-enhancing substances. Also, Keats had mentioned the 'real deal' product for his clients in the Bronx.

While drug problems were an issue in any city, areas of the Bronx were still among the most socially deprived in the United States, and so vulnerable to drug dealing, as Harlem had been with heroin and crack in the Seventies and Eighties respectively. Rick had seemingly balked at involvement in the harder drugs Keats was peddling. It indicated that whatever the boosters were, they were lower-level substances, something that Rick's conscience, such as it was, could tolerate.

Jake could feel his temper starting to boil as he considered the implications of what Rick had been doing. If he already had an established system of supplying his clients and collecting money, then tonight wasn't his first waltz. He had been dealing drugs for weeks, perhaps even months, and had been spinning a yarn to Casey about extra work hours. The recent ready availably of cash indicated that he was doing a brisk trade. That ended tonight.

Jake drew his pistol from the shoulder holster under his jacket, firmly gripped it in both hands, and advanced towards the shed. He assumed that Rick was alone, but without sure knowledge of what he would find inside, he again decided to err on the side of caution. Even if Rick was alone, Jake hoped that the impact of seeing an armed law enforcement officer burst in would sufficiently scare the hell out of him, at least enough that Rick would drop his usual belligerence and provide Jake with some answers.

Jake braced himself in front of the main door to the shed. It looked reasonably solid, but was old and wooden, with peeled paint and some visible wood rot suggesting it would not pose too much of an obstacle. Jake raised his leg and booted it hard. The door flew open, and Jake pounced inside, his weapon raised.

'Freeze, sheriff's department!' he roared.

The interior was lit up by several battery-powered camping lamps, providing just enough illumination to spot Rick crouched down over a hole in the ground towards the rear of the shed. Its walls were lined with dust and cobweb-covered boxes and tools long since forgotten. Rick sprang up and launched his hands into the air.

'Don't shoot, Jesus, please don't shoot!' he screamed.

'Walk forward, slowly,' ordered Jake, his tone hard and unforgiving.

'Wait, Jake?' said Rick, as realization slowly dawned as to who was pointing a gun at him. 'There's been some kind of mistake here,' he continued, lowering his arms.

'Get those arms back up!' shouted Jake.

'Okay, okay,' said Rick, meekly, as his arms shot back up again.

Jake approached Rick, turned him around, pulled his arms down behind his back, and handcuffed him. All the while, Rick was breathing rapidly, quickly assessing that he was in a hole, and it was getting deeper and darker with every passing second.

'Look, Jake, I told you, there's been a mistake.'

'Don't give me your bullshit. It may work on Casey, but I see you for what you are. I know all about your little arrangement with Keats.'

'What, how-?'

'Never mind how. Don't worry, he'll get his, once I'm done charging you.'

'For what?'

Jake forced Rick down to his knees, holstered his pistol, and walked over to the hole in the ground. A large metal cover had been dragged to the side, revealing a small open safe buried a foot under the surface. Inside was a plastic Ziploc bag. Jake slipped on a leather glove, grabbed the bag, and held it up to the light of a nearby lamp. It contained half a dozen clear capsules, easy to swallow, that held what looked like brown powder. Jake turned to Rick.

'What's this? And don't for a second try and be cute. You're sure as hell not stocking up on candy to sell.'

'I want a lawyer,' spat Rick.

'Fine,' replied Jake calmly as he pulled out his phone. 'I'll just give Casey a call, explain the situation, ask her to get a hold of-'

'Okay, okay,' said Rick, resigned. 'We call them boosters. They give your body a… well, boost. Helps build muscle mass, gives you more energy.'

'So steroids then?'

'No! Well, not exactly. It's supposed to be all-natural ingredients.'

'Jesus Rick, does Keats seem like a hippie herbalist to you?'

'Look, he's a smart guy, with chemistry and stuff. He says he refines a bunch of natural ingredients to get the end product. I took him at his word.'

'Yeah, because a guy who lives like the Unabomber and has a drug lab in his barn is so damn trustworthy. How did you hook up with him?'

'We met at college. I'd been injured one time and needed more pain meds than I was allowed. Keats said he could get them for me. Eventually, he was thrown out for dealing weed. Then a few months ago, he turns up out of the blue at the gates to the mill, waiting for me to finish my shift. He tells me that he'd heard I'd moved back to Independence, so he'd traveled up, asked around, and found me.'

'What would he want with you after all these years?' asked Jake.

'Well, I wasn't the only one on the football team he fixed up in college. I'd kind of helped spread the word about what he could provide.'

'You 'kind of helped'? In other words, you were his damn PR agent. Let me guess, he knew you were a sports hero in this town, that young players would still come up to you for advice. All you needed to do was nudge them in the right direction, and he'd be able to provide the goods to make them better, faster, stronger.'

'He proposed a partnership. He said things had gotten too hot for him back home, somewhere down south, I didn't ask. He was looking for new opportunities up here, a backdoor into the New York City market. I knew the old Moorcock farm was abandoned and that no one would bother him there. He agreed to supply me with the boosters, and then I'd sell them on at a profit.'

'So how does your system work?'

'If they ever came to me for advice and I was alone with them, I may have suggested to some players that a little extra help wouldn't hurt their prospects, that they could find natural choices on certain websites. They didn't know that I was behind those sites. There was a number for a prepaid phone on them, along with instructions. Clients would text me what they needed, I'd reply with a price. If they were fine with it, I'd send another text with the location and a code for the safe.'

Jake kneeled down and raised the lid of the safe. There was a keypad on it.

'I see,' he said. 'So they'd come here, enter the code, take what they'd ordered and leave you the money. Then you'd restock for the next client and reset the code. If they ever screwed you with the money, you'd know it was the last person who'd opened it, and you'd cut them off.'

'Exactly. I'm their exclusive supplier, so no one's taken that chance.'

'Very cloak and dagger, Rick. I'm almost impressed. These kids must have known there was nothing 'natural' about this crap to have to go through that whole process.'

'They just want to win, Jake. They'll do anything to win. See no evil, hear no evil. That's what they say, right? Hell, I doubt it's just football players now. Word spreads. It could be basketball kids, members of the swim team, even the damn chess club for all I know.'

Jake sighed, tossed the bag of capsules back into the safe for later evidence collection, and rubbed his hands on his sleeves as if the stain of cheating had somehow transferred through the bag. There was nothing he could do about Rick's clients. It was true that his system had kept everyone anonymous to each other. But that system was now broken. Jake couldn't stop any of the users potentially trying to find a replacement elsewhere. However, he could remove Rick from the chain of supply, and he'd admit to finding no small pleasure in doing so.

'You asked what you could be charged for, Rick,' said Jake. 'How about intent to distribute illicit substances, actual distribution, aiding and abetting criminal elements. Hell, by the time I'm done with you, you'll go down for stealing Christmas presents from orphans.'

Rick shook his head, part in despair and part in frustration.

'You're loving this, ain't you, you son of a bitch? Drag me down in front of the town, in front of Casey, show her what a worthless asshole I am compared to a Captain America like you.'

'You brought this on yourself, Rick, plain and simple. But why? Why risk everything?'

'Because I'm about to lose it all anyway!' Rick yelled.

'Don't be a drama queen,' said Jake dismissively. 'Casey told me you guys had some money problems, but nothing can be so bad that you're forced to deal drugs to kids.'

'You don't get it, Jake. She doesn't know just how in deep we are. My credit cards were maxed out, my savings account was gone. I blew through it all just to keep our heads above water, even with her wages coming in.'

'How the hell did things get so bad?'

'Cutbacks at work. And, well, I had a bad run at the bookies a few times.'

'Jesus,' said Jake, shaking his head in both pity and disgust. 'You really are a piece of work. Some football players end up bankrupt and in prison, but at least they do it after a few years of success. I guess you just decided to save time and skip that part.'

'Hey, screw you! I know I'm no angel, but I was trying to clear up my own mess. We were weeks away from losing the house. I was desperate, and then Keats came along like a golden goose.'

'A lot of people have it bad, Rick, but you don't see them turning to crime, poisoning kids, lying to their wives.'

'I was trying to protect her, Jake,' said Rick, his lip quivering. 'She's got enough to worry about in her condition, she doesn't need the stress or the disappointment. She needs a husband and a home!'

'What are you talking about? What condition?' pressed Jake.

'She's pregnant!' yelped Rick, and the tears started to flow.

They were two simple words that hit Jake like a heavyweight boxer's fist to the stomach. For a moment, he thought he would actually physically crumple to the floor. Once that passed, a wave of nausea overcame him instead. Jake swallowed hard and covered his face with his hands. He wanted time to stop, for the world outside the shed to cease to exist. If he had been able, he would have shrunk to a small enough size to leap into Rick's drug safe and close the lid behind him, never to be disturbed again.

But reality did not allow such luxuries. Time did not stop, and the world outside kept turning. Seconds ago, he had been triumphant in his hunt, ready to pose with a defeated Rick and later stuff and mount him on a wall. Now he felt lost in the dark without a map, helpless.

'How far along is she?' asked Jake, numb.

'Almost two months. We didn't want to tell anyone until after the first trimester.'

Jake nodded. Looking back, the signs had been there. Casey's abandonment of alcohol and her upturn in exercise were all designed to become a healthier carrier for a new life.

'I know how you feel about her,' said Rick, sniffing back his tears. 'I've known it ever since the night we won the state championship, the way you were looking at her. Now I was a drunken asshole that night, I hold my hands up to that. I said some terrible things to you. Maybe it put you off coming to college with us, maybe it didn't. I know it broke the bond we had. But if not now, we were like brothers back then, and so I'm asking you-'

'Shut up! Just shut the hell up!' screamed Jake.

'You know what's gonna happen, Jake!' raged Rick as he managed to stumble up onto his feet. 'You arrest me, I'm going away. Casey'll divorce me, but she'll have no house and no support. She'll be forced to raise our baby by herself, another kid without a father. She'll probably have to quit the job she loves. She'll become trailer trash, just like her mom, and the cycle will start again. The bottom line is, Jake, you put me away, and Casey's gonna be homeless, crushed, and alone. Do you really want that future for her?'

Jake crouched down and closed his eyes. He rubbed his temples hard. He didn't like it, but Rick probably presented a reasonably accurate forecast of what Casey's life had in store if her husband went down. It was one thing to destroy Rick when it was just Casey and him. She would cry, rage, separate, and eventually move on to a new life.

But with a baby, an unbreakable connection to Rick, whatever he was guilty of? That changed the situation entirely. At the same time, how could Jake let Rick go, knowing what he had done? Could his conscience and sense of duty allow such a thing?

Whatever justification Jake could offer himself for letting Rick go, no matter which way he sliced it, it was a corrupt act, a betrayal of his oath. It wasn't meant to be like this. Policing a small community should have been a pure thing, easy, a world away from the dark savagery and moral compromises he had been forced to make on an almost daily basis in the sweaty hellholes of Afghanistan and Iraq. But at what price his honor? A divorced and ruined single mother and a shamed, fatherless child?

Jake stood and quickly walked up behind Rick. He undid the handcuffs and roughly spun Rick around to face him.

'Give me the rest of your stash.'

'Does this mean-?' started Rick.

'Shut the hell up and do as I say, quickly,' said Jake, keen to get the dirty business over with before he had second thoughts.

Rick dug into his jacket pockets and pulled out half a dozen more Ziploc bags with the same powder-filled capsules. He handed them over to a waiting Jake, who paced over to the drug safe and tossed them in. He turned to Rick and stabbed a finger at him.

'This is over, Rick. No more peddling this crap. You ditch the phone, you close the websites, you never even think of Keats again. If someone comes up to you for advice and you suggest anything stronger than a protein shake, your ass is mine. I've got your fingerprints all over those bags. If I wanted, I could bring your world crashing down. You tell Casey that you've had less shift work than you'd hoped. You take the pain, but you make it work, and you do what's right like a real man should. You want to be a father? Fine. Then set an example. Otherwise, I'll make an example out of you. Am I clear?'

'Yeah,' replied Rick, his head bowed, eyes to the ground like the chastened child he had become.

'Now get the hell out of here,' sighed Jake. 'Casey'll be home soon.'

'But what about Keats? If I stop showing up and he's busted, he'll guess it was me that snitched on him. He's dangerous, Jake, he's not right in the head. He'll find me and cut my balls off!'

'What a loss that would be for the gene pool. Look, don't worry about Keats, or anything else that ties you to this. I'll take care of it.'

'Thanks, Jake. I appreciate this so-'

'Don't thank me. I don't want your thanks. In fact, don't even look at me. Christ knows how I'll even be able to look at myself in the mirror. Just get out of my sight.'

Rick nodded humbly and beat a swift retreat out of the shed door. Jake eased himself to the ground and sat on the metal plate that had covered the safe hole. He was suddenly desperate for a cigarette, despite never having smoked regularly. It was only something he had done while on tour, before and after stressful encounters. While the evening's events came nowhere close to a combat environment, he still felt he had earned a smoke.

He shook the thought from his mind. He hadn't earned anything. He had disgraced himself. He had put his personal feelings for Casey and concern for her welfare ahead of his principles. Maybe there was a kind of honor in such an act, he didn't know. But that was the point. No one would ever truly know the burden of his choice except him. At that moment, he was the loneliest he had ever felt.

CHAPTER TWENTY-THREE

Amanda sat at her desk in the sheriff's office. Jake and Casey stood before her waiting to report.

'We're collecting the pieces, guys,' began Amanda, 'but we need more if we're going to put together something solid out of them. Jake, anything?'

At the mention of his name, Jake switched his focus from the park outside Amanda's window to her face. It had been a long night with little sleep. He wasn't as focused as he usually was, susceptible to letting his thoughts drift. It was going to be a three-cups-of-coffee morning, he could tell. He'd need all his wits about him if he was going to deal with the Keats problem, and it was one that needed tackling immediately before it could cause any more damage.

'We're still waiting on the court order for Judy's phone records,' he responded. 'I put in another call to the judge's office, so we should get that today. Where we have got actionable info is from her car's GPS. We managed to retrieve-'

Casey playfully cleared her throat. Jake rolled his eyes.

'Casey managed to retrieve a list of the destinations Judy recently searched for. Most are outside the county, places she'd likely never visited or was unfamiliar with. The one place locally that did come up was this address.'

Jake handed Amanda a post-it note with an address scribbled on it. She scanned it and raised an eyebrow.

'Cabin One, Dry Lake Road. I've probably driven along it from time to time in my years here, but I can't say I recognize it.'

'There's no reason you should,' interjected Casey. 'It didn't exist by that name until a couple of years ago. It was just a standard numbered road that passed by the forests up in the north-west of the county limits.'

'So why'd they name it?' asked Amanda.

'Because two years ago, it became residential. Well, kind of. I did some digging, and apparently, several cabins have been built nearby, right in there with the trees. You need to turn down a small side road from the main one. Then that side road itself splits into smaller tracks, each with a designated cabin. There are planning requests for a dozen more. Nothing too ostentatious, just small to medium-sized log structures, suitably rustic. They're new enough that they don't show up on maps yet, but you still need mailboxes for them, and an easily identifiable address, so Dry Lake Road was born.'

'A little patch of paradise,' Amanda thought aloud. 'Well, if Judy paid it a visit, then it would be rude for us not to as well. Those cabins seem pretty ideal for discrete business. The fact she had to search for it makes me even more curious. Anything else to add?'

'I heard back from Judy's life insurance provider,' said Casey. 'They said that she last renewed her policy two years ago.'

'Two years exactly?' asked Amanda.

Casey consulted her notepad and flicked through a few pages, running her pen down a list of scribbled-down facts until she found what she was looking for.

'The policy hit the two-year mark last Friday. Is that important?'

'Usually, life insurance policies become forfeit in the event of suicide,' replied Amanda. 'The exception is that if two or three years have passed, depending on the provider, then the policy will still often payout, even if suicide is proven, with mental health considerations especially taken into account. What we have here is Judy Sterling and her last letter attempting to convince the world that she'd taken her own life due to mental anguish. Conveniently she decided to do it two days after her policy could no longer be forfeited. So, yeah, I'd say that's pretty important. Good work.'

Casey nodded in quiet satisfaction.

'What's our plan now?' she asked.

'Well, we go check out Cabin One and see what there is to see.'

Jake seized the opportunity to put his plan into motion.

'How about Casey goes with you? She did discover the address, after all.'

'Bored of my company, Jake?' replied Amanda playfully.

'Actually, duty calls. We had an anonymous phone call from someone saying they thought they saw some activity last night at the Moorcock farm. Some lights, a little noise, things like that. Well, unless Old Man Moorcock's relatives have pitched up to check on their inherence, it could be squatters. I thought I'd check it out to be sure.'

'That sounds fine to me,' said Amanda. 'Though why would anyone call in anonymously for that?'

'Who knows?' shrugged Jake. 'Maybe it's a prank, but no harm in patrolling out that way anyway, show some of the farmers that we're not just sitting here eating donuts.'

'Perish the thought,' said Amanda as she rose from her chair. 'This is purely a muffin department.'

She led Jake and Casey into the main office area where they collected their hats and jackets from the hooks. Amanda turned to Jake.

'I'll radio you if we come across anything of interest. Otherwise, we'll meet back here later.'

The trio exited, saying goodbye to Wayne en route. Casey joined Amanda in her patrol car, while Jake took his. He started it up and headed out of town in a southerly direction, towards farming country.

There has been no anonymous call, of course. He had made it up, but the desired effect had been achieved. Jake needed to be alone for his plan to work. He would scope out the farm and wait for Keats to leave to collect his supplies, as he had told Rick he needed to do to finish the booster order. Jake could then check out the house and if he found nothing immediately incriminating, move on to the barn, where he was sure he would find that Keats had been cooking up something foul.

Jake would then wait to make the arrest, radio Amanda and Casey for backup, and break up Keats's little operation without any mention of Rick, or that Jake himself had prior knowledge of the whole setup. From both Amanda and Keats's perspectives, Jake had simply stumbled across criminality while investigating possible squatting. A piece of good luck for the sheriff's department and bad luck for Keats, but those were the breaks.

Overall it wasn't pretty, and he hated misleading Amanda. However, Jake's priorities were to prevent Casey's ruination by keeping her husband out of jail, while at the same time making sure Keats ended up there. It was possible that Keats would seek to make a deal by naming those he was supplying, whether in Independence or the Bronx. At least Jake had confiscated all incriminating evidence against Rick, so it would be his word against Keats's, a drug-producing dropout who could be offering Rick's name because he had known of him in college and was desperate.

For all Jake knew, the Drug Enforcement Administration would want a piece of Keats depending on what he had been cooking. If matters escalated in that direction, then there was probably little Jake could do to keep Rick's nose clean, but he would cross that bridge if and when he came to it. For now, Jake was reasonably confident that his current plan would work. But at the same time, he was all too aware from his combat experience that even the best-laid plans rarely survived the first contact.

CHAPTER TWENTY-FOUR

It took almost half an hour for Amanda and Casey to reach Dry Lake Road. It really was on the periphery of the county. A mile or so further, and they would have found themselves in the next one and out of their jurisdiction, which was a headache Amanda was glad to avoid. She reduced her speed to be sure that they didn't miss anything obvious. However, the road was so quiet Amanda could have slowed to crawling speed and presented no issue for any traffic coming from behind.

'Keep an eye out,' she said to Casey, who focused on the right side of the road, while Amanda concentrated on the left.

'It doesn't get much more secluded than this,' observed Casey. 'Perfect if you wanted to meet up with someone away from curious eyes.'

'Isn't it just,' nodded Amanda. 'The question is who she met so discreetly?'

'We find Cabin One, and you might get your answer.'

After a minute of driving, Amanda spotted a small assemblage of color positioned next to the entrance to a side road on the left. She slowed to a stop in front of a collection of mailboxes, each painted a different color and labeled with a single line. The first said Cabin One, the second Cabin Two, and so on up to Cabin Six.

'Looks like our place,' said Amanda.

She swung the patrol car onto the side road. She slowly proceeded up the gentle incline, large fir trees casting a continuous shadow with hundreds of random beams of sunlight penetrating their foliage. While initially asphalt for a few dozen yards, the smooth surface quickly gave way to gravel and then to hardened mud and small pebbles.

Maybe the developer intended to finish the road properly at some stage or leave it as was to preserve the 'entrance into nature' theme. Amanda guessed, however, that any cabins built out this far for such expense would have enough creature comforts to allow the enjoyment of nature, while at the same time keeping its discomforts at bay. She doubted she would see any outhouses next to the main buildings.

After a minute of slow progress along the increasingly bumpy trail better suited to an SUV, Amanda spotted a turn-off to the right. A wooden sign was erected next to it, the words 'Cabin One' artfully burned into the short plank of lighter wood. Amanda turned onto it and proceeded up a slightly steeper incline that gradually curved along a ledge.

Through her natural sense of direction, Amanda could tell they were ascending in a north-westerly direction, no doubt to allow a spectacular view of the surrounding forest and the Catskills in the distance.

Eventually, the trail flattened out, the curve became straight, and the ledge to the left and trees to the right opened up into a large grassy clearing. At the center was a wooden cabin, though lodge would have been a more appropriate term given it was three times the size of a typical forest log cabin.

The two-story structure was built on a foundation of stones and mortar. A porch ringed the entire ground floor, while solar panels were fixed to the roof. Large patio doors belonging to the main bedroom upstairs opened out onto a balcony that did indeed offer the stunning view that Amanda had supposed would be found. In front of the building, a sleek Mercedes was parked alongside a tank-like SUV. Whoever lived there was certainly not surviving on food stamps.

Amanda parked up on the side of the clearing, allowing her and Casey more observation time as they slowly walked towards the front door.

'Do you recognize those vehicles?' asked Casey.

'No,' replied Amanda. 'But at least someone's home for us to talk to. And this is clearly their home, or at least one of them, not a rental.'

'How can you tell?' asked Casey.

Amanda pointed to a large stack of chopped wood piled high against one of the stone foundation walls. A tree stump and wood ax were located nearby.

'They've been chopping wood for some time, probably stocking up for the winter. If you were renting this short-term, why bother? If you're here to relax, why spend days on hard, repetitive work when you could just as easily buy wood in? Also, look at the tire tracks.'

Amanda indicated the tracks on the surface that led to both parked vehicles. There were far more leading to the sporty Mercedes than there were to the SUV, with much of the grass around it having given way to exposed dirt. The latter only seemed to have a couple of deeper gouges in the dry mud leading to it.

'The Mercedes is a regular feature here, the SUV less so. Maybe a few times in the past couple of weeks. It leaves deeper groves, so there'd be noticeably more of them if it'd been here as often. What does that tell us?'

'That the SUV either belongs to a visitor, or it's a second rarely-used vehicle,' continued Casey, catching the theory ball Amanda had tossed her. 'The Mercedes is more active. Whoever owns it has been coming and going regularly, so probably lives here.'

'Very good, Sherlock,' smiled Amanda.

'Thank you, Watson,' replied Casey with a returned grin. 'The bottom line is whoever lives here, the owner of the Mercedes is most likely the person that Judy came to meet.'

'Exactly,' said Amanda. 'And with a place this out of the way, I doubt it was for a book club.'

'Sex, money, or politics, I wonder?' asked Casey aloud.

Their gentle stroll to the cabin stopped as they heard the front door open. The occupant stepped out from the shade of the covered porch and descended the short row of steps onto the grass of the clearing. Gary

Brennan possessed a look that blended surprise, curiosity, and no little anxiety.

'Perhaps all three,' replied Amanda.

CHAPTER TWENTY-FIVE

Jake had parked his patrol car down a small side road a hundred yards from the entrance to the Moorcock farm, a far less noticeable spot than the night before. His car was parked on a slope just out of sight of the main road, so any passing drivers would not spot it. Jake hoped that Keats would leave the farm soon, but as he couldn't be sure which way the aspiring drug lord would turn upon reaching the main road, he had wanted to keep his sheriff's vehicle out of sight. One hint of a law enforcement presence nearby and Keats would likely return to the farm in an instant, pack up his equipment, and bolt for good.

Without cover of night, Jake had cautiously advanced down the farm's entrance road. He kept a keen ear out for any approaching engine noise, ready to dive into the adjacent bushes in an instant. Thankfully he had heard no such thing and emerged into the grounds of the Moorcock farm. Crouched low, Jake stuck to the nearby bushes and patches of trees that formed a wide arc around the front and side of the main farm buildings, the perfect cover at least a hundred yards out.

Jake slowly and discreetly made his way to an advantageous viewpoint, being careful not to rustle the foliage too much. He found the perfect angle to monitor the farmhouse and the barn and pulled out his pocket binoculars from his jacket. Now all he could do was wait until Keats left for his supply run.

Jake hoped that he hadn't done so already, though Keats didn't come across as someone who regularly woke up at the crack of dawn with an energetic vigor to begin a day's work. At the same time, if Keats still intended to meet Rick's order by that evening, then he wouldn't wait for it to get too late to head out either. Just as long as Jake could collar Keats before Rick's anticipated arrival, his plan could still work. If Rick failed to show up, then it would potentially arouse Keats's suspicions.

There was also the other consideration that Jake simply couldn't sit out in the bushes all day. Amanda was under the impression that he was checking out potential squatting and paying some friendly visits to local farmers, activities that wouldn't last more than a few hours.

Jake kept his eyes on the farm buildings but allowed his mind to drift back to his second tour of Afghanistan. One of his best friends had been a Marine sniper who had impressed a still relatively enthusiastic Jake with tales of taking out insurgent commanders from incredible distances. Brett 'Radar' Reilly, so nicknamed due to his uncanny ability to sense potential threats from a distance, had chalked up numerous kills and wasn't modest about his score.

Jake had been toying with the idea of undertaking sniper training himself at the time. His marksmanship was undoubtedly good enough for him to stand a realistic chance of making it. By way of a taster, Reilly had offered Jake the opportunity to join the sniper team on a mission to conduct surveillance on a suspected enemy compound. They were to wait for a notorious local insurgent commander to turn up and dispatch him with extreme prejudice if he did appear.

For two days, they had lain prone at a respectable distance from the compound, enduring the scorching heat of the day and the sleepless cold of the nights, taking in food and water and passing out both in the same two square meters. Finally, the commander had appeared with his entourage, which had been larger than expected. Upon reporting this detail to command and control, they were asked to standby. Word soon came back that the Air Force was going to deal with this matter and that Jake's team could pull back.

Ten minutes later, the compound vanished in a massive blast of fire and earth. An airstrike had taken out the commander instead of a sniper's bullet, along with a dozen of his comrades. Unfortunately, the strike had also taken out a similar number of women and children who had been hiding out of sight in the compound buildings and basements, likely to avoid surveillance from American troops. It was the kind of surveillance that would have saved their lives by taking the airstrike option off the table to prevent collateral damage. While it still took several more years to complete the journey, the events of that day set Jake on course to a dark place.

Jake shook his head and snapped back to reality. It was never a good idea to dwell on such things. Though what else was there to distract him? Casey's pregnancy? He wondered when she would tell him. He hoped she would do so before it became physically obvious. It would be a mark of trust, a trust they had always shared, whether during their senior year in high school when she confided in him her despair over her drunken, womanizing father, or the evening before last when she had raised her and Rick's money troubles and apparent salvation.

Well, Jake had played no small role in making that salvation a short-lived one. While he had rarely lied to Casey, he had deliberately kept the big things from her, for the sake of their friendship. He would just have to add his handling of the Rick situation to the list.

Jake squinted as he thought he saw movement from within the farmhouse. He snapped the binoculars to his eyes as the front door opened. Keats stepped out onto the porch, cigarette in mouth and a cup of coffee in hand. In the daylight, Jake was fully able to see Keats's features. He wore a checked red and black lumberjack shirt, jeans torn at the knees, and scuffed leather boots. He was a short, weaselly-looking man, with an uncombed mullet of dark brown hair and an untrimmed beard. While physically less than imposing, even from a distance, Jake could tell that Keats had an alley-cat viciousness to him, that he would smile at you one minute and lash out the next.

Keats finished his cigarette, tossed the butt away, and poured the remaining coffee on the ground. He retreated back inside for a moment and then reappeared. Keats twirled a set of keys around his finger and walked over to his battered pick-up truck. He hopped in, finally started it up after a few failed attempts, and drove up towards the entrance road. Jake watched Keats disappear from view and waited a few moments until he could no longer hear the pick-up's groaning engine.

Jake pocketed the binoculars and slowly made his way towards the farmhouse. He cautiously checked in all directions just in case Keats had any accomplices that he had somehow missed. Jake navigated the rusted farm machinery and headed straight to the barn, the site of Keats's self-proclaimed lab.

A large padlock and chain sealed the main door, forbidding entry. Jake pulled on the handles enough to create a small gap to peek through, but the interior was so dark he could barely make anything out. While it was probable that Keats had taken the padlock key with him, it was still worth checking the farmhouse for a spare and for other incriminating evidence.

Jake headed over to the main house and stepped onto the porch. He drew his pistol and pointed it downwards. It was worth being cautious, but not too paranoid. He knocked on the door, again testing as to whether Keats was truly alone. There was no response from inside. Jake gently pushed the door open and stepped forward.

The interior was significantly darkened by the windows being blacked out, either with paint brushed over the glass, or black garbage bags taped across them. Still, enough ambient light from the bright sun outside managed to shine through the open front door, or missed patches of blackout. Jake's eyes quickly adjusted, and he took in the layout of the house.

To Jake's right was a large living room area, with several dusty couches that looked like 1950s props but were probably the genuine article, as was the washed-out floral wallpaper. A huge widescreen television, a box rather than a flatscreen, dominated the far corner.

To Jake's left was the dining room, which led on to the kitchen. Empty pizza boxes, soda bottles, and dozens of crushed beer cans dominated the scratched dining table. Directly ahead of Jake was the staircase that led upwards to what he assumed were the equally messy bedrooms and bathroom. The Moorcock farm had the feeling of a temporary base, disposable and easily abandoned.

Jake advanced through the dining room and headed for the kitchen, his weapon raised in standard practice. He pushed against the door, which he discovered swung both ways. He entered the kitchen and ripped away a garbage bag that covered a window above the sink. With the added illumination, he was greeted by exactly what he had expected, a mass of unwashed saucepans and the pungent smell of decomposing food.

Jake scanned the walls in the hope of finding some hooks for various keys, something he had often spotted in other houses and indeed his own. Luck was on his side, and he spotted a small bundle hanging on a bent nail near the back door. He retrieved the keys and quickly studied them. One of them looked like it could be a padlock key, but the only way to know for sure was to try it out.

He reached for the back door handle, pulled it, but the door wouldn't budge. Jake checked the keyring, but couldn't see anything that looked like a deadbolt key. He would just have to return to the barn through the front entrance. He turned back and pushed the swing door out into the dining room and stepped through.

Jake instantly froze as he saw Keats standing a few feet in front of him. The initially bemused look on Keats's face quickly turned to one of rage. He raised the pump-action shotgun he had been holding and swung it like a club in Jake's direction, knocking the pistol from Jake's hand before he could get a shot off. In an instant, Keats lunged forward and booted Jake square in the chest, sending him flying back through the swing door and crashing onto his back on the grubby kitchen floor.

Winded, Jake attempted to struggle up, but Keats's booted foot planted itself on his shoulder and forced him back down, pinning him to the ground. Jake heard the shotgun cock and looked up to find the barrel point-blank to his face. The feeling of power must have hit Keats like a drug, as his angry expression instantly twisted into a rictus grin, thrilled at having Jake at his mercy.

'We got ourselves a fox in the henhouse!' screamed Keats.

He flipped the shotgun around and slammed the wooden stock into Jake's face. Everything went dark.

CHAPTER TWENTY-SIX

'Good morning to you, Sheriff, Deputy,' said Gary hesitantly, nodding in turn to Amanda and Casey. 'I have to say this is a surprise.'

'Likewise,' said Amanda dryly.

The three of them were standing in the clearing, a dozen yards from the cabin. Amanda instantly felt another piece of the puzzle drop into place. However, she did not know what part of the overall image it revealed. It appeared that Judy Sterling had, at one point, visited this secluded place, most likely to meet with someone. Unless some bizarre coincidence was occurring, that someone appeared to be Gary.

The evidence was not conclusive, but at first glance, it appeared that Councillor Judy Sterling might have been having an affair with Mayor Gary Brennan. It would explain Mary Brennan's evident passive aggressiveness towards her husband. Also, if that headline-grabbing revelation turned out to be accurate, it was little wonder they had wanted to keep it quiet. But had the need to keep that secret, if it was real, cost Judy her life?

Amanda looked at Casey.

'Casey, could you give the Mayor and me a few minutes alone, please? Take a little walk.'

'Sure,' acknowledged Casey with a nod. She turned and headed off towards the ledge that overlooked the forested landscape and the Catskills in the far distance.

Amanda had not been intentionally rude with her last remark. She had signaled to Casey to further explore the area and see if there was anything of interest while Gary was distracted by conversation. Amanda started a slow walk with Gary alongside her.

'I didn't know you lived here, Gary. This place is yours, right?'

'Yes, but I don't live here. It's kind of a little retreat, a way to get out of town without having to leave the county.'

'Speaking of which, you told me at your office that you were away on business today.'

'It's a private matter,' said Gary, visibly stiffening up.

Amanda decided to stop circling and cut to the chase. She was getting tired of vagaries and was growing impatient for some clarity.

'I'm going to be honest with you, Gary. I'm here because this was the one place in the county that Judy

Sterling searched for on her car's GPS. That makes sense, as these cabins are new. Even I wouldn't know where to find them unless I was told. My question is why she came here, to a nice, quiet, out of the way location? Were you having an affair with Judy, Gary?'

'What?' scoffed Gary. 'Not at all. Jesus, there are other reasons she'd come here, Amanda!'

'Such as?'

'If you must know, Mary and I hosted her and Ray for a weekend towards the start of the year. A couple's retreat, if you want to call it that. That's probably why Judy had the address. We'd just taken ownership of this place, and she hadn't visited before. She was driving as I recall, since Ray had had a few drinks at a work event.'

'That's well-remembered of you,' remarked Amanda, not entirely convinced.

'It's true,' said a female voice from above.

Amanda looked up and saw Mary Brennan standing upon the balcony that the main bedroom opened onto. She was wearing silk pajamas and a dressing gown. Amanda also noticed she wore the same scarf around her neck as the previous day.

'Forgive my appearance, Sheriff,' said Mary. 'I was about to get changed when I overheard you and Gary talking. But yes, Judy and Raymond spent the weekend with us in January. As you said yourself, this place isn't easy to find at the best of times, never mind with the winter snows. I'm afraid you've had a wasted trip if you expected to find any juicy gossip. Now, if you'll excuse me, it's a little breezy up here.'

With that, Mary reentered the bedroom and closed the glass doors behind her. Clearly, there was no appetite for the conversation to continue on her end. Amanda lowered her head back down to face Gary, who looked at her with a self-satisfied smirk.

'You see? Perfectly innocent,' he said.

'Maybe so. By the way, which car is yours?'

'The SUV, why?'

'And that's your only vehicle?'

'The only one I drive anyway. Mary finds it too big for her tastes. Again, your point?'

'My point, Gary, is how long have you and Mary been separated?'

'Excuse me?' he asked, trying to feign surprise and failing.

'There's nothing illegal about marital troubles, but on a personal level I don't take kindly to being lied to, so I'd rather you didn't. If the SUV belongs to you, then you've been here only a handful of times recently. The Mercedes, on the other hand, is a regular visitor. Maybe Mary has been living here alone, for a little while at least. Plus, I'm not stupid. The tension is obvious.'

Gary thought for a moment and then frowned.

'Fine. Mary and I have been having some problems recently. I bought this place as a surprise, thinking that it would help if we had a little project to work on. Hell, this used to be an old logging camp anyway, already cleared, so I was even sensitive about her tree-hugging crap. It only papered over the cracks, though. She moved out of our place in town last month.'

'I'm sorry to hear that. You kept it well hidden.'

'Yeah, well, it's no one's business but ours. If you must know, we're trying to figure things out. That's why I came here today, in the hope of a little peace and quiet. Thanks for shattering that by the way.'

'I'm sorry, but I had a lead to follow up.'

'For God's sake Amanda,' Gary fumed, exasperated. 'Can't you just accept that Judy was simply a messed up lady who killed herself? I respect your work ethic, I really do, but this is it, the end of the story. Case closed.'

'Thanks for the compliment, but I'll be the judge of what constitutes a closed case or not,' replied Amanda, calmly but cooly.

An awkward silence hung in the air. Gary glanced back to the cabin and sighed.

'Look, you've been told what brought Judy here. I hope that satisfies you, but I've got nothing else if it doesn't. If we're done here, I'd like to get back inside and pick up where Mary and I left off.'

'Okay. Thank you for your time,' said Amanda as she tipped the front of her hat with pinched fingers. This freed Gary, who nodded and returned to the interior of the cabin.

Amanda spotted Casey hovering at the edge of the clearing. She beckoned the young deputy over and walked towards her so that they met halfway, pivoted, and continued towards the patrol car.

'How'd it go?' asked Casey.

'Both the Brennans say that Judy and Ray paid them a visit here early in the year and that's why she had the address on her car's GPS.'

'Do you believe them?'

'There's nothing to say that they're lying, but I'll check with Ray when I go see him later. It's time to let him in on our suspicions about how Judy died.'

'Even if he might be a suspect?'

'Who knows, he might admit it there and then. Worst case, we shake a tree and see if any cats fall out.'

They got into the patrol car, and Amanda started it up. Casey reached into her jacket pocket and pulled out her phone.

'Well, while you were distracting Gary, I think I may have shaken a tree of my own, and a big, black kitty fell into our arms,' said Casey as she unlocked her phone and opened the photo album.

'I was walking the outskirts of the property when I came across these,' she continued.

Casey tilted her phone screen towards Amanda. It displayed a photo of some tire tracks in the dried mud.

'Looks like there was a third car here in the last few days, and from what I could see, it sped off pretty quickly from where it was parked. Someone floored the accelerator and spun its ass around so that it pointed towards the exit road before taking off.'

'Interesting,' said Amanda, suitably intrigued.

'It is, but that's not what's *most* interesting,' said Casey with a grin.

She used her finger to swipe backward through her photos.

'Do you remember that I took photos of those skid marks on the Saratoga Bridge?'

'Yes,' replied Amanda, 'but it was difficult to make out the tread pattern.'

'True, but if we had something to compare it to, we might be able to spot at least some similarities.'

'Let me guess, you've made a comparison?' ventured Amanda.

Casey's finger continued swiping back in time to the morning of the previous day. She stopped on a photo of the tire tracks left on the bridge asphalt.

'I've compared both sets of photos,' confirmed Casey. 'I'll admit, we're not talking laboratory levels of accuracy here, but I can spot enough similarities in the impressions of the tire treads. They strongly suggest that the third car that visited this cabin is the same car that screeched to a stop right where Judy was probably pushed.'

Amanda let the implications soak in for a moment.

'So whoever was driving that third car left here in a hurry and headed out to the bridge to confront Judy. We find that car and who owns it, we find our probable killer.'

'It's a solid theory,' nodded Casey. 'Of course, that would likely mean that something happened here to set things in motion. Whatever Gary and Mary told you, I doubt they're as clean as they tried to make out.'

'Of that, I have no doubt,' acknowledged Amanda. 'We need to get Jake back to the station and come up with a plan of action.'

Amanda reached down and grabbed the car's radio mic.

'Jake, this is Amanda. Come in, over.'

CHAPTER TWENTY-SEVEN

Jake slowly regained consciousness and almost immediately wished he hadn't. What had been a low throbbing in his temples gradually increased in pressure and pain. Keats had certainly done a number on him, a concussion at the very least. Jake tried to move but found that he couldn't. He forced his eyes open and looked around to find himself tied to a rickety wooden chair. He struggled, but the ropes that bound his wrists to the back of the chair were tightly secured.

Jake scanned his immediate environment. He guessed he was in the barn based on the size and shape of the wooden interior and remnants of straw scattered around the ground. A few weak beams of sunlight managed to shine through cracks in the roof, showing up the dust that hung in the air.

He strained his eyes and just managed to make out some farming and horse-riding equipment hung from one of the vertical wooden support beams to his left. Jake turned his head to the right and quickly focused on the small collection of sickles, scythes, axes, and saws that were neatly arranged on another beam.

Jake's heart started thumping with increasing speed as adrenaline flooded his system. If the situation hadn't been so severe, he could have almost laughed at the horror-movie cliché he had become. He was the overly-curious cop who searches the spooky abandoned property by himself, only to be captured by the unstable psychotic and subjected to God-knows-what treatment.

Jake breathed deeply, attempting to regulate his heart-rate as best he could. He tried to brush away such dark imaginings. He looked around to assess his situation when suddenly half a dozen lights snapped on. Jake winced slightly as his eyes adjusted to the brightness. He instantly spotted Keats leaning against the far wall, a small remote control in his hand, and a sly smile on his face. He had been waiting patiently in the darkness, just out of Jake's sight until the moment had been right.

Now that the barn's interior was lit up, Jake could see what Keats had been up to. While it was not a huge drug manufacturing facility with an industrial capacity, it was still reasonable for one man. Three large workbenches were lined up in a row, each playing a part in the manufacturing process. The raw ingredients seemed to be stacked up on the first bench. The main tools and chemistry set dominated the second, while the finished product was arranged on the third bench.

Alongside several small packages of the brown-colored booster powder Keats had been supplying Rick, were several larger Ziploc bags holding a white crystalline substance. Jake guessed that it was methamphetamine, crystal meth, bound for contacts in the Bronx, or further afield. If it was, then no wonder Keats had moved his operations into the barn. The cooking process for meth was a notoriously risky proposition, liable to cause explosions if performed incorrectly. It was also another reason why Keats had clearly valued an isolated location and the privacy that came with it.

'Yep, them's the fruit of my labors,' said Keats calmly.

He walked forwards and stopped a few feet in front of Jake. He squatted down a little so that they were both at eye-level.

'So I'm drivin' along nice and happy, when this thing starts to ping.'

Keats retrieved his phone from his back pocket and showed the screen to Jake. It was split into four small quarters, with each quarter showing a black and white camera image. One was from the inside of the farmhouse, two had wide views of the outside, and the final quarter showed a high-angle shot of Jake tied to the chair with Keats before him. Jake glanced in the likely direction of the feed and quickly spotted a small web camera fixed to one of the barn's wooden beams. Keats smiled and replaced the phone in his pocket.

'I may not look like I got brains, but I do know my tech. These days a man's gotta be certain that his property is secure, without ideally spendin' a fortune on such peace of mind. So those little cameras link to an app on my phone. Soon as they detect motion, they ping me a live feed. So when you started snoopin', my screen lit up, and I hauled ass back asap. Managed to sneak up on you mighty nicely, didn't I?'

Jake simply stared at Keats impassively, not willing to give him the satisfaction of a reaction. Keats shook his head and sighed.

'Had me a nice little thing goin' here,' he said casually as he scratched his beard. 'Mindin' my own business, doing no one no harm. Then you showed up and complicated things. A lot.'

The last two words were laced with clear menace. Keats had left a pause, expecting Jake to take over from him.

'What do you want me to say?' asked Jake. 'Sucks to be you, I guess.'

'You got that half right, boy,' chuckled Keats. 'The other half bein' that it sucks to be you too. You see, in case it escaped your notice, I've got you at my mercy. Now, we can have a nice, civilized conversation where I ask you some questions, and you answer 'em. Or I can kick your ass all over this here barn. One of those options is how it's gonna go down, and I think it would be best for the both of us if you decided on the first. Don't you?'

'Depends on what kind of questions you have,' replied Jake.

He had no idea where things were going but decided playing for time was his best option in the hope that something, anything, might turn up.

'Oh, nothin' too taxin'. The simple facts o' life, such as the why, the when, the how, those kinda things.'

'And if I give you the wrong answers?'

'Don't. That would be my advice.'

Keats stood up and stretched himself out. He cricked his neck and clapped his hands together.

'So then, first question. What you doin' here?'

'We had a report of potential squatters, so I was sent to check it out,' Jake lied as convincingly as he could. 'This farm is supposed to be abandoned. You were bound to attract attention sooner or later.'

'Oh, no doubt,' said Keats. 'I knew this was a short-term deal. Why do you think I treat it like such a crap hole. I'm outta here next week, ain't my problem. But what *is* now my problem is you turnin' up and messin' with the timetable before I had my next place ready. I still got orders to meet and deliveries to make. No sir, this timing does not work out well for me at all.'

Keats was trying to conceal his anxiety, but Jake could tell that the thought of the law rolling down the entrance road and encircling the barn was playing on the man's mind. If Jake could push that button, it might convince Keats to make a run for it and forget him. That was, of course, providing Keats wasn't of the mind to simply kill Jake and then run. Still, if Jake could somehow convince Keats that his time was better spent clearing out than on interrogation, he might stand a chance of making it, a slim one though it was.

'You're right, the timing sucks,' said Jake. 'So wouldn't it make more sense for you to get your ass out of here before the rest of my department shows up and really ruins your day?'

Keats eyed his produce nervously and checked his wristwatch. He scratched his beard again, more vigorously this time. A sign of stress, perhaps? Jake kept pushing.

'My people, they know I'm here. Probably on their way right now, wondering why I've not radioed in. So you can keep asking me questions you probably already know the answers to. Or you can grab all your crap and bolt. Because I'd say a twenty to thirty-year break in the joint would put a bit of a dent in your delivery schedule, wouldn't you? Tick tock. It's one or the other, Keats, make your choice.'

A sweaty Keats slowly turned his attention away from the drug pile and looked Jake square in the eyes, a fire burning in his pupils.

'How'd you know my name?'

Crap. Jake had been in such full-flow, pressing Keats, that he had not checked himself. He had indeed used Keats's name, despite trying to sell the story that he simply stumbled across the operation on a routine patrol.

Keats delivered a mean right-hook to Jake's jaw. For a second, he saw stars and instantly tasted blood. Keats shook his hand and rubbed it against his shirt.

'Now I was pretty good at math, so I can add two and two together well enough. You knowing my name either means you've been scoping me out, or my contact has loosened his lips. Yeah, I bet I know which it was. My only link to this place. Either way, you know a hell of a lot more about me than you would simply by stumblin' on this place. And I don't like people knowing all that much about me, no sir!'

The rage was visibly bubbling up in Keats. Jake wondered if he had sampled some of his own product, but whether it was that or a natural temper, it seemed that Keats had crossed the point of reason, and there was no talking him down. There was electricity in the air, the same kind that Jake had felt before a schoolyard brawl or a firefight in a dusty desert street. Things were coming to a head, a climax, but it wasn't going to be a good one, that was certain.

Keats stomped over to the collection of farming tools and grabbed a sickle. He gripped it so hard that his knuckles turned white. He started advancing towards Jake, who began pushing the chair backward with his feet, scraping the legs along the barn floor in a desperate and futile bid to keep Keats at a distance.

'Think what you're doing, Keats! If it's murder, you get life!'

'They'll have to catch me first, lawman, and they ain't been so good at that lately,' retorted Keats through gritted teeth. 'You be sure that I'll clear out, but not before I take care of your ass and that ex-jock son of a bitch who I know's been talkin'!'

Jake pushed back hard, but it was too much, and the momentum tipped him over onto his back with a crash. Pain shot through his hands and forearms as all his weight landed on them. That was the least of Jake's problems as Keats bared down upon him, his eyes wide and hate-filled, his mouth open in a defiant roar as he brought the sickle up high and cleaved it downwards towards Jake's head.

CHAPTER TWENTY-EIGHT

Three gunshots.

Jake saw Keats's chest take two hits, followed by the left side of his head, which blew itself out on the right side and covered a small patch on the nearby wooden wall in blood and brain matter. The force of the impacts sent Keats spinning and crashing to the ground. The sickle was still gripped tightly in his hand.

Jake let out a held breath with a loud gasp. That had been as close as it had ever come. He heard Amanda call his name, and a moment later, she appeared in his line of sight as he stared up at the ceiling, attempting to process all that had transpired in the last few moments.

Amanda held her gun and quickly holstered it. She looked over to the side and beckoned someone Jake could not see toward her. A few seconds later, Casey appeared, also holding her pistol. She looked pale and shocked in contrast to Amanda's calm demeanor. Jake knew from personal experience that Amanda was not blasé about what had just happened, but was simply compartmentalizing it to be dealt with later. Her priority right now was Jake's wellbeing, assessing whether he was hurt or not.

By contrast, Jake recognized that Casey's expression was of someone who had been changed by what they had just witnessed. Seeing someone die before you, especially through violence, wasn't like on television or the movies. It never was.

Casey holstered her pistol and helped Amanda grab the back of the chair and heave Jake up. He saw Casey walk to his rear and start to undo his binds as Amanda checked him over, paying attention to his eye movements. He briefly squeezed his eyes shut and shook his head, trying to reestablish focus on what was being said to him.

'Jake, look at me,' said Amanda. 'Give me a sit rep.'

She had asked him in the shorthand to briefly give her any information about his condition and the situation that he thought was important.

'The guy knocked me out. Slugged me too. That was the worst it got, I think. Just him as far as I know. Drug producer working out of this place. He dead?'

'I put three in him,' said Amanda. 'Didn't have a choice. We heard him screaming, burst in, and saw him about to cleave your head off. If I'd been a second slower on the trigger, he just might have.'

Jake glanced down at Keats's body, his eyes half-closed as if he was about to doze off, the exit wound from the head mercifully pointed in the other direction.

'I think it was pretty clear that he wasn't having the best day. Now that confirms it,' said Jake, attempting a black-humored laugh and grimacing as pain shot through his jaw and forehead.

'We better get you to the hospital. You've got a nasty gash above your right eye, blood all down your face. Jesus, if you say that was the worst he did to you, God help you if things had gotten serious.'

Casey finally untied Jake's hands. He brought them to his front and flexed them, before gingerly touching the area above his right eye. It stung fiercely, and he hissed.

'That's where the son of a bitch landed his shotgun stock on me. You'd better look around, make sure he hasn't got any other toys waiting to surprise us.'

Amanda stood up and looked to Casey.

'Casey, get an ambulance out here. Ruth Chalmers too.'

Casey quietly nodded and headed out of the barn, opening the doors wide as she exited, allowing natural sunlight and a cool breeze to enter.

'She okay?' asked Jake.

'I think so,' replied Amanda. 'She drew too, but I took the shots. It's easy to forget that you and I have done this before. It can't have been easy for her to see that.'

'It's never easy, no matter how many times you've seen and done it,' said Jake as he gently rubbed his temples. 'How are you feeling?'

'Not great,' said Amanda flatly. 'But better him than you. How the hell did you get into this mess anyway?'

'It's as I said. I was checking out the place for squatters, came across his little operation, and he ambushed me. Who he is, what this whole setup is all about, I just don't know.'

It was a blatant lie, but Jake's immediate pain temporarily smothered his guilt, though he had no doubt it would play on his mind in due course. He would have to process the exact consequences of the morning's events, but what was certain was that he wouldn't have to worry about Rick being implicated. That connection had died with Keats.

'How'd you know I was in trouble?' he asked, looking to move the conversation on.

'We didn't,' replied Amanda. 'We discovered something up on Dry Lake Road and tried to radio you. There was no answer on that or your phone, so we started to worry. You'd said you were checking this place out, so that was our first logical stop. We parked on the grounds and were taking a look around when we heard the commotion coming from inside. We drew, kicked the door in, and, well, you saw the rest.'

'That was pretty damn fine timing,' said Jake as he attempted to stand. A wave of dizziness and nausea overcame him, and he slumped back down.

'Easy,' said Amanda as she placed a reassuring hand on his shoulder. 'You're not going anywhere except the hospital. And even if they say you're fit to run a marathon, you're still taking the rest of the week off.'

'But what about the Sterling case?' Jake protested.

'Casey and I have it in hand. Don't worry, I'll keep you up to speed. We need to clean up this mess first, though.'

Amanda stepped over to Keats's drug production benches and leaned in to examine the packages of white and brown substances. She shook her head.

'Crystal meth, right under our noses. So much for the picket fences dream. I guess nowhere's immune these days.'

'He said he was moving on soon, so this was probably just a short stop to help get himself started up,' said Jake, hoping that providing Amanda with some of the truth would contribute in a small way to balancing out his lies about the bigger picture.

'Any idea what this brown powder is?' asked Amanda.

'He said that it was some kind of performance booster,' said Jake, again slipping in a little truth.

'Like steroids? He told you that?'

'He was boasting, telling me all kinds of things. I guess he was looking to kill me anyway, so what did it matter what he said?'

'Well, I won't take his word for it. We'll have this analyzed as a priority. If he's been distributing this stuff in my county, I want to know what we're dealing with.'

'And the rest of it?' probed Jake.

'This looks bigger than us. With the amount of meth here and the ingredients to make more, I'd say he'd set his sights beyond Independence. I'll call the DEA in New York, get them up here.'

They both looked to the main doors as Casey returned.

'Ruth and the ambulance are on their way.'

'Thanks,' nodded Amanda. 'Looks like Ruth's hope was for nothing. I'm seeing her again all too soon.'

**

It was getting dark by the time Amanda left the Moorcock farm. Once Jake had been taken to the hospital for further examination, Amanda had spoken with Ruth about what had happened, while Casey had cordoned off the farmhouse and the barn and proceeded to take crime scene photographs. While Ruth conducted her initial examination of Keats's body, Amanda had called the Drug Enforcement Administration branch office in New York City and explained the situation. They had dispatched a team immediately.

They were led by an agent named Monica Diaz, who had transferred from her native Texas to New York. By comparison to the Mexican cartels' operations she had previously uncovered, Keats's first steps in empire building were modest but no less concerning. Amanda left Diaz and the DEA team to continue their work, offering them the use of the guest desk back at the sheriff's department. She doubted it would be needed, though, based on the mass of equipment they had brought themselves.

Before the DEA's arrival, Amanda had given one of the brown powder packages to Ruth, keen to discover what it was without being reliant on the Feds. She had asked it to be chemically examined as a priority. Ruth had promised to pull some strings and see what she could do about obtaining the results as quickly as possible.

By the time Amanda and Casey's duties on the farm had come to an end, the sun was setting. She had asked Casey to return to the office to make a start on the necessary paperwork. Amanda had debated joining her, but there was not much she could do beyond supervising. The break-up of a potentially major drug operation had fallen into her lap and dominated the day.

However, Amanda was still keen to finish that day as it had started, by making further inroads into the Judy Sterling case and putting other distractions to the back of her mind temporarily.

The local news, perhaps even state media, would quickly descend on Independence as word got out about Keats's operation, but more the fact that a female sheriff had gunned down the bad guy before he had killed one of her captured deputies. No doubt there was a 'movie of the week' producer somewhere out there who would jump on such a story.

Amanda had no appetite for such sensationalism, though. The fact was that she had killed someone. Even if it had been necessary to save Jake, it was still not something that made her proud. It had not been the first time she had taken a life, nor was it possibly the last, but it was certainly not something to be celebrated.

She found herself craving a beer, but decided that she would put in some decent miles on the treadmill instead when she returned home after paying a visit to Ray Sterling. Before either of those events, though, she had a more important place to be.

CHAPTER TWENTY-NINE

Jake sat up in the hospital bed and groaned. His head still pounded, though the pain had eased somewhat. The cut above his eye had been cleaned and stitched, and after one of the doctors had examined him, Jake had been advised to take it easy for a few days.

The doctor had wanted to keep him in for overnight observation, but Jake had waved him off. He had suffered worse injuries on tour and had still been expected to fight during the more intense engagements. Besides, Jake didn't want to take up the room he had been placed in any longer if someone more deserving needed it. However, it seemed a quiet night in the Independence Community Hospital.

Dressed in a standard patient gown, Jake hopped off the bed and opened the door into the main corridor. He instantly winced as the florescent lighting hit his eyes. He quickly closed the door again and retreated into the darker room and the wall lamps' gentler lighting. Jake stepped back and sat on the bed with a sigh.

While it was true that he had hurt more in the past, that had mainly been during his early twenties when the feeling of indestructibility had yet to fade. Now he was a stone's throw from thirty, and while his age wasn't so much the problem, the physical mileage was. Aches and pains took longer to stretch out, and his collection of scars, big and small, had just acquired a fresh one.

As Jake sat staring at the floor, he felt morose thoughts beginning to intrude once again and knew the black dog was back on the prowl. He doubted running would be a good idea for a few days, at least to the degree he usually pushed himself. Neither was alcohol an option to throw the dog off the scent. Even during his darkest days following his military discharge, Jake had simply been too wary and aware of his own weaknesses to dare drowning his sorrows too much, lest he never resurfaced. He would just have to fake-grin and bear it.

Perhaps he deserved to in some small penance for being so stupid in handling the Keats situation. He had narrowly avoided decapitation and had unwittingly placed Amanda and Casey in danger in their search and rescue of him. Two lives put at risk for his own. No. Three lives, one tiny.

Jake broke away from such thoughts and looked to the door as he heard a light tapping. It opened, and Amanda poked her head through and grinned.

'That a backless gown?'

'Affirmative,' replied Jake, unamused at Amanda's amusement.

Amanda stepped through and closed the door. She carried a roll of clothes under her arm.

'Well, as much as I'm sure the nurses would like to catch a glimpse of a bare Marine Corps ass, I stopped by your place and grabbed these.'

Amanda placed the rolled-up pair of jeans and black sweater at the foot of the bed next to Jake. She dragged the visitor chair from the wall towards the bed and sat opposite Jake.

'They're actually wrapping to smuggle in what I know you really want.'

A curious Jake unrolled his clothes to find a brown bag cocooned inside. He opened the top and pulled out a burger wrapped in greasy paper. He raised a questioning eyebrow at Amanda.

'I also stopped by Glenn's. Bacon cheeseburger, pepper jack with mushrooms, just how you like it. Truffle fries too. How much do you love me right now?'

'You know you're not supposed to bring stuff like this in here, right?'

'Are you seriously going to tell them?' scoffed Amanda.

'Hell no,' said Jake as he unwrapped the burger and took a large, satisfying bite.

'Whoa there horsey, it's not all for you. And my condition for this is that you take it easy for the next few days. I'll take you home and expect you in bed before I leave.'

'Yes, Ma'am,' said Jake with a soft salute.

Jake removed a box of fries, balanced them on his lap, and passed the brown bag to Amanda. She pulled out her own burger, unwrapped it, and started eating. She sighed, satisfied.

'I haven't eaten all day. Dammit, even more treadmill later. Glenn has his price.'

'More?' asked Jake between munches.

'Yeah,' responded Amanda, her tone slightly deflated. 'The first few miles to clear my head. You're not the only one who tries to outrun the dark.'

While unsatisfied, Jake had decided to bury his guilt as best he could. However, he still felt obligated to offer some form of apology, no matter how small.

'I'm sorry about what happened, Amanda, about what you had to do.'

'Why sorry? It wasn't your fault.'

'I rushed in there. I could have gotten myself killed, not to mention you and Casey. It was stupid and reckless.'

Amanda stared at Jake a moment as she chewed on several fries. Then, without a word, she placed her food on the floor, unknotted her tie, and unbuttoned the top half of her shirt. Jake looked on awkwardly for a few seconds, unsure what his friend and superior was doing. Amanda pulled her shirt collar to the right to expose her shoulder area and moved her bra strap a few inches. It revealed the circular scar of an old bullet wound.

'You know what this is, right?' she asked quietly.

'Of course,' replied Jake with a nod. 'I never knew, though.'

'Yeah, well, I try not to acknowledge it myself most times,' said Amanda as she pulled her shirt back up and re-buttoned herself.

'What happened?' probed Jake.

Amanda stared into space, lost in a momentary daydream, then locked eyes with Jake.

'It was Ninety-One. Desert Storm was well underway. I'd just been promoted to Corporal and was a field medic for my unit. We would go in our Black Hawk and rescue any crashed pilots. Well, the call came in that an F-16 had gone down. So we scrambled, headed right on in, armed with plenty of enthusiasm and not nearly enough intelligence. A freak sandstorm hit, threw us off. By the time we got out of it, it took a while to get our bearings back and head for the pilot. But the delay was okay because we'd been told that Iraqi resistance was minimal, barely even there. I guess the soldier who hit our tail rotor with a heavy machine-gun didn't get the memo. We went down hard, but we all survived the crash. Not all of us made it home, though.'

'How come you've never told me this before?' asked Jake gently.

'It was a visit to hell, Jake, not one I'm inclined to relive with anyone, even family. And I don't want to talk about it now either. All you need to know was that people died, I got off lightly by comparison, and we were only saved when the ground invasion reached us. But it all started with rushing in. My point being, we didn't see it coming then, and you didn't see it coming today. It took me a long time to come to terms with my experience, but what happened at the farm isn't worth weighing you down. We both know you're carrying more than enough already.'

Jake looked down at the floor and nodded. A silence developed between them, not uncomfortable, just thoughtful. Eventually, he looked up.

'So, did you bring any dessert?' he inquired with a grin.

Amanda screwed up her burger wrapper into a ball and threw it at him. They both started laughing.

CHAPTER THIRTY

Ray Sterling's face instantly dropped as he opened his front door and saw that it was Amanda waiting on the other side.

'This is becoming a bad habit, Sheriff,' he said.

Amanda was unsure as to what degree he was serious versus blackly humorous.

'I'm sorry to bother you again, Ray, but I need to talk with you about what happened to Judy. It's a serious matter.'

Ray nodded and opened the door for her. She stepped through, and he led her to the lounge, almost an identical repeat of the scene they had found themselves in previously, even in their seating arrangements. Amanda noticed the cracked television on the wall. She was curious, but wanted to press on.

'Where's Jason?' asked Amanda as she sat down.

'Still at practice,' replied Ray. 'I've barely seen that boy, but it is what it is. If that's what's helping him keep his head while all this crap is going on, then fine. He's still got his future to think about.'

'And how are you holding up?' asked Amanda. Ray sighed.

'How do you think I'm doing? You've been in the exact same place with losing a loved one if I remember rightly. Tell me, does it get any easier?'

'A little,' said Amanda. 'But easier doesn't mean easy. Not totally, not ever.'

'Thanks for not sugar-coating it. I respect that. Better to be honest with someone rather than patronize them.'

'Well, that's exactly why I'm here,' advanced Amanda. 'To be honest with you. There have been some developments in Judy's case.'

'Oh?' said Ray as he leaned forward, instantly engaged. 'Like what?'

'I know it'll be difficult to hear, but we increasingly have reason to believe that Judy was murdered.'

Amanda gave Ray a moment for her statement to sink in as he stared at her blankly. He raised an eyebrow and shook his head, evidently less than convinced.

'I'm sorry, but I don't follow. It was clearly a suicide. Abandoning her car, her things. Hell, the note she wrote doesn't get much more black and white.'

'I know all the initial evidence points that way, but new things have come to light, things I needed to look into before coming to you. There are signs on Judy's body that she was pushed rather than jumped. It's also likely a second car and person was at the scene.'

'But who'd kill her if she was going to do it herself?'

'Exactly, it doesn't make any sense. Unless, of course, she actually didn't intend to kill herself. It's possible that she was aiming to fake her own death instead. As you say, the abandoned possessions, the unambiguous note, they're both strong evidence. With no body, we'd have put two and two together, concluded that she'd jumped and been lost in the river. She would have been free to walk away, safe in the knowledge that her life insurance would see you and Jason looked after. I'm guessing that's why she hadn't updated it after two years had passed, so that it wouldn't have been forfeited by a suicide clause.'

Ray waved a dismissive hand and stood up. He started pacing around the sofa.

'I'm sorry, but this smells like bullshit. A conspiracy to fake her own death? Please! For what reason? Ever heard of Occam's Razor, Sheriff? It's the principle that to explain something, you should make no more assumptions than are necessary or, put another way, sometimes the most obvious answer is the right one. Now I loved Judy, I really did, but she clearly had issues she kept from us, and she dealt with them by punching her own ticket. It's there in her own handwriting! End of story!'

'You know, Ray, you're the second person today to use those exact words to discourage me.'

Ray stopped pacing and looked at Amanda, curious. He waited expectantly.

'I paid a visit to Dry Lake Road this morning,' she continued. 'Have you ever been there?'

Ray thought for a moment then shook his head.

'Can't say that I ever have.'

'Well, that's funny,' said Amanda with zero levity. 'Because Gary and Mary Brennan have a cabin up there, and they both told me that you and Judy spent the weekend with them in January. So either they're lying, or you are.'

Ray maintained eye contact with Amanda. He licked his lips slightly.

'Yes, I remember now, we went to visit their new place, enjoy some walks in the snow, food and drink, that kind of thing.'

'And how close were you and Judy to the Brennans?'

'Close enough, I guess. It was more Judy, really. The three of them had politics in common, whereas I felt like a bit of a fifth wheel at times. It just isn't my thing.'

'If that's the case, then why did you and Judy have a fight over her vote against the Riverside Road development a couple of weeks back?'

'Excuse me?'

'The night my deputy showed up here, you and Judy had been screaming at each other. I checked her recent voting record, and that day she had gone against her entire previous pattern. Fast forward to that evening. A coincidence? I doubt it. Or maybe you'd discovered she was having an affair and was planning to leave you?'

'What!' Ray thundered.

Amanda had deliberately rolled the dice with her last comment. Her entire conversation flow had been designed to rattle Ray, shake the tree, and see what fell out. Based on the degree of red Ray's face began to turn, she had succeeded.

'How dare you come in here and-!'

Ray paused in mid rage and narrowed his eyes.

'Oh, I get it now. That's why you were asking about our connections to the Brennans. You think maybe Judy was having an affair with Gary. Very clever. Bait the hook, and I might bite. Well, not this fish. Now, unless you have anything to discuss that isn't supposition on your part, I'd like you to leave.'

Amanda grabbed her hat and headed to the front door, eagerly herded by Ray behind her. She opened the door, stopped, and turned.

'There is one last thing. Where's your car tonight? It's not parked outside.'

'Jason took it to practice,' replied Ray. 'I didn't want him walking home late. Why, more conspiracies?'

'No, just that I have photographic evidence of tire tracks at the Saratoga Bridge that most likely figure in Judy's death. Those same tracks appeared near the Brennan cabin earlier. I'd just like to check the tread on your tires and see what we can see.'

'I don't know what you're talking about,' said Ray stiffly.

'In that case, you'll have nothing to worry about if I come to visit tomorrow, will you?'

Amanda put her hat on and gently tipped the front with pinched fingers.

'You have a good night now.'

Amanda stepped off the porch and headed towards her car. She heard the door close behind her, not a word from Ray.

***

Ray closed the door and squeezed his eyes shut. He silently pleaded to wake up from the nightmare but knew all too well that this was reality. Carter had called the previous night to warn him that Sheriff Northstar had been probing Gary, gathering clues, and was running with them. Ray and his associates had thought she had been getting closer to the Riverside Road plot. However, she was actually getting closer to much worse. If she checked the tires on his car, there would be no way to avoid the truth eventually coming out. Ray felt the walls closing in on him. He was out of time and options. Only drastic action would do.

CHAPTER THIRTY-ONE

As Amanda had predicted, several news crews had gathered outside the sheriff's department by the start of the next morning. She pulled to a stop in her usual parking space. Amanda stepped out, trying to look as authoritative as she could as the throng of reporters advanced towards her, their microphones leading the way. She walked towards the main entrance and met the group half-way.

A cacophony of questions erupted. They all revolved around the same issue, that of a major drug find in the county, and that a man had died in the process of that discovery. Amanda stopped in front of the entrance and decided to give a statement to satisfy the reporters as best she could, though she knew that it would be a vain hope.

'Good morning,' she started, pausing for effect and to allow the cameras and microphones to assume their positions. 'Yesterday, while conducting a routine patrol, one of my deputies accidentally stumbled upon a drug manufacturing operation run by a single individual. The deputy was held hostage for a brief period before another deputy and myself, aiming to locate our missing colleague, also came upon the operation. Unfortunately, to prevent the serious injury or even death of our captive colleague, it was necessary to fire upon the suspect and end his life. I am confident that the county medical examiner's report will find events unfolded exactly as I have described. My deputy suffered minor injuries, was discharged from the hospital last night, and is now on leave for the remainder of the week. My department will be releasing a more detailed statement in due course. Should you have any questions relating to the illicit drugs discovered on the site, please direct them to the Drug Enforcement Administration. They have taken over the investigation regarding those matters. Thank you for your time.'

Amanda turned around and headed inside, ignoring the barrage of additional questions that were fired her way. There was nothing else she could really add without either repeating herself or going into more detail than she wished until the full report was made available. She found Wayne sat at his desk.

'Good morning, Amanda,' he said. 'Not a great start to the day, huh?'

'They're just doing their jobs. I may as well be annoyed at the rain for being wet.'

'How were your mother and Max about the whole thing?' he asked, peering over his spectacles.

'Worried about me, but I told them what they needed to hear.'

'I get you,' Wayne nodded. 'I don't think the big guy upstairs will hold a few white lies against you if it helps keep the home front sweet.'

'Casey in yet?' asked Amanda. Wayne nodded.

'Yep. Jake too.'

Amanda rolled her eyes at hearing that Jake wasn't at home resting, but then she wasn't surprised either. She thanked Wayne and entered the main office to see Jake and Casey sitting at their desks, though only the latter was in uniform, while Jake wore his biker jacket and jeans. Jake raised his hand in an effort to speak first.

'Dammit Jake,' said Amanda, beating him to it. She tried and failed to keep her voice down. 'You're on leave. That was an order, not a suggestion.'

'I am, I swear,' said Jake, raising both hands in defense. 'I'm sure as hell not sitting at home though, and the doc says I can't drive for a few days on account of my head. So I'm just saying a quick hello.'

'Yeah, but your version of hello translates into wanting a case update, am I right?' said Amanda as she raised a wary eyebrow.

'Indulge me, I'm a wounded man,' said Jake, throwing in a playful smile for effect.

'Fine,' replied Amanda, shaking her head. 'But you really need to get a life.'

'Duly noted,' said Jake as he stood up and walked to the coffee maker to pour three mugs. 'I'm actually going to watch Max practice later, offer him some of that advice we talked about the other night.'

'Be sure to have some Eighties power ballads ready for your training montage,' teased Casey.

'Hey, if it ain't broke, don't fix it,' retorted Jake with a grin. 'Need I remind you I have a state champions ring to prove my Yoda-like credentials?'

'No, I don't need reminding thanks. Rick still wears the damn thing everywhere he goes. Where's yours?'

'Not sure,' shrugged Jake. 'Hanging above my father's toilet, I think.'

Jake handed a mug of coffee to Amanda and Casey as he returned to his desk.

'So, moving on swiftly,' began Amanda as she sipped her coffee. 'I paid a visit to Ray Sterling last night. It did not go well.'

'How hard did you shake his tree?' enquired Casey.

'Hard enough. He knows more than he's letting on, I'm sure of it.'

'Think he's our killer?' asked Jake.

'I'm more doubtful of his innocence than I was, put it that way. But whatever he's hiding, I'm squeezing it out of him today. No more playing around. Whether it was an affair on Judy's part or something about her Riverside Road vote, Ray was pissed. If he didn't kill her, then something he knows might help us find out who did.'

'So what's our play?' asked Jake.

'I told him I'd be calling to check his tire treads against the ones we found on the bridge and at the Brennan cabin. They might be completely unrelated, but it's pressure on him all the same.'

Casey held up a sheet of paper.

'I've got the lab analysis of that brown powder we seized at the farm yesterday.'

Amanda perked up, while Jake subconsciously raised his mug high to sip from, almost as if he was trying to hide behind it.

'Go on,' said Amanda, nodding to Casey. 'If this crap has been getting out there, I want to know what we're dealing with.'

'Jake said the guy called them boosters. Well, get that brown stuff into your system, and it'll certainly give you a boost, like a rocket in your pants. According to the lab report, a lot of the ingredients seem natural, including vitamins and caffeine. But there's a major steroidal component, no doubt about it. Great for the metabolism, rapid muscle building, bursts of intense energy. Not so great for your long-term health, your testicles, or your state of mind. Part and parcel of the energy bursts is heightened aggression and then epic downers once it wears off. All in all, a hell of a recipe for mood swings.'

'Do we have any idea who this stuff would appeal to?' Amanda asked the room.

'Whoever has an ego to nurture or a competitive advantage to find,' offered Jake. 'Could be athletes under pressure, or gym monkeys looking to impress. I saw it in the Marines from time to time, guys looking to build themselves up like Spartans. Some opted for the natural route, others chose the short cut. It was illegal, of course, but out in theater, you've often got nothing better to do than patrol, read, or work out, so after enough time, everyone looked equally ripped.'

'Either way, I'd better let the school board know, get them to inform parents to be on the lookout,' said Amanda.

'Well, I'm sure the press will find out sooner or later, spread the word,' said Casey. She craned her neck to look out a nearby window. 'Hey, where have they all gone?' she wondered aloud, puzzled.

Amanda walked over to the window that looked out upon the park in front of the sheriff's department. She opened a gap in the blinds and peered out.

'Looks like they're all moving towards the town hall. Some are running. Casey, can you put a call in and ask-'

Amanda was cut off as Wayne burst into the room, wide-eyed and breathing heavily. He looked around the office momentarily and quickly fixed on where she stood.

'Amanda!' he squawked urgently. 'We've just had a report of gunshots at the town hall.'

CHAPTER THIRTY-TWO

The trio sprinted towards the town hall. Amanda and Casey had responded immediately, while Jake had grabbed a shotgun from the weapons locker and followed them a moment later. By virtue of his height and fitness, he had quickly caught up with them, ignoring all medical advice to avoid exertion.

When the trio reached the town hall entrance, they found the assorted journalists had pitched up behind trees or walls to cover the scene without getting too close. Passers-by outside had scattered. A dozen municipal workers were evacuating out the fire exits either side of the building. Amanda and Casey drew their pistols while Jake cocked his shotgun and covered their rear as Amanda gently pushed the main door open and entered.

Amanda quickly scanned the main lobby and signaled Casey and Jake to follow when she spotted no threat. They spread out with their weapons raised, Amanda advancing centrally with Jake to her right and Casey to her left. Amanda heard whimpering coming from behind the reception desk and headed towards it. She peered over the side and found the young female receptionist she had met previously tucked underneath, lying on her side, curled up as much as she could.

'It's okay, the sheriff's here,' said Amanda soothingly. 'Can you tell me what's going on?'

'Gun, upstairs, mayor's office,' the girl squeaked, her eyes darting around, looking in every direction except Amanda's.

Amanda was tempted to ask why the girl hadn't evacuated, but it was clear that the young lady had panicked at the sound of gunfire and had dived for the nearest cover. With mass shootings almost a scheduled occurrence on news network coverage, it was no surprise that she had thought the worst and reverted to 'deer in the headlights' mode.

'Okay, you go with my deputy, she'll look after you.'

Amanda looked to Casey and nodded towards the receptionist. Casey returned a nod of acknowledgment, stepped behind the desk, and gently raised the girl off the ground by the arm.

'You're safe now, let's get you out of here,' said Casey gently as she led the girl towards a nearby side fire exit.

Amanda knew that Casey wouldn't have an issue with escort duty. Though Amanda had hoped that a shooting incident would never occur in Independence, the possibility had always existed. So, she had discussed roles with Casey and Jake if the unthinkable became a reality. Casey was to take charge of any evacuations and subsequent crowd control. At the same time, Amanda and Jake, with the best part of two decades' military experience between them, would deal with any shooters. Now, with Casey and the receptionist safely out of the building, Amanda glanced at Jake and indicated the stairs that led up to the mayor's office.

They both advanced step by step, their weapons trained on the top of the stairs in case any nasty surprises emerged. It was all quiet, though. They reached the top and took the left turn that led towards the mayor's office. The secretary's desk was abandoned, and the door to Gary's suite was ajar.

'This is the sheriff!' Amanda called out authoritatively.

'You can come in, Amanda, you're not the one I had my sights on,' a male voice responded. 'Besides, I need you to bear witness.'

Amanda instantly recognized that the voice belonged to Ray Sterling.

'What's going on, Ray? What do you want me to witness?' Amanda called back through the door.

'Just come on through,' replied Ray with an eerie calm. 'I promise no more shooting.'

Amanda weighed up the risks in her head. She was conscious that she only had a few seconds to make a decision as to whether to burst in and take Ray down, hopefully with a shoulder shot, or enter Gary's office and mediate whatever situation she found herself in. It was the unknowns that convinced her to go for the second option. She had no idea what lay beyond the door and didn't want to risk making things worse.

If Ray was in Gary's office and had fired shots, it was possible that Gary was wounded and needed medical attention. If Gary was dead, then it wouldn't make any difference. At least she could try and discover why a man she had met only some twelve hours previously had suddenly acted so out of character.

'Okay, Ray, I'm going to holster my pistol and come on in,' she said loudly and clearly to leave no room for misunderstanding.

Jake understood all too well and glanced over to her across his raised shotgun, his expression incredulous. *Are you serious?* he mouthed silently. Amanda nodded, holstered her pistol, raised her arms, and slowly advanced towards the door.

'I'm coming in. Now I've got your word that there'll be no more shooting, right? Because I'm entering in good faith.'

'Don't worry, I promise. You just need to hear the truth, then I'll come quietly.'

Amanda paused at the threshold of the door, breathed deeply, and gently pushed it open with the tip of her boot, keeping her arms raised as she stepped forward. Gary's office looked no different from her previous visit, except that the large window behind his desk had been shot several times, a spiderweb of cracked glass emanating from each bullet hole. In the seating area to the right, Ray sat on a chair. He held a 9mm pistol in one hand and a tumbler of whiskey in the other, care of Gary's drinks tray that rested on a nearby side table.

On a second chair to Ray's left sat Gary Brennan, his right hand pressed tightly against a bullet wound in his upper left arm. He was panting, pale, and sweating.

Amanda wouldn't have been surprised to see him vomit or pass out. Still, he was managing to keep things together, even as his wide-eyed stare in her direction seemingly pleaded for her to take out her gun and blow Ray's head off. The chair nearest to her, directly opposite Ray, was empty. Ray indicated it with his whiskey-holding hand.

'Please, take a seat,' he said, more as a suggestion than an order.

Amanda lowered her arms and cautiously sat down, keeping her eyes fixed on Ray's pistol. Her focus on it did not go unnoticed by its owner.

'I have to admit that this has been a little drastic on my part.'

'A little?' she replied, raising both eyebrows. 'Jesus, Ray, what have you done?'

'What I had to do to get the truth,' answered Ray as he downed the tumbler of amber liquid in one gulp.

'What truth, Ray?' pressed Amanda, sensing that, finally, the answers she sought were only seconds away.

'The truth about Judy's betrayal and who with,' said Ray as he stared intensely at Amanda. 'The reason I had to kill her. To make her pay for seeing this piece of crap behind my back.'

Ray had admitted murder flatly and dispassionately. Amanda attempted to absorb his words but was immediately distracted by a yelp from Gary to her side.

'I don't know what the hell you're talking about, you crazy bastard!' squealed the mayor. 'I never touched her!'

'Bullshit,' said Ray coolly. 'As soon as the sheriff here told me about the photos she had of my car's tire tracks, I knew the game was up. The same tracks that I left outside your cabin after I'd finished spying on you and Judy. The same tracks I left after I stopped next to her on the bridge and forced her over. The same tracks that Amanda would have matched if she had checked them today. I was careless, I guess. But if I'm going down for it, I figured I may as well take you down with me, Gary.'

Ray eyed Gary with a piercing gaze, causing the latter to look away after a moment, unable to sustain eye contact, though whether it was out of shame or fear Amanda couldn't tell. She leaned forward, trying to get things straight in her head.

'So if you knew Judy was having an affair with Gary, why wait until the night she was leaving before acting?' she asked.

'Don't you get it?' replied Ray impatiently. 'I only found out *on* the night Judy was going to leave me. I followed her to the Brennan cabin, then it all made sense. I tailed her to the bridge and confronted her. She told me she was going to fake a suicide so she could escape from me. Well, if she wanted to escape so bad, I made her wish come true.'

'And after killing Judy, you were just going to sit on all this and let Gary get away with it?' pressed Amanda.

She wanted to believe Ray, wanted an elegant solution to present itself, but skepticism still gnawed at her. That said, Gary was bleeding three feet away, and Amanda doubted Ray had simply shot the man on a whim, without cause.

'Of course not,' said Ray, his irritation growing. 'I was just waiting for the right opportunity to get him. Accidents happen all the time. You just forced my hand, that's all.'

'I swear Amanda, I have no idea what he's talking about,' said Gary, his voice cracking.

'Then why shoot to wound and not to kill, Ray?' probed Amanda.

'Jesus Christ, don't encourage him to finish the job!' screamed Gary, who then gasped in pain and squeezed his bleeding arm tighter.

'What can I say?' shrugged Ray. 'I'm a bad shot. And I've scared him enough. The truth will come out after this, his career will be finished. I certainly didn't plan on having all those reporters hanging around your building, but why look a gift horse in the mouth? They'll help me finish the job. Sometimes you can destroy a man without killing him.'

Ray suddenly stood up. Amanda went against instinct and stayed her hand from reaching for her gun. Ray extended his own hand, offering his weapon balanced on the palm.

'I've made my point,' he said with a sigh. 'Take me in, and I'll offer a full confession. Let's just put all this behind us and move on with our lives.'

'You make it sound so simple, Ray,' said Amanda as she stood and gently took the gun away from him. 'Like you only need to pay a parking ticket, and we can forget the whole thing ever happened.'

'There's a certain clarity that comes with knowing that life as you know it is over,' said Ray as he looked down at a whimpering Gary. 'Things that were complicated enough to make you scream can become simple pretty quickly when you don't have to worry anymore.'

Amanda reached for the handcuffs behind her gun belt. Without any prompting, Ray turned around and placed his hands behind his back expectantly. She clipped the cuffs on and made sure they were secure.

'And what about Jason? Sounds like life's just got a whole lot more complicated for him,' observed Amanda.

She didn't see it, but as Ray's head tilted downwards and he exhaled a heavy sigh, Amanda could tell he had squeezed his eyes shut.

CHAPTER THIRTY-THREE

After reading Ray his rights, Amanda handed him over to Jake and helped Gary up from his seat. They quickly made their way down to the main lobby and outside, where an ambulance was waiting. The paramedics attempted to make their way through the same throng of reporters, photographers, and video cameramen who had greeted Amanda earlier.

She stepped forward, parting her hands like Moses before the Red Sea, an action which, accompanied by a deliberate cold stare, silently communicated to the bustling journalists to make way for the medics.

The paramedics gently took Gary and led him to the back of the ambulance, where they started to tend to him. Knowing that he was secure with them, Amanda scanned for Casey. She spotted her swiftly advancing towards the throng, away from a small group of town hall workers comforting the young receptionist. Casey knew she would be needed for crowd control as they escorted Ray to the jail cells.

Amanda had debated keeping Ray inside and bundling him into a patrol car when the opportunity presented itself. Driving between two buildings within easy sight of each other would have appeared ridiculous, though. It would also have allowed more time for curious onlookers to gather outside. Better to get Ray into the sheriff's building as soon as possible.

Amanda turned to Jake behind her, who firmly held onto Ray. She nodded towards the sheriff's building. She led the way, joining up with Casey as they cleared a path for Jake and Ray to follow. As they advanced, what hope Amanda had naïvely held that the media would patiently wait for a statement was quickly dashed. Numerous questions were fired either at her or at Ray, clashing and mixing until they almost became a white noise of indiscernible babble.

'There will be no comment for now,' yelled Amanda above the din. 'A statement will be issued later today.'

'Gary Brennan slept with my wife!' cried Ray, clearly determined to make his own statement right there, right then. 'He's a disgrace to his office and deserved what he got, just like she did!'

'Are you confessing to the murder of Judy Sterling?' quizzed one of the journalists Amanda recognized as a writer for The Independence Star.

'I loved her, but it had to be done! She deserved to die, to pay for what she did, and I don't regret it,' screamed Ray.

Amanda instinctively felt that it was play-acting of the highest order. No one ever came clean as melodramatically as that in real life, only in neat police procedural shows or old-fashioned black and white detective movies.

Finally, the circus came to an end as they reached the entrance to the sheriff's building. Jake led Ray inside, followed by Casey. Amanda hung back and turned to face the pursuing journalists. She raised her hands, palms like a barrier, and they halted. She slowly stepped back towards the entrance doors.

'I've told you guys, whatever Mr. Sterling has said, there will be an official statement released later today. So before you go reporting things that may have to be retracted, I'd advise you to have a little patience and wait for the official version of events.'

Amanda turned and entered the building. She usually had a genial relationship with the media. She was even prone to exchanging light-hearted conversation or jokes, especially with the local press. Amanda had no time for such pleasantries today, however.

Jake and Casey were waiting with Ray in the lobby, with a slightly mystified Wayne gazing upon the scene from behind his desk. Amanda looked at Ray, who stared at the ground silently, avoiding eye contact with anyone. His taste for spontaneous public confession had seemingly dissipated now that the cameras and audio recorders were no longer directed at him. She looked at Jake.

'Take him to the cells. We'll draw up a confession for him to sign if he's so eager.'

Jake nodded and led Ray into the main office and the direction of the holding cells towards the building's rear. Casey turned to Amanda.

'Want me to draw up that confession?' she asked.

'No,' replied Amanda, shaking her head. 'I want you to head straight back to the town hall, make sure everything has calmed down there. Find out who's sticking around or heading home early, just to be sure they're okay. Then I want you to go to the archives and speak with Shelly Goodwin.'

'But what for? What if she's gone?'

'She'll be there, I guarantee,' reassured Amanda. 'Bless her heart, but she enjoys her dramas, and this has been a dramatic morning, to say the least. She'll be keen to soak it up, I'm sure. But I need you to ask her for everything she has on Gary Brennan's expense claims.'

'Can I ask why?' probed Casey as she raised an eyebrow.

'I know what you're thinking,' replied Amanda. 'We have Ray Sterling in custody prepared to tell the entire world that he shoved his wife off the Saratoga Bridge. So why keep digging?'

'My question exactly.'

'Ray's justification was that Judy was having an affair with Gary. Well, that could be true. There's certainly the cabin we found where they had their supposed liaisons, but it's still circumstantial. There has to be more evidence, a connection.'

'More evidence beyond a full confession?'

'Jesus, are you having a problem with this, Casey?' snapped Amanda, her frustration and the delayed adrenaline comedown from the morning's events mixing together into a cocktail of irritability.

Casey lowered her head and shook it, giving the impression of a scolded child. Amanda sighed and instantly felt guilty.

'I'm sorry, that was uncalled for. I appreciate everything you've been doing, I really do. Just do this last thing for me, okay? If nothing comes of it, then we'll focus on Ray.'

Casey raised her head and offered a lukewarm smile. Amanda's apology had been accepted, but the wound caused by her temper was still fresh.

'And what are you going to do?' she asked.

'I need to get to Jason and tell him what his father's done before social media does it for me.'

CHAPTER THIRTY-FOUR

Amanda gently tapped her knuckles on the door to the football team's meeting area. It was a medium-sized windowless room, large enough to hold two-dozen chairs and plenty of standing room for any unfortunate latecomers to team strategy lectures. A ceiling-mounted projector beamed video onto the smooth, white-painted wall at the front of the room where Coach Booth and his assistants would play, freeze, and play again footage of the Independence Rebels, analyzing movements in fine detail.

On this occasion, Amanda found Jason Sterling educating himself. He sat at the front row, a notepad resting on his lap and remote control in his hand, though the room was so dark, Amanda wondered how he could see any of the thoughts he had jotted down.

Jason's attention was entirely on the game footage unfolding on the wall before him, his focus blocking out everything else so that Amanda had to knock a second time to gain his attention. His trance broke, and he turned to face her. His eyebrows rose in surprise at seeing the sheriff, and he instantly paused the video.

'Hi Jason, sorry for interrupting,' said Amanda, pleasantly. 'May I join you?'

'Uh, sure thing, Sheriff,' he replied, slightly confused.

Amanda entered the room and flicked on the lights, causing Jason to squint slightly as his eyes adjusted. She grabbed one of the free chairs and pulled it over so that she could sit facing him, close enough to be a comfort if needed, but not so close as to dominate his personal space.

'I was going to go to your house, but then I remembered Max telling me that the coaches let you come here to the team area, rather than class.'

'Coach Booth and the principal are okay with it,' said Jason, attempting to get an explanation in early in case trouble was further down the road.

'That's not a problem, not at all,' said Amanda. 'Times are tough, and sometimes you just need to escape into what you enjoy the most.'

'It's the first game of the season next week, against the Warriors. That's why I'm watching the game from last year, get a little reminder of their strengths and weaknesses.'

'Everybody has them,' said Amanda with a shrug.

She wasn't delaying the breaking of bad news, just making Jason comfortable with her presence before she delivered what would undoubtedly be a hammer blow to the young man. Within barely a week, he would have lost both parents, the first to death, and the second to prison.

'Sorry, but you're wrong, Sheriff,' replied Jason with deadly seriousness rather than jocular self-confidence. 'I'm all strength and no weakness. This is my year, my time to shine. No distractions, just victory.'

'But Jason,' said Amanda gently, trying to contain her shock, 'it's not a weakness or a distraction to feel pain. Anyone would in your position.'

'I know that!' he replied, his voice rising. 'I'm not a damn robot. But my mom made her choice, and it was to walk out on me, to leave me.'

'Jason, that's what I'm here to talk to you about.'

Amanda's comment seemed to instantly dissipate Jason's temper, as his expression changed from somewhat embittered to a mixture of curiosity and concern.

'Is something wrong?'

'It's about your dad, Jason,' said Amanda as neutrally as she could.

'Oh God, is he okay?'

Jason made to stand, but Amanda eased him back down with a hand gesture.

'Don't worry, your father's fine, he's not hurt or anything. But I've still got some bad news, and it's going to be tough for you to hear.'

Jason leaned forward expectantly, his eyes widening, desperate for her reveal.

'I'm so sorry, but your dad has confessed to killing your mom.'

Amanda had expected to see Jason sigh, close his eyes, lean back, cover his face with his hands, or numerous other reactions she commonly witnessed when she had to give someone bad news. Jason did none of those things. Instead, he exploded.

Jason launched himself from his chair with such force that it slid along the linoleum floor and tipped over. He threw the remote control against the football game's frozen image, where it smashed into a dozen pieces of black plastic and circuitry. Jason gripped his head in his hands and roared a terrifying cry of fiery rage and dark despair. Amanda was so shocked that she too leaped from her seat and backed away nervously. She held out her hands, trying to calm him down.

'Jason, please! Just breathe!' she appealed.

It was to no avail as he grabbed a chair and flung it across the room where it clattered against the back wall.

'Jason Sterling, shut up and sit down!' screamed Amanda, as she reached back into her life experience and momentarily accessed the disciplinarian in Staff Sergeant Northstar, the bane of rowdy recruits.

Trying to calm Jason through gentle persuasion had evidently failed, and so she had had little choice but to deliver the verbal equivalent of a slap to the face. It seemed to do the trick as Jason stopped his tantrum and looked at her blankly. She followed through to make sure he wouldn't flare up again.

'I'm sorry, I know this is hard for you, but I won't tolerate that kind of behavior.'

Jason's eyes started to water, though Amanda suspected it was the reality of the situation sinking in rather than her chastisement.

'Please, Sheriff, tell me what happened. I've had my phone switched-off all morning. I haven't heard anything.'

'Look, all I know is that your father went into the town hall this morning and injured Mayor Brennan. I don't want to say anymore. I think it best if you come back to the sheriff's office with me and talk to your father, let him explain in his own words.'

Jason wiped the sleeve of his white and blue football jersey under his nose and sniffed back his tears.

'This wasn't supposed to happen,' he said as he stared into space.

'I know, honey,' said Amanda, but she quickly suspected that he had been talking to himself rather than to her, as he continued to stare blankly ahead and repeat the sentence.

As he did so, he seemed to be working himself up again as Amanda could see his fists start to clench up, and the pace of his words increase. Amanda stuck her head out of the door, hoping to spot one of the team coaches that could help her bring Jason back down to earth.

'This wasn't supposed to happen, this wasn't supposed to happen!' he continued rambling. 'She said it would all be okay!'

'What?' said Amanda as she snapped her head back to face Jason. 'Did you just say 'she'? Jason, who are you talking about?'

'I need to get out of here, I need to think!' he cried and burst towards the door. Amanda attempted to reach out and stop him, but there was no way she was going to stop a young man who regularly barged through players twice her size. Jason pushed past her, and though it was not a deliberate blow, he knocked Amanda to the floor and sprinted off down the corridor.

'Jason, stop!' she called out.

She struggled to her feet and set off after him. As athletic as Amanda still was, the almost thirty-year age gap quickly made itself apparent as he pulled out a growing distance and disappeared around a corner. Amanda heard some doors being thrown open. When she rounded the corner herself a few seconds later, she was confronted with an open fire exit.

Amanda ran outside and looked in every direction, hoping to spot Jason so that she could continue the pursuit. All she found were dumpsters, the entrance to the school garage, and several candy-bar wrappers blowing in the breeze.

Jason had vanished and with him the answer to a new burning question. Who was the 'she' Jason had mentioned? Judy herself? Had Jason known what her plans had been, or at least known more than he let on? The web of speculation started to weave itself once more, but Amanda had to concentrate on what she could find out in the here and now.

Breathing deeply, she let her heart rate ease and pulled her phone out of her pocket. She dialed Casey's number, and it was answered after a couple of rings.

'Casey, it's Amanda. I'm at the high school. Jason Sterling just bolted.'

'Oh my God,' came the reply. 'Why would he do that? Are you okay?'

'Yeah, I'm fine. He just blew a gasket as soon as he heard about Ray.'

'Should Jake and I head out and look for him?'

'No, stay tight for now. I think Jason just needs time to calm down and get his head straight. I'm willing to bet he'll come and see his father before the day is out. He seems to have just as many questions as we do.'

Amanda decided not to mention Jason's reference to a mystery woman. She was conscious of not wanting to appear like she was making too many conspiratorial leaps. Plus, Jason had hardly been clear-headed when he had said it. If there was anything to it, then she could burrow deeper when she saw Jason again, hopefully in a calmer and more cooperative state of mind.

'How's Ray?' Amanda asked, wanting to divert from the subject slightly.

'Jake brought him some lunch, but he hasn't touched it. He just stares up at the ceiling,' answered Casey.

'A man with a lot on his mind, I'd say. Mentally liberated, my ass,' said Amanda, biting her lip. 'Say, did you see Shelly about Gary's expenses?'

'I've just come back from the archives. I didn't want to be away from the office for too long, so I had Shelly email me the documents. I was going to print them out for you.'

'No, it's okay, could you just forward them to me, please?' asked Amanda.

'Sure, just give me a sec.'

Amanda heard the tapping of a keyboard as Casey accessed her desktop terminal.

'Shelly's actually been too efficient and sent both Gary and Mary Brennan's expense claims. I'll send Gary's over now.'

'No,' said Amanda after a momentary pause. 'Send them both, please.'

'Okay. You should have them now.'

Amanda lowered her phone and heard a ping. An envelope icon appeared at the top of the screen, indicating that her inbox had a new resident.

'Got it, thanks,' she said.

'When can we expect you back?' asked Casey.

'Not too long. I just want to catch my breath.'

'Sure you're fine?'

'I think I can just about get over an emotional footballer outrunning me,' replied Amanda. 'If a bruised ego is the worst I have, I can't complain.'

'Okay then,' said Casey with a brief chuckle, reassured. 'See you soon.'

Amanda hung up and started walking back to the team meeting room. She thought about how she would explain to Booth why his 'war room', as he called it, actually looked like a conflict had taken place in it.

Amanda entered the meeting room and sat on one of the chairs. She wanted five minutes of peace to study Gary's expenses before dealing with Booth. She tapped through to her inbox, opened Casey's email, and downloaded the expenses documents. She opened Gary's and immediately set about looking for a pattern.

Amanda had virtually memorized the dates for out-of-county trips Judy had claimed expenses for. It stood to reason that if she had been having an affair with Gary, another political high-flier, then they could have used the excuse of work to take joint trips together, at least a few times, to avoid the risk of being spotted in or around Independence.

But no pattern stood out. All of Gary's trips outside Independence had taken place at completely different times from Judy's work-related excursions. Amanda weighed up two possibilities. Either Gary and Judy had been exceptionally cautious as an illicit couple, or there had been no affair to conceal. Amanda knew which option her gut favored.

It was true that her suspicions had been raised when she had discovered Gary's cabin and Judy's connection to it. However, Gary's reaction to Ray's accusations of infidelity earlier that morning had instantly cast doubt on those initial suspicions. Amanda had seen enough people stare death in the face to be able to tell when they were lying or speaking the truth. She was sure that Gary had been truthful in his denials. But if that was the case, then where was the logic in Ray's actions, whether in shooting Gary or murdering Judy?

Frustrated, Amanda closed Gary's expense claims and stared at the email. She sighed and tapped on Mary's document, more out of curiosity than expectation. Amanda did not expect to find anything of interest. She could not have been more wrong.

CHAPTER THIRTY-FIVE

Mary Brennan was startled by the knock on the cabin door. It was evening, and the sun was on course to set within a couple of hours. She never had visitors at this time of day. In fact, she never had visitors at all. That was the point of the cabin.

Mary placed her glass of wine on the nearby coffee table, got up from the sofa, and headed towards the front door. She peered through one of the nearby side windows to identify who stood upon the porch. Her heart started to beat a little faster when she saw that it was Amanda Northstar. Mary quickly glanced at a nearby mirror to make sure her silk scarf was properly in place, took a deep breath, and opened the door.

Amanda nodded and raised a slight smile.

'Good evening, Mary. I'm sorry to bother you, but we need to talk. Now.'

'Of course, come in,' replied Mary, slightly taken aback by Amanda's forthrightness.

Amanda's tone had been polite but insistent. She was going to enter the cabin no matter what, because she knew beyond the threshold were the answers she sought.

Amanda stepped through, and Mary closed the door behind her. They stood in the center of the main room, the wood paneling and plush sofas complementing the crackling fire to add a comforting warmth to the feel of the place. There were no animal trophies mounted on the walls, of course. Not in the house of Mary Brennan.

'Can I get you anything, Sheriff? Coffee, glass of water?' Mary asked.

'No thanks, I'm just here for the truth,' replied Amanda flatly.

'I'm sorry, I don't understand,' said Mary. 'The truth about what?'

'The murder of Judy Sterling.'

Mary stared at Amanda a moment before shaking herself into a response.

'I heard the news that Ray confessed to it. It's awful, but I don't know what I can add to it. I just hope that justice is done.'

'Don't we all,' said Amanda, her eyes narrowing slightly. 'In fact, that's what Ray claims as his motivation, both for killing Judy and shooting Gary. Justice, for himself. He claims that they were having an affair. Did you know anything about that? I'd be surprised if you didn't given how frosty things have been between you and Gary.'

Mary simply stared at Amanda in silence.

'How is Gary, by the way? Have you visited him?' Amanda asked.

'No, I have not,' replied Mary, visibly stiffening.

'I thought you were trying to work things out, to reconcile? That's what he said.'

'Gary says a lot of things, not all of them true,' she replied cooly. She then sighed. 'I thought about it, about giving us another chance, but there's simply too much distance now.'

'Well, I'd agree that Gary's record on truth-telling is probably less than shining,' said Amanda with a tilt of her head. 'On this occasion, though, having watched him when he thought he was about to die, I'm inclined to believe Gary when he denies ever being involved with Judy, even if Ray was technically right that she was being unfaithful.'

Mary shot a puzzled look at Amanda.

'But if Judy wasn't having an affair with Gary, then who was she seeing?'

'Judy *was* having an affair with a Brennan,' confirmed Amanda. 'It's just that it wasn't Gary. It was you.'

Mary raised an eyebrow and waved her hand with a dismissive scoff.

'Ridiculous. Honestly, Sheriff, I have a lot of respect for you, but I'm incredibly disappointed. Where did you get this crazy idea from?'

'I just followed the money,' replied Amanda. 'I took a look at your and Gary's council expense claims today. Suppose Gary and Judy had been seeing each other. In that case, there might have been a pattern of away trips taken simultaneously, attending the same conferences, symposiums, trips to Albany, things like that. Perfect opportunities for some alone time, away from suspicious local eyes, but for legitimate political reasons. But there was nothing in his claims that matched up with hers. So imagine my surprise when I looked at your claims as an afterthought and found the pattern I was looking for right in front of me. Same mileage claims, same hotels, at the same events.'

'Of course Judy and I would go to the same events,' protested Mary. 'We were both on the same committee.'

'Well, that's funny,' said Amanda. 'Because after I reviewed your expenses, I revisited the town hall archives, which is where I've been most of the afternoon. Let me tell you, Shelly Goodwin can be a little too eager sometimes, but I can't fault her attention to detail. We found more expense claims going further back to the early days of you and Judy serving on the Planning and Environment Committee together. Same committee, same tasks, but you rarely attended the same events together. That seems to be the case for most of the other members, too, since I guess sending one representative from the committee to events to report back is usually enough. But then since March of this year, you and Judy seemingly took every opportunity to go away together.'

Mary crossed her arms over her chest and sighed in frustration.

'Again, there's nothing suspicious in that. Judy and I worked well together, and many of the events held mutual interest for us.'

'You're absolutely right. There's nothing illicit or even suspicious about such trips. Especially when the submitted receipts show that at each hotel you both stayed at, you booked and paid for a room with two single beds. The official paperwork confirms everything you've said.'

'That's because it's true,' said Mary frostily.

'But now we come to the part where I used the information on the receipts to contact the hotels you stayed at to confirm your arrangements.'

Upon hearing those words, Mary's face started to drop. Amanda could tell that she knew what was coming.

'When I identified myself as law enforcement, they were happy to help. They all confirmed that payment was made for the rooms on a credit card, and receipts were given. However, they were mystified when you requested the honeymoon suite at the same time and paid in cash with no receipt. So on paper, it looks like you and Judy shared a nice sensible hotel room. In reality, though, you left it untouched to stay somewhere far more colorful and off the books. We both know what typically goes on in honeymoon suites, Mary.'

Amanda paused, her point made. There was no need to press harder, as she could see Mary's lower lip starting to quiver as she desperately attempted to hold back tears. It was to no avail. Mary burst into sobs and collapsed to her knees with the suddenness of a marionette with severed strings. She bawled into her hands.

'Why couldn't you just leave this be!' wailed Mary.

Amanda slowly approached Mary and kneeled down in front of her. It would have been unprofessional to physically comfort Mary, now a potential suspect. Still, Amanda was not without sympathy and soothed her tone of voice.

'I'm sorry, but I need to know the truth. Sex, money, politics, or all three, played a role in Judy's death, and you know more than you've told me.'

Mary wiped the tears from her eyes, though more still trickled down.

'Fine, there's no sense living a lie anymore. Not now that she's gone. You're right. Judy and I were seeing each other. It started not long after that weekend Gary and I hosted her and Ray in January.'

'So that did actually happen?' probed Amanda.

'Oh yes, but it wasn't wine by the fire and snowy walks. It was purely business.'

'Let me guess,' said Amanda. 'Riverside Road.'

Mary nodded.

'It was such a neat little arrangement. Ray has made so many bad investments lately that he's drowning in debt. The Sterling's are months from losing everything they have. But there was one last roll of the dice available to him. Ray kept it quiet to avoid accusations of a conflict of interest when Judy gained a seat on the committee, but he'd invested in the Riverside Road development a few years back. But with the delays in approving it, his money was just sitting there. He couldn't sell it on, because, with all the associated risks, it would have been at a loss. The only way for him to cash in was to get the development approved, but the vote was deadlocked when the committee met in January.'

'Yes, I saw the voting records,' noted Amanda. 'So this little business meeting you all had was to chart a path to get Riverside Road approved and save Ray's bacon?'

'Exactly. Gary's star may be waning, but he knows all the right strings to pull to get things moving. He talked to a few committee members to see what he could do to improve life in their wards. Better street-lighting, extra money for fixing potholes, all the little things that the councilors could claim credit for come election day.

Most of the committee members weren't for moving, except one.'

'Will Richardson,' continued Amanda. 'The one guy who voted against Riverside Road in January then flipped to voting in favor a couple of weeks back. That should have been enough to get the development through on a 5-3 win, but no one saw Judy going completely against type and making it a tie again.'

Mary raised a slight smile.

'She knew what the consequences would be, but by that time, she didn't care. Like me, she just wanted to escape and stick it to our husbands while doing so. Our friendship had grown before the January meeting, though I think there was always a spark between us that we tried to ignore. But you can only suppress those feelings for so long. After that meeting, we both felt like passengers, with Gary and Ray in the driving seat. That bond brought us closer together. Then one night in February, things just… happened. We still went along with their plan at first. True, Judy loved her lifestyle, but more than anything, she didn't want to see Jason lose his home and see his world come apart, not during such an important time in his life.'

'And you?' asked Amanda. 'What was your motivation? Your record is pretty solid on the environment, Mary. You may have voted against the development, but you knew the plan was to get it through in the end.'

'There was no point in changing my vote to be in favor. It would have looked too suspicious given the stand I've taken on so many other environmental issues. But for a time, I convinced myself that it was a small loss that would help win the greater battle. If Riverside Road had gone through, Ray's financial worries would have been over. He would have been able to make a significant donation to Gary's reelection campaign, and the economic boost to the community might have been just enough to get him back into the mayor's office.'

'Where you could use his power and influence to help advance your own agenda.'

'That's politics for you, Sheriff. Don't misunderstand me, I'm no Lady Macbeth. I loved Gary once, I really did, back when he had genuine principles and zeal. But the years have just worn him down, made it more about holding power than putting it to use. Our relationship has been a purely functional one for some time. If that makes it easier to get my own projects through, then so be it. Well, that was the plan anyway, before Judy and I realized what we had with each other. We also realized that we, not the men, were in the driving seat. They were reliant on us to help get their plan through. We were being used, plain and simple. I had nothing to lose by leaving Gary, and in time Judy came to realize that she'd grown unhappy with Ray too, trapped in a marriage rather than committed to it. Like I said, Sheriff, we both just needed to escape. If we could inflict a little pain on our selfish husbands too, then life has its little bonuses.'

The picture was becoming clearer to Amanda with each passing moment. She stood up and began slowly circling Mary, offloading her thoughts.

'You both wanted a clean break, to run away together,' she said. 'But unlike you, Judy had a son, and she wanted to make sure he'd be looked after. So you both cooked up her fake suicide. It would allow her to cut all her ties and start fresh, and the life insurance money Ray and Jason would receive meant that they wouldn't become destitute if Riverside Road failed. She had to wait to hit two years on her policy to make sure it couldn't be denied to her family, but even then, the timing still worked out. The second vote on Riverside Road caused her and Ray to have a huge falling out. Together with what seemed like mental health issues in her suicide note, it made it all the more credible that she'd take her own life. I suppose you would have met her soon after?'

'We'd arranged to meet that night, on the Saratoga Bridge,' confirmed Mary with a nod. 'I was to take her to a place where she could lay low until we could be sure it had all gone to plan. Then I would leave Gary and embarrass him in my resignation statement so that he could never recover politically. I'd have left everything I knew, but it would have been okay because Judy and I would have been together, and that's all that mattered. We'd have started a new life, on the West Coast perhaps. Anywhere really. The slate was truly blank.'

Mary started sobbing again. Amanda gave her a moment to allow a little emotional release. As she looked on at the sorry sight, Amanda had obtained the answers to so many of her questions, except the most important one. She knew that Mary's story didn't simply stop there, that she had only set the scene for the tragedy that had transpired and not revealed how it had actually unfolded.

Even if Mary had not pushed Judy off the bridge herself, and Amanda could not see why their romance would have taken such a dark turn, then she would surely have an idea or even confirmation of who did.

Amanda's phone pinged, and she pulled it out of her pocket to find a text message from Jake. Before driving up to the Brennan cabin, she had contacted the office to tell Jake and Casey not to call her phone, just in case it interrupted her questioning of Mary, which she knew would be vital. [Jason's just walked in. Orders?] read Jake's text. [Have him wait in the interview room, back soon.] Amanda tapped in response.

Amanda pocketed her phone and kneeled back down in front of Mary, who had managed to compose herself enough to meet Amanda's gaze with reddened eyes. The time had come for Amanda to press on with a question that had started forming ever since Mary had looked down upon her from the cabin balcony the previous day.

'Your scarf, Mary. What are you trying to hide?' probed Amanda.

Mary instinctively brought a hand up to touch the silk scarf around her neck.

'I don't think it's a fashion statement,' Amanda continued. 'Every time I've seen you this week, you've been wearing it, no matter what else you've got on.'

'It's nothing,' protested Mary, her hand still stroking it.

'Then you won't mind removing it,' replied Amanda. 'Because no matter how long we need to sit here, it's coming off.'

Mary's lower lip started to quiver again. Still, she resisted crying, instead squeezing her eyes shut as she gradually unwound the loops of silk that covered her neck until the freed scarf fell gently to the ground.

Amanda couldn't help but let out a brief gasp. A strip of Mary's throat and sides of her neck were badly bruised, a sickly mix of dark blues, blacks, pinks, and yellows.

'Jesus, who did this to you?' asked Amanda, shocked.

'I can't,' said Mary, fighting back tcars as she shook her head. 'I promised it would be okay.'

Amanda slid forward a little and gently placed a hand on Mary's forearm. Whatever professionalism demanded, Mary clearly needed support, any support, to continue.

'I need you to tell me everything,' urged Amanda.
And Mary did.

CHAPTER THIRTY-SIX

Amanda opened the door to the sheriff's department interview room and closed it behind her. Much like any room of its type, its grey-painted walls, fluorescent lighting, and simple metal chairs and table were designed not to comfort or stimulate, but to provide answers. Sitting at the table was Jason Sterling, who immediately rose to greet Amanda, his arms raised in repentance.

'Oh my God, Sheriff, I'm so sorry for what happened!' he said with what Amanda felt was genuine conviction. 'My head wasn't straight, not after what you told me. I just needed to get away, to breathe, to think.'

'Well, Jason, I'm not going to say it was okay how you reacted, but perhaps it was understandable given the circumstances,' she replied. 'Are you calm enough to talk now?'

'Yeah, of course. Look, I just want to see my dad, speak with him.'

Amanda tapped a knuckle on the door. It opened, and Ray Sterling entered, followed by Casey. His hands were cuffed in front of him, and his face wore a saddened expression that vanished as soon as he saw

Jason. Casey removed Ray's handcuffs, and father and son rushed to each other and hugged tightly.

'Dad, what the hell is going on! Are you insane? It's all over the news, what you said.'

'Don't worry, we'll figure it out. Just as long as you're okay,' replied Ray as he cupped his son's head in his palms and looked upon him with moistening eyes.

Amanda looked at Casey and nodded towards the door. Casey retreated back out and closed it behind her. Amanda crossed her arms and sighed. She wasn't prepared to let the charade she was witnessing carry on any longer than it needed to.

'Ray, I'm sorry, but the only thing that needs figuring out is why you lied about killing Judy.'

Ray turned to face Amanda.

'What are you talking about? I killed her, I shoved her off that bridge. I take full responsibility,' he insisted.

'I understand, I do,' said Amanda honestly. 'There's nothing I wouldn't do to protect my family, to protect Max. But there's no use pretending anymore. I know the truth. I know that you didn't push Judy off that bridge.'

Ray glanced back to Jason, who took a step away and fixed his gaze on Amanda.

'Jason did,' she continued.

Her statement left the room so silent that only a sharp intake of breath from the young man could be heard.

'This is ridiculous!' protested Ray, his head turning from Amanda to Jason and back again like he was at a tennis match. 'I did it, I confessed, case closed!'

Amanda said nothing and once again tapped her knuckles on the door. The lock turned, and the door opened to reveal Mary Brennan. She stepped through, with Casey again bringing up the rear. As soon as Jason saw her, he fell onto one of the metal chairs, a vacant look spreading across his face in realization that the game was up. Mary started to well up and shook her head despairingly.

'I'm so sorry, Jason.'

'What is this!' demanded Ray.

'The truth,' replied Amanda. 'And we're about to hear it all.'

.

CHAPTER THIRTY-SEVEN

Jason sat in his father's car, brooding, nursing his rage. His hands gripped the steering wheel so tightly that his knuckles were white. He had been waiting outside the Brennan cabin for almost an hour, and his mother was still inside. He knew what she was doing with Mary Brennan, though he wished he didn't. He tried to push the images out of his mind, but seeing them share a passionate kiss on the cabin porch had done nothing to douse the fires of his imagination. He should have confronted them there and then, but he had just about managed to keep a lid on his impulses. It had become harder to do so lately.

Jason knew it was the boosters he'd been taking. He wasn't so naïve that he thought he could take them without consequences, but the physical results had been clear to see. In conjunction with daily gym sessions, they had helped him bulk up enough to be truly competitive on the field this season, to eliminate all weakness. This was a scouting year, his best chance to land a college scholarship. There could be no failure. It was as simple as that.

They had tried to keep it from him, but he knew his parents were having money problems and that they wouldn't be able to send him to college. His only hope was a football scholarship, and if that meant making a few sacrifices in the here and now, then so be it. He'd give the boosters up as soon as he had secured a place. He didn't need them. He could stop whenever he wanted.

While the boosters had made him more on edge and quicker to anger, he would have grown suspicious of his mother even without them. Maybe his father was too wrapped up in work or had stopped caring due to them fighting so much, but Jason could sense that his mother was up to something. Too many nights away, or late returns at the end of a day. Too many times, he had heard her conducting whispered phone conversations, hanging up as soon as he or his father made their presence known.

His parents' marriage had been in trouble for a while. That much was obvious, even if they both tried to carry on as if it wasn't. But Jason wasn't having any of it. His father was no saint, but if his mother was having an affair, then it wasn't just a betrayal of her marriage vows, it was a betrayal of her family too, including Jason.

His mother's behavior that evening had been strange, almost as if she had been desperate to get somewhere, but at the same time reluctant to leave. Jason and his father had been watching television when she stood in front of them. She claimed she was going out to meet a friend from the council for a drink and for them not to wait up. Then she had kissed Jason tenderly on the forehead and squeezed his father's shoulder as she walked past him. Jason then made the decision to find out what exactly was going on, whether the supposed drink with a friend was real or an excuse like he suspected.

He had borrowed his father's car, as he was occasionally allowed to do, under the pretense of meeting CJ Townsend, and had discreetly followed his mother's vehicle. The black paint of his father's car had made the perfect camouflage under cover of night. His lights could have belonged to anyone.

When his mother turned off Dry Lake Road, Jason had been mystified as to where she was going. He had had to kill his lights to avoid arousing suspicion, but slowly made his way along the trail, what ambient light there was from the moon just about penetrating the tree branches above to help him see. He had followed his mother's taillights up another side-road until it opened up into a clearing with a large cabin in the middle.

Jason had immediately turned the engine off to silence any noise and pulled to a quiet stop. He had been far enough away to avoid easy detection and so had simply watched as his mother parked up in front of the cabin, bounded up to the porch, and was met by a woman he recognized as Mary Brennan. That was when he had seen them kiss. He had almost vomited, and his heart had started racing, but he had forced himself to calm down.

He had not been known for it lately, but patience was the order of the day, to wait and watch and decide what to do. It was possible that he could use his mother's secret to convince her that what she was doing was wrong and that her marriage was worth a second chance. He had stepped out and quietly pushed his car to the far side of the clearing, unnoticeable unless someone had been looking for it.

That had been an hour ago, and it was close to midnight. While Jason had tried to keep calm and think strategically, the thought of what his mother was up to inside had started to make his blood simmer. Much longer, and it would reach full boil. Just as he was about to burst out of the car and kick down the front door, it opened, and his mother stepped outside, holding hands with Mary Brennan. Jason had left the driver window down and strained to hear what was being said between the two women.

'Get going and make everything ready. I won't be long behind you,' said Mary.

They shared a tender kiss, touched foreheads, and separated. Judy headed back down the steps to her car, started it up, executed a J-turn, and drove out of the clearing as Mary looked on.

Jason debated what to do, whether to follow his mother or confront Mary. He could see his mother any time, though. If he was going to get the truth from Mary, it had to be now, while the element of surprise was in his favor, and her denials would be meaningless.

He leaped out of the car and stormed towards the front of the cabin. He was quickly noticed by Mary, her shock evident.

'Oh dear God, Jason, it's-'

'Not what it seems, right?' he roared.

He bounded up the stairs towards Mary, who had backed up against the front door in fear. She reached for the handle, but Jason swatted her arm away.

'I saw everything!' he screamed into her face. 'How could you both? It was you, wasn't it? You're the one who messed my mom up! And what the hell was all that about making things ready?'

'Jason, I know this is hard, but you have to understand that we didn't plan this, it just happened,' pleaded Mary. 'Your mom and I were both so unhappy!'

'Bullshit!' cried Jason. 'She has everything she wants!'

'But not the love she needs!' snapped Mary.

In an instant, Jason was overcome by red mist. It took him a few seconds to realize what he was doing, but by then, he had grabbed Mary's throat with both hands and was squeezing as hard as he could. Mary tried to prize his hands away with her own, but the difference in strength made it impossible. She managed to pull his fingers away just enough to croak out a last, desperate plea.

'Please, Jason! We can go see her right now!'

Her struggle for breath hit home with Jason just in time for him to release his grip. Mary slid down to the decking and clasped her throat, greedily inhaling as much air as she could. Jason backed off and looked at his trembling hands. They had come close to taking a life before he had been able to snatch enough self-control out of the fire of his impulsive rage. But the anger remained, tempered, not extinguished. He shook his head, snapping himself back to reality.

'Where is she? Tell me!'

'You're not seeing her alone, not after what you just did,' said Mary between deep breaths. 'I'm coming with you. I'll show you as we go, that's the only way I trust you.'

'Fine,' sneered Jason. 'Let's go.'

Jason didn't wait and hauled Mary up. He dragged her to his father's car, bundled her into the passenger seat, and then got behind the wheel. He started up the engine and floored the accelerator, executing a half-donut so that the front pointed at the exit road. He sped off back towards Dry Lake Road. For the next twenty minutes, he and Mary sat in silence. Their only exchanges were his demands for new directions and her meek replies.

Eventually, they found themselves on the road leading to the Saratoga Bridge. As he raced towards it, Jason spotted his mother's car parked to the left of the road. She was close. Mary hadn't been lying, which had been a wise choice.

The lighting on the bridge provided just enough illumination for Jason to spot a small figure half-way across. He dipped his headlights but maintained his speed until he was close enough to see his mother standing on the bridge sidewalk. Jason slammed on the brakes and almost lost control of the front of the car, but managed to stop only a few meters away from a clearly shocked Judy.

Jason leaped out of the car, quickly followed by a frantic Mary.

'Oh God, Judy, he found us out!' she cried.

Judy raised a hand to her mouth as Jason reached her. He simply stood there, at a loss for what to say, his eyes wide and intense. After a moment, a tearful Judy lowered her hand.

'I'm sorry,' was all she could muster.

Jason slapped her hard across the face, then, instead of carrying on any abuse, he slumped to his knees.

'Why?' he wept.

Judy knelt down next to Jason and took him in her arms, resting his head under her chin. Mary stood to the side, looking on, trying to suppress her own emotions as she and Judy's carefully laid plan unraveled with each passing moment.

'I'm so sorry baby, I didn't mean for this to happen. You're the most important thing in my life, but I just couldn't do this anymore. It's just become too painful.'

'What, being with me?'

'No, of course not. It's your father and life and… oh, I wish I had the words to explain, to help you understand, but I just don't.'

Jason sniffed back his tears and slowly peeled himself away from Judy.

'What are you doing here, Mom, on the bridge?'

Judy's eyes darted around as she tried to manufacture a plausible explanation. Her hesitation did not go unnoticed by Jason, for whom realization quickly dawned.

'Wait, that's what Mary meant about getting things ready, that she'd be along soon. This is the main road out of the county. You're leaving, aren't you?'

They both stood as Judy tried to reassure Jason, only to have him bat away her hand.

'I… I don't know what to…' struggled Judy.

'I'm right! You were going to leave tonight, to walk away from everything and everyone. You were going to leave Dad. You were going to leave me!'

Jason felt the fire build up in him again, the anger about his mother's lies and the growing pain of her apparent rejection adding ever more turmoil. Judy slowly advanced towards Jason, her arms raised in an effort to embrace him.

'Please understand, I had no choice. I love you, but I-'

Before she could finish, Jason seized her by the collar of her cashmere coat.

'Fine, if you want to leave, then just leave, you bitch!'

Jason shoved her away. Judy was propelled backward at speed but managed to stay afoot. It was just as she was about to regain her footing that her shoe clipped the curb of the sidewalk and unbalanced her once again. She kept flailing backward until she hit the sidewalk barrier, hard, the momentum still enough to tip the upper half of her body over. Jason and Mary looked on in ever-increasing horror as they saw what was unfolding.

'Oh, shit!' cried Jason as he launched himself in Judy's direction.

Judy's fingers clawed at the smooth black paint on the barrier, but could not find any purchase. Her momentum carried her over the side. Jason dived and managed to grab her right foot just as Judy went fully over. For a moment, Judy dangled, screaming, as Jason tried to get a grip with one hand while holding the barrier with his other to prevent himself from also tumbling over.

'*I've got you!*' *he screamed.*

Mary joined them and tried to grab Judy's other foot, but simply didn't have the reach. Jason started to pull Judy up, his teeth gritted with the effort.

'*We've got this, we've got this!*' *he yelled.*

Suddenly Judy's right shoe started to slip off, the pull on it too strong.

'*Oh my God!*' *screamed Judy.*

'*No, stay with me, we're almost there!*' *pleaded Jason.*

But the shoe continued to slip as more and more of Judy's sock was exposed. Jason wouldn't be able to raise her up in time, and she knew it. Judy stopped screaming as a moment of eerie clarity descended upon her. She glanced at Mary.

'*Protect him, promise me.*'

The shoe slipped fully off. Judy plunged screaming towards the water as Jason and Mary grabbed for the thin air she had occupied half a second earlier. They both cried out as they watched Judy fall, her arms and legs flailing, before hitting the water headfirst and disappearing beneath the inky blackness of the Hudson.

A stunned Jason started shivering uncontrollably. He dropped the shoe into the river and slumped to the ground. He curled up on his side, knees to his chest, and started moaning. Mary stared down into the water, unable to look away in the hope that Judy would break the surface and gasp for air. But all she saw was the moon's reflection shimmering on the dark surface.

Mary slumped to the ground, her thigh almost touching Jason's head. For a few moments, she sat in silence, trying to process what had just happened, rewinding and replaying everything to try and make some kind of sense out of a senseless event.

For a second, she felt the temptation to fling herself over the side and join Judy in oblivion, anything to escape the pain she would feel once the shock had worn off. But the thought swiftly passed. This wasn't just about her anymore. The devastated young man weeping only inches away from her had an even bigger stake in what happened next.

Mary's thoughts became a jumble of desire for instant revenge, of considered action to inform the sheriff about what had happened, and the need to start forming a plan that would extract her and Jason from the mess they were in. The battle raged in her mind longer than it probably should have, given how exposed they both were on the bridge, with the possibility of passing traffic at any time. Eventually, she settled on an escape plan.

In truth, there was no other option. Judy's last words had been a plea not only to protect Jason from any immediate fallout, but to safeguard his future, which had been her primary consideration after her own had been secured. If their love had meant anything, then Mary needed to honor Judy's request, as much as her gut demanded retribution for seeing her own prospects for a new life vanish in an instant.

Mary looked down to a still-weeping Jason, a physical beast of a young man reduced to a pathetic, curled-up child. What sliver of maternal instinct Mary possessed asserted itself, and she placed a hand on his head and gently started stroking his hair. She would need to soothe him as quickly as possible, to get his head clear enough to explain what had been going on and how circumstances were still ideally arranged in their favor. The secret she and Jason would both need to carry would be the heaviest of their lives, but both their futures depended on bearing that burdensome load.

'It's going to be okay, Jason,' said Mary. 'I promise.'

CHAPTER THIRTY-EIGHT

Amanda and Mary sat at the interview room table, with Jason and Ray opposite them. The story had been told, the truth had been outed. Now there was only the aftermath to reveal. Jason was desperately trying not to cry. Whether he was in despair after reliving his and Mary's joint account of the night of Judy's death, or seeing his future dissolve before his eyes, Amanda could not tell. He shook his head.

'I didn't mean to kill her. It was an accident,' he said mournfully.

'I know,' said Amanda gently. 'I didn't say you killed her, just pushed her. You never meant for it to happen, but it did. You didn't realize your own strength after a summer taking those boosters. The lab report I have on the stash we found at the Moorcock farm tells me that it was nothing but bad stuff, for your mind, as well as your body.'

'Jesus, Jason,' said Ray, as he ran his fingers over his head, trying to absorb the fresh hell the news had revealed.

'I had no choice, I needed the results!' responded Jason, pleading for understanding.

'So you didn't know he'd been using, Ray?' asked Amanda.

'Not that part, no,' he replied.

'But you knew about everything else.'

Ray nodded.

'I need the truth from you too,' requested Amanda. 'It's useless to lie anymore.'

Ray sighed and looked up to the ceiling, as if for guidance.

'I'd been waiting up most of that night, chain-smoking with worry,' he said. 'Things hadn't been great between Judy and me for a while, but I still worried when she didn't come back. On top of that, for Jason to be out all night without notice was a new one. I even called the Townsend house, but CJ claimed not to have seen him all evening. I started thinking that maybe Jason had crashed the car and was lying injured or dead somewhere. Then about two in the morning, give or take, he turned up. I was furious at first but could tell he'd been upset, even though he tried to hide it. He told me it was nothing, that he'd broken up with a girl he'd been seeing, though it was news to me that he'd been dating anyone. There was no use arguing about it, so I let him get to bed and carried on waiting for Judy. But she never came back. I had no idea what had happened until you showed up at my door.'

Amanda turned to Mary.

'What happened after Judy fell?' she asked.

It was Mary's turn to sigh.

'We needed to act, fast. I didn't go into the whole story, but I told Jason about the fake suicide plot. It was a lot to lay on him, but I had no choice. It was our best shot at getting through it all. Everything had been set up ready, so even though it was an accident, it would still seem like her death had been her choice. All we had to do was keep quiet, and that part of the plan would hopefully unfold, leaving people like you none the wiser.'

'I'm afraid there aren't many people as curious as me,' responded Amanda.

'Yes, Independence is lucky to have you, Sheriff,' retorted Mary with a trace of bitterness.

Amanda turned back to Jason.

'But the flaw in the plan, other than my suspicious mind, was that it was a secret just too hard for you to keep.'

'I tried to block it out, to become hard to it, to focus on my football and nothing else,' said Jason, as tears trickled down his cheeks. 'But it was just too much. After Dad collected me from the field to tell me about Mom, we went home. He was in a bad way, blaming himself, asking questions about why Mom had done it, what he could have done differently. Whether it was guilt or the boosters messing with my head, I just exploded.'

Jason held up his bandaged hand.

'I punched the TV and let it all out. I told him everything that happened before the bridge and on it.'

'It floored me,' interjected Ray, as he tried to spare Jason the pain of more recollections. 'But what could I do? Turn him in, destroy my son's future? So I made a choice. Mary and I didn't discuss it. We didn't need to. I'm not sure I could have even looked at her anyway. But her plan was sound. Just wait for the whole thing to blow over.'

'Until I came calling and promised to analyze your tire treads,' said Amanda.

'I knew then that it was only a matter of time until your investigation led right up to our door. I had to divert your attention, to offer you an easy arrest, anything to protect Jason. You'd been right that Judy had been having an affair, but with the wrong person. Your suspicions about Gary meant that it would be easier for me to convince you I had a vendetta against him.'

'So you put on a show at the town hall to leave no room for doubt. You never intended to kill Gary.'

'Of course not,' scoffed Ray. 'I had to do just enough to be convincing. I'm no murderer, Sheriff.'

'But you're still going to prison,' said Amanda.

'It was a small price to pay for my son's freedom.'

'Yeah, without both parents. It would have been freedom, Ray. The loneliest kind.'

'But with enough money from the life insurance and sales of my assets to put him through college, to set him up for a bright future. That's all that mattered to me.'

'And now he has neither,' said Amanda with regret.

She stood up.

'I'm afraid that none of this ends well. I hope you'll believe me when I say that I genuinely feel for you all. Nobody should have to experience such things. But the fact remains that you're all still alive to experience them at all, and Judy isn't. And for that, the scales need to be balanced.'

Jason burst into tears and moved to hug his father, who eagerly embraced him. Mary sat in stony silence, emotionally drained, her thoughts her own.

Amanda had solved a crime that almost everyone had claimed was anything but. However, she held no sense of satisfaction nor felt victorious, not at the sight of such misery. All she felt was pity. Justice would be done, but the personal pain and regret being endured by the three broken people sat in front of her was perhaps the worst kind of punishment there was.

CHAPTER THIRTY-NINE

Amanda sat at her kitchen table and gratefully received the cup of coffee Maggie had poured for her. The past week had been a whirlwind, all amplified by voracious state-wide media coverage. Jason had been charged with second-degree manslaughter. Mary with aiding and abetting. Ray with a double-whammy of aiding and abetting along with aggravated assault for his attack on Gary.

Gary Brennan himself had resigned as mayor. Although he had not been charged with a crime, it was clear that he was jumping before he was pushed, whether by council pressure or the ballot-box. Being so close to the scandal had dragged his reputation down with the rest of those involved. Media attention and town gossip had finally subsided enough that some form of normality seemed to be returning, much to Amanda's relief.

Boomer sat next to her and laid his chin on her lap. Amanda smiled, despite the dog hairs he would leave on her uniform. She started scratching his ears. Maggie placed a plate of bacon and eggs in front of her daughter and sat down opposite with her own coffee.

'Thanks, Mom. I keep saying that you don't need to do this.'

'And I'll keep ignoring you,' Maggie replied. 'You've barely had a break this past week, and on top of that, you're policing the football tonight. Rustling up some breakfast is the least I can do.'

'You're still coming to the game, right?' asked Amanda as she started eating.

'Are you kidding?' scoffed Maggie. 'I wouldn't miss it for the world. I haven't been to a game since we used to go and watch Max's father work his magic. It'll be nice to see his son complete the circle. Though, I guess the question is how you feel about it?'

'I'll be okay. It's time to move on. Truthfully it was time to move on years ago. It's only a field. What happens on it is what counts. If Max enjoys himself, then that's all that matters to me.'

'I'm glad to hear it. That said, I hope you stocked up on the aspirin.'

Amanda looked up from her plate at Maggie, unamused, and was met with a mischievous smile. They both turned towards the kitchen entrance as Max bounded down the stairs and took a seat next to Amanda. Boomer, in search of the ear-scratching that Amanda had abandoned, moved over to Max and successfully tried his luck.

'Breakfast, dear?' asked Maggie.

'Yes please, Grandma,' confirmed Max. 'And don't spare the eggs. I'll be needing the protein later.'

Amanda finished her own plate and sipped her coffee.

'How do you feel about the game?' she asked Max.

'Pretty good, considering. I won't lie, Mom, what happened with Jason still has everyone in a spin. Coach Booth threw his playbook out the window, literally, and had to switch to a passing rather than a running game. We've been practicing morning and evening, over and over.'

'Well, we'll look forward to seeing you out there,' said Maggie encouragingly.

'Don't get too excited, Grandma,' urged Max. 'I'm still only the backup receiver, so it's pretty certain the only place you'll be seeing me is on the bench.'

'Ye of little faith, Maxie,' said Maggie, pointing a wooden spoon at him.

Amanda finished her coffee, stood, and kissed Max on the top of his head.

'Remember, your dad's spot was always near the bench.'

She headed towards the hall to collect the rest of her uniform items.

'Early start today?' asked Maggie, curious.

'No choice,' responded Amanda. 'The new mayor calls.'

CHAPTER FORTY

The mayor's new assistant opened the door to Gary's old office, and Amanda stepped through, nodding her thanks. The door closed behind her, and she slowly walked forwards. The new mayor was sat in a new high-backed chair behind his new, opulent, and intricately carved polished wooden desk. He was facing the other way, gazing out of the newly restored main window.

In short, almost everything was new, from the seating area furniture to the conference table design. Gary's presence had been erased in the space of a few short days. Amanda stopped in front of the desk. With calculated timing, Carter Townsend slowly spun his chair around to face her.

'Good morning, Amanda,' he said with a flawless smile. 'So good of you to come.'

He stood and offered her his hand, which she shook politely.

'No problem, Your Honor.'

'Please,' he said with a dismissive wave of his hand. 'Stick with Carter.'

He sat back down and indicated the chair opposite him in front of the desk. Amanda sat, her hat resting on her lap. While it was a stylish chair, it was also hard and nowhere near as soft as Gary's old ones had been. It seemed that Carter wanted his visitors in slight discomfort from the very beginning, to establish an early edge over them, whatever the reason for their visit.

'I'm sorry you had to come in so early,' he said. 'But ever since I took over, my diary has been crazy. I had to do all the creative scheduling I could just to make it to CJ's game tonight. But I still thought it was important that we formally met.'

'This isn't our first waltz,' said Amanda.

'No, but it is to new music,' replied Carter as his hands formed a pyramid under his chin. 'When we last saw each other, I was just Head of the Council. I had no expectations of higher office, but if the mayor resigns or dies, then it falls to the Head to take over until the next election. I was very humbled.'

'I'm sure,' said Amanda dryly. 'You'll have quite a busy year ahead of you, campaigning for re-election, I mean.'

'Well, let's not get too ahead of ourselves now!' Carter chuckled.

A moment of awkward silence emerged.

'Still, a shame about Gary,' said Amanda, breaking it.

'Yes, he was quite the fixer,' responded Carter. 'But all good things must come to an end.'

'Do you have any idea what he'll do?' she asked.

'I think he's going to take some time upstate, get away from this place, do some teaching maybe. He's qualified, you know.'

'Well, you wouldn't want him hanging around like a bad smell now, would you, Your Honor? And Ray Sterling's incarceration takes care of the rest of the equation.'

'I'm not sure I follow your logic, Amanda,' Carter retorted. 'But I certainly follow your tone. Not feeling very happy, are you?'

'My happiness has nothing to do with it. What I am, though, is curious. Curious about many things.'

'Such as?' probed Carter.

'Well, I'm curious why, when we had a chance to look at Ray Sterling's accounts, a large payment was made to him by your company for supposed legal services.'

'He was a lawyer,' Carter shrugged.

'You already have several.'

'You can never have too many, especially for a company as large as mine.'

'Uh-huh,' nodded Amanda. 'I'm also curious about why Ray Sterling made a sizable donation to Will Richardson's campaign fund for next year.'

'He's a fine councilor, a credit to his ward. I'm sure Ray felt the same way.'

'Despite how close he was to bankruptcy?' Amanda commented skeptically. 'That was very generous of Ray. Almost as generous as the donation he made to Gary's fund too. It's funny, but it was interesting to note how you could add up those donations, plus allow Ray some funds to keep his head above water, and pretty much reach the amount that you paid him for his, uh, legal services. A cynic might suppose that Ray Sterling was used to funnel campaign contributions to help grease the wheels for approving the Riverside Road development, for which your company is set to be the primary contractor.'

Carter slowly leaned back in his chair, his eyes narrowed.

'Yes, a cynic might indeed suppose that, but a supposition is all it would be, due to a complete lack of evidence. Are you a cynic by any chance, Amanda?'

'I have my moments,' she replied, raising a tight smile.

'Well, it seems to me that Ray was simply exercising his democratic right to support whichever pubic figures he deemed worthy,' said Carter with a shrug. 'As a businessman and public figure myself, it would have been unethical for me to indulge in such direct support. How Ray Sterling chose to use the money he earned was completely his affair. I suppose you could always ask him to clarify.'

'I did,' replied Amanda. 'He stated that he was merely exercising his democratic rights to support people he believed in. Now, where did I just hear something like that?'

It was Carter's turn to smile.

'Public support is an important thing, Amanda. It's the lifeblood of people like you and me. We shouldn't forget that. I certainly won't should I decide to run next year.'

'By which time the inevitable Riverside Road build will provide a handily-timed boost to your economic record, not to mention your wallet,' noted Amanda.

'In fact, I'm stepping down from the day-to-day running of the Townsend Group. Leaving it to the board. The good people of Independence are my priority now.'

Amanda pursed her lips, genuinely surprised.

'You're truly a man of the people, Your Honor.'

She checked her watch and stood.

'I'm afraid I have to head off, but thank you again for inviting me.'

'Any time. We'll be doing this a lot more, I'm sure. It would be better if we were friends, I think. Better for the town and county. Better for the people. Better for you.'

His last remark was not an implicit threat but flirted dangerously close to being so. If not a warning, it was advice. Never become an obstacle to Carter Townsend.

Amanda placed her hat on her head and tipped the front with pinched fingers.

'You have a good day now, Your Honor.'

As she turned and headed for the exit, Carter called out.

'I'm looking forward to working with you, Amanda.'

Amanda paused at the open door, thought for a moment, and looked back.

'That's Sheriff Northstar if you don't mind.'

She closed the door gently behind her.

CHAPTER FORTY-ONE

It was a warm evening, and the gentle breeze was refreshing on Jake's face as he jogged down one of the many walking paths that ran alongside the Hudson.

'Slow down, where's the fire!' Casey called out from behind him.

Jake eased off and let her catch up before they both stopped. Jake's heart rate was little different from when he rose out of bed each morning, whereas Casey was breathing heavily, and her t-shirt was drenched with sweat.

'What's the matter?' he teased. 'I thought you were supposed to be killing it at pilates?'

'You're killing me!' replied Casey as she leaned back against a nearby tree.

'Okay then slowcoach, we'll jog back to town nice and steady. Unless you want me to carry you too?'

'It would be a nice demonstration of that *Semper Fi* attitude.'

Jake raised an eyebrow.

'I think I've shown enough faithfulness by promising to try one of those cheerleader backflips of yours. After proper instruction, of course.'

'I thought you were joking,' said Casey, an incredulous expression on her face.

'I did say that I'd give it a try if you came out running with me. A deal's a deal.'

Casey nodded approvingly and smiled.

'You're right, it is.'

She turned to face the tree and used it to brace herself for a calf-stretch.

'Anyway, it was good to get out, with or without the prospect of you falling on your ass. Hopefully, I can get my head down properly tonight after the game.'

'Not sleeping well?' asked Jake.

'Sleep has not been a friend lately,' she replied with a sigh. 'Rick had his hours cut last week. It's typical. As soon as it looks like things are going okay, something comes along and knocks us back down again.'

Jake hadn't had any contact with Rick since the night in the old maintenance shed. He'd been waiting for Casey to give him some indication as to whether Rick had kept his word. If the couple had still been flush with cash, then Jake would know that Rick had reneged on his promise to walk away from peddling drugs and would have crushed him accordingly, regardless of the consequences.

However, it sounded like Rick had, surprisingly, done the right thing, even if satisfying that promise had involved further lies to Casey about his work situation. Clearly, the prospect of future financial worries was not sitting well with Casey, given the costs of raising a family. While she had been open with Jake about Rick, she had offered no indication that she was pregnant.

'Well, I think it'll all work out in the end,' said Jake, trying to sound optimistic. 'With Mary Brennan's resignation, it doesn't take a degree in political science to realize that Riverside Road will be approved sooner than later. When it is, there'll be plenty of work coming in at the lumber mill.'

Casey smiled at his effort.

'This is true. At least we managed to put a little away from all the extra work he did get. Should keep the rain out for a bit.'

It irked Jake that the little financial buffer that Casey was so grateful for was comprised of drug money rather than the fruits of Rick's labor, but there was nothing he could do except to try and ignore the sense of injustice he felt and hope it went away.

Casey finished stretching and ran a hand through her hair. She bit her lower lip and turned to Jake.

'Listen, Jake, there's something I've been meaning to talk to you about. It's not easy, but I feel I need to tell you and get it off my chest.'

Jake could tell from her tone that it was serious. The easy mood from a few moments earlier had evaporated. He saw that Casey needed to say something, but her eyes darted to various points on the ground as she tried to figure out what those words would be. She was finally going to tell him about the baby, he knew it.

'It's about what happened in the barn,' she said.

Jake desperately tried to conceal his disappointment. He crossed his arms and nodded to her.

'Go on, it's okay. What about the barn?'

She thought for a moment more, then sighed.

'When Amanda and I burst in, the first thing we saw was that maniac Keats about to cleave your head off. It was obvious. No room for doubt or debate. There were a couple of seconds to save you, if that. Amanda and I both drew at the same time. We both took aim at the same time. But I froze. I just couldn't pull the trigger.'

'Don't worry,' said Jake genuinely. 'Amanda took care of it.'

'But what if she hadn't been there?' Casey snapped. 'What if I'd been alone and the only thing that could have saved your life is if I'd taken the shot, but just couldn't. You'd be dead.'

Casey's eyes started to water. Jake stepped over and placed his hands on her shoulders, offering them a reassuring, gentle squeeze.

'Look, it didn't happen that way, so there's no sense beating yourself up about it. I've seen it before, in genuine war zones, never mind small-town USA. People just freeze. All the training in the world can't prepare you for the actual moment when you can end a life. If the ability to kill without a second thought was an entry requirement for law enforcement, then all the psychos out there would be walking the beat.'

'But Amanda didn't hesitate,' noted Casey as she sniffed back tears.

'Because she's done it before and, believe me, only when she absolutely had to. Now I can't promise that you'll never have to draw your gun again or never pull the trigger. What we do has its dangers, like you've seen. But take it from me, and Amanda would agree, you're no less valued just because you found it hard to kill someone. It's never supposed to be easy.'

Casey raised a slight smile and surprised Jake by wrapping her arms around his back and hugging him tightly. He returned the gesture, closing his eyes to enjoy the intimacy as much as he could before it inevitably ended. After a moment, they parted, and Jake gave her upper arm a supportive rub.

'Is there anything else you want to tell me?'

Casey thought for a moment, then shook her head and smiled.

'No, I'm good. Thanks for that.'

Jake gazed at her a moment, then raised his own small smile.

'Then let's head over. Football waits for no man.'

They started up a gentle jog and headed back towards Independence in contented silence.

CHAPTER FORTY-TWO

Max finished strapping on his padding and ensured his laces were tightened for the third time in as many minutes. The locker room was a hive of activity, the atmosphere buzzing with electricity, and the air thick with testosterone. Max made sure that he had everything in order, the simple act of mentally checking things off helping him to keep calm. His kit was clean and well-kept. Even if he spent no time on the field tonight, he would take pride in looking his best for his team, school, and himself.

Coach Booth stood at the center of the locker room, with the expectation that the team would form a circle around him as he offered his rallying speech. Max was hoping for something a little more inspirational than just a call to kick ass and take names. He had been too busy with classes and practice to find the time to dig into the videotape archives of his father's coaching days, but promised himself he soon would, to listen to his pre-game speeches and on-field coaching. For now, Max was content with an old photograph found in the family album to provide him with a pre-game emotional boost.

He retrieved it from his school bag that rested at the bottom of his locker. It was of his mother and father, laughing at the camera in a lush and sunny garden. The taller Max Sr stood behind the younger, shorter-haired Amanda, his arms wrapped around her, his hands clasped together just above her prominent baby bump. It was the only complete family photo Max had, taken a few weeks before his father had died, but it was enough.

He smiled, choosing to take inspiration from it rather than sadness. It was a part of his past, but he wouldn't let that past, with all of its heartache for his mother and he, define his future. Max returned the photo to his bag and used the symbol of his potential future to safeguard it, as he tucked it securely within the pages of an application guide to the United States Military Academy at West Point.

**

Amanda sat in the middle of the bleachers, the uniform confirming the official nature of her presence, but her anticipation that of any other fan. Maggie sat to Amanda's right, with Chelsea Bannerman alongside her.

Amanda smiled and shook her head as she overheard her mother gently teasing Chelsea about how her strictly-platonic relationship with Max might change once she saw how handsome he looked on the field. Chelsea seemed to take it with good humor.

Amanda scanned the corner of the field near the main entrance gate. She spotted Jake and Casey standing together, overseeing the line for entry. They spotted her back and waved, a gesture she returned.

To Amanda's left sat Glenn, who was devouring a burger.

'You seem to be enjoying that a little too much given that they're your competition,' she said, nudging him with her elbow.

'I can appreciate a good burger as much as the next man,' replied Glenn as he finished the bun and licked his fingers. 'Besides, what competition? Where do you think all these folks are going to go celebrate after we've won tonight?'

'I hear there's a nice little sports bar somewhere in town,' said Amanda.

'Damn right,' he declared.

'The owner is a crusty old fart, though.'

'Damn right,' he said with equal conviction.

A moment passed until they could no longer maintain their mock-seriousness and burst into laughter.

'Thanks for coming,' said Amanda, once her giggles had subsided. 'I appreciate it, and I know Max does too.'

'Well, you guys are like family to me,' said Glenn.

'No, we *are* family to you,' corrected Amanda.

Glenn smiled tenderly, and for a moment, Amanda thought she noticed the tiniest hint of moisture in his eyes. Any poignancy was blown away by the deluge of rock music that rang out across the field as the pre-game ritual commenced, and the announcer began his hyperbolic commentary to whip-up home crowd passions.

After the visiting Warriors team had entered the field to a mixture of cheers from their traveling supporters and polite if restrained applause from the home crowd, it was the turn of the Rebels. CJ Townsend led them out in a single line to a rapturous greeting. After a moment, an excitable Maggie repeatedly tapped Amanda's arm and pointed out Max when she spotted him.

Amanda looked on quietly, but proudly. She found her gaze drifting down towards the side of the field, where the coaches were assembled. Almost two decades had passed since she had sat in the same place and looked down upon Max Sr doing what he did best.

In her mind's eye, she saw him again, wearing his coach's jersey and baseball cap, silently scanning the field, visualizing how his plan would come together. She had aged, but he would remain forever young. Max Sr turned away from the huddle of players to which their son now belonged, looked up to her, and smiled warmly.

Amanda smiled back.

Amanda Northstar returns in...

HEADS WILL ROLL

As Independence prepares for Halloween weekend, houses and streets are decorated with carved pumpkins, fake tombstones, and fun monsters. The town also plays host to a festival celebrating the best of horror literature. Authors, poets, and academics from around the country mix with fans, with an open-air theatrical production of *The Legend of Sleepy Hollow* launching the event.

Sheriff Amanda Northstar and her deputies, Jake Murrow and Casey Norris, police proceedings as audience anticipation builds for the Headless Horseman's appearance. When the Horseman finally rides in, everyone enjoys the show until the pumpkin-headed actor falls to the ground, and it is discovered that he has been genuinely decapitated inside his mask.

As the weekend unfolds, more bodies are discovered around Independence, each murder influenced by a famous horror tale. With the clock ticking down to Halloween night, Amanda, Jake, and Casey race to discover what links the victims and stop an insanely imaginative killer from realizing a truly devilish design.

In the same shared universe…

QUEENS OF THE STEAL:
THE NAME OF THE GAME

Sometimes vengeance isn't just taken - it's stolen.

Axel Archer was a retired soldier, family man, patriot... and the king of thieves. He used his training and expertise to pull off heists throughout New York City. First, it was out of necessity to support his family, but then because no other thrill could hope to rival it.

That was until the day a single gunshot rang out and what was supposed to be a routine bank job spiraled into disaster. His four daughters - Cassidy, Delilah, Bethany, and Angie - were forced to scatter and assume new identities, trying their best to live new lives and forget about the past.

Five years later, tragedy causes the Archer sisters to return to New York to pick up the pieces of their shattered lives, reunite in a quest for vengeance, and uncover a conspiracy which has cost them dear.

They will take their father's training, their own skills and qualities - from infiltration to marksmanship to getaway driving to hacking - and adopt their own style. They will show New York that the heirs to the king of thieves are back in town and that the queens of the steal are just as worthy of the throne...

Queens of the Steal - Volume One is an eight-part series of action-thriller novellas ideal for fans of the crime and heist genres who enjoy quick and entertaining reads.

ABOUT THE AUTHOR

IJ Benneyworth is a British writer with a long academic and personal appreciation for American history and culture, strengthened by repeated visits to the U.S. He has been writing creatively in one form or another since he was a child, first practicing his story-craft by improvising adventure tales around the fireplace with his grandfather, to having his stories read out in class during his school years.

He moved into screenwriting and filmmaking after graduating from university, and worked in various production office and crew roles in the film and television industry for several years. In recent years IJ has moved back to writing short stories and novels, as well as becoming an academic in the field of International Relations and Security Studies.

Dark River was his first published novel, and the first to feature Amanda Northstar, the sheriff of Independence, a fictional town and county on the banks of the Hudson River, inspired by his wonderful visits to many of the towns and villages of the region, as well as the Catskill Mountains. The second book in the Amanda Northstar mysteries series, *Heads Will Roll*, soon followed, and he is working on the third in the series, *Blindsided*.

Over time IJ will be expanding the fictional universe Amanda inhabits with novels following other characters who occupy the same world but operate in different parts of the United States, following their own adventures and story arcs, such as the *Queens of the Steal* series of novellas. IJ is also launching a new fantasy action series in the style of a comic-book adventure, entitled *Legends of the Wraiths*, beginning with *Storm-Wraith*.

Printed in Great Britain
by Amazon